T0246179

THREE BURIALS

THREE BURIALS

Anders Lustgarten

HAMISH HAMILTON
an imprint of
PENGUIN BOOKS

HAMISH HAMILTON

UK | USA | Canada | Ireland | Australia
India | New Zealand | South Africa

Hamish Hamilton is part of the Penguin Random House group of companies
whose addresses can be found at global.penguinrandomhouse.com.

Penguin
Random House
UK

First published 2024
001

Copyright © Anders Lustgarten, 2024

The moral right of the author has been asserted

Lyrics on pages 56–7 from 'I'm Coming Hardcore' by Kieron Jolliffe and Lee Hudson

Set in 12.25/15pt Fournier MT Std
Typeset by Jouve (UK), Milton Keynes
Printed and bound in Great Britain by Clays Ltd, Elcograf S.p.A.

The authorized representative in the EEA is Penguin Random House Ireland,
Morrison Chambers, 32 Nassau Street, Dublin D02 YH68

A CIP catalogue record for this book is available from the British Library

ISBN: 978–0–241–63879–8

For all the Cherrys. And all the Omars.

PART ONE

The First Burial

Chapter One

OMAR

There are seven of them in the boat.

An Afghan who swears he can steer it across the sea. Weird for a man from an entirely landlocked country, but no one else knows how to, so he gets first shot. Three Iranians and a Senegalese. They're just cash cows, chipping in for the vessel. It's Omar and Abdi Bile who made it happen. Omar and Abdi Bile who picked through the camp for the likeliest candidates. Who went to see the French fishermen and returned with all they could afford: a rowboat with a rusty engine which has never been further than the harbour wall. It's Omar and Abdi Bile who have the courage and the conviction, who make the rest believe it's possible.

It's party time at first as Omar and Abdi Bile push them out from shore, giggling at the cold shock to their legs, splashing the others with foam like kids. All the weeks of lassitude and frustration and uncertainty, blowing away with the sea breeze. They're going to do this. They're going to make it.

The elation lasts until they hit deep water, and the currents grab them.

The tiny boat rocks and judders and leaps out of the water like a salmon. They grab for something solid but there is no solid, only surges and wrenches and twists. The currents rip the tiller from their feeble hands and steer the little engine this way and that. They squat low to the wooden floor and panic swamps them. Total powerlessness. The realization that life is no longer in their hands. The men stare ahead like sprinters in their blocks, fingers digging into the wood, trying to winch themselves across the sea with the force of their eyes.

Omar's job is lookout. He kneels in the prow, shielding his eyes from the spray. Abdi is next to him, the navigator. He has Google Maps open on his phone, the blue dot of them surrounded by endless lighter blue. The wind picks up like a giant hand pushing them back. Warning them to turn around.

All at once Omar is back home, training with his father. The wind like an elbow into his heaving chest, sand eddying across the dusty track. His father standing by the finish line, glaring at his stopwatch as if it was talking back to him, shouting out split times. Promises of scholarships to America, talk of international races and agents and a way to support his family, all of which disappeared when his father got sick and died two days before Omar's fifteenth birthday.

It was Omar who gave Abdi Bile his nickname. It comes from his resemblance (in face, if not in stocky body) to Somalia's most famous athlete, 1500m world champion in the 1980s, Omar's father's hero. His father trained Omar in Bile's style: the killer burst around the top bend, negative splits. Negative splits – running the second half faster than the first, the last lap fastest of all – is the hardest way to win a distance race. It requires the most determination. Your lungs explode, the lactic burns, all you want is to make the pain stop, but against all your instincts you go harder. It's emotional as much as physical. The key is not to panic. Omar has learned not to panic.

A wave of homesickness and loss sweeps over him. He pushes it down. The future is coming. Asha is waiting.

The boat struggles on.

JAKUBIAK

He shivers and hunkers down into his thin denim jacket. DI Barratt had told him it was gonna be a warm dry night. That's why they're here. Warm and calm is perfect crossing weather for the illegals and so it's the time for Defenders of the Realm to do their job, the job the government should be doing: intercepting migrant boats and sending them back. But instead the rain is spitting and hissing like a spiteful cat, his jacket is wet through and the wind is blowing hard. He watches the fat raindrops blend into the soggy cotton and wonders yet again why he can't manage a similar trick.

Andy Jakubiak is a drifter, and he hates himself for it. For whatever reason he was not allocated his place in the world, dropped into one of the random school categories which become our identities: funny, sporty, brainy, hot, bad boy, even nerd or freak which at least puts you somewhere. He has his gym-built physique these days, his muscle armour against the world, but still he has no *place*. He is an illegal item in the bagging area of life.

His father in Poland with his real family. His mother a doormat. Overlooked at school: not praised, not criticized, merely ignored. The teachers *looking* for the black boys, the Asian girls, pushing them forward for prizes, picking them out when his own hand was raised. The careers officer telling him not to set his sights 'unrealistically high'. Girlfriends hard to come by, stumbling cumbersome in the presence of women. The anger building, the bile simmering. Taking out his frustrations in the weight room, the rough music of crashing iron. The hulking man hides the bruised child within.

He joined the police straight from school. Wanting an identity off the peg, somewhere to fit in. The nods of respect (or even fear, whatever, just *notice me*, pay attention to me) in the street. The solidarity, the banter. But it was the same again. There were the cool kids and the smart kids and the popular kids, and Andy was none of them. There's some joy to be had in cracking heads now and again, but the job is eighty per cent admin and Andy is lying to himself if he thinks that's enough for him anyway, he's not a true headbanger. What he really wants, yearns for, though he doesn't know it, is love. A social love, a sense of belonging.

He marinated slowly in the bitter brine of the canteen, imbibing the loathing, soaking up the prejudices. Passed over for promotions, fast-track schemes for which he wasn't eligible cos minorities and women only. Years as a street plod while people half as good as him shot up the ranks. All the time swallowing his bile, it'll just make it sweeter when you get it in the end Andy, but the resentment building and building until it came up his throat and choked him in his small bed at night but nowhere to put it, nothing to alleviate it with.

Until now. Until DI Barratt picked him out.

The pride Andy felt when Barratt invited him on the mission. Being chosen. Trusted. Asked to be part of something meaningful. A thousand illegals a day coming over. Fifteen hundred. Two thousand. The government, elected on the open promise of the baton and the barbed wire fence, doing fucking nothing. This is our country. This is a white country. So if they won't, we have to do something about it. A volunteer force to turn the illegals back. Defend our borders. Protect our souls.

A rumble in his guts. He looks up. Barratt has started the engine. He gives Andy a big wink. Andy salutes back. Aye aye, skipper.

'Get your camera out!' bellows Detective Inspector Freddie Barratt. This is Andy's task for the night. Record the migrant invasion. Show the world the scale of the problem. Wake people up. He pulls out his mobile. The latest in the range, incredible camera quality. Set him back most of a month's wage, but you have to look the part.

He presses the red square. Barratt laughs and flexes his biceps.

They lift together. More lower body than upper, as a matter of fact. Split squats, RDLs. Olympic lifts: power cleans, snatches. Lower body is where all your base strength comes from.

The rigid-hulled inflatable moves out to sea. A taut string twangs somewhere in Andy's heart. Maybe, finally, he has his place.

⌘

OMAR

He sneaks another look at Asha's picture, sent when she first made it to London, her grin so wide it almost splits her head. He was already leaving the village, the hunger and heat and militias, but most of all his mother sobbing in the dark and his promise to his father never to let her starve. But Asha decided the destination.

He puts his lips to the peeling plastic around her photo. His good luck charm. Abdi Bile gave him endless shit when he first saw it.

'Laminated? I'm sorry, I didn't realize it was 1997.'

'Anything can happen to a phone. Lost. Stolen. Dropped in the water. We are crossing the ocean, you know. And then pooof, all your photos and memories gone. Can't go wrong with a laminated printout. Plastic is for ever, brother.'

The boat has stopped. Omar thinks the engine's seized up again, but the rest are all looking his way. He cranes over his shoulder and his heart stops. The tanker is coming from the right. It's like watching a moving city coming towards them. Trying to see to the end of it gives Omar a dizzy off-balance vertigo feeling, like peering down a bottomless dark hole. He saw it a few minutes ago on the horizon, far away. Three kilometres, four? And now here it is, looming and looming and looming.

There's an earthquake. Omar has been in earthquakes before. The vibrations batter your ears, the rumble mangles your guts, everything is suspended and you can't move. And yet the sea doesn't change, the waves don't pick up. Suddenly a deafening silence and his ears hurt and a crushing weight lifts off his chest, and he realizes the earthquake was the ship's horn.

They all gasp in air at the same time and they're freed from the spell. The engine coughs like a dying mule, then hums again. They kick out over the surface of the water and out of the tanker's path, everybody laughing and taking the piss out of Omar. 'What kind of lookout can't see a boat that size?? Are you blind, dickhead?!' But I can see something, he tells them, on the horizon: a blue-green smear. Land. England.

And over it, a huge dark cloud.

꩜

JAKUBIAK

The wind berates Andy for his stupidity. A howling tongue lashing rips barbed wire salt across his cheek, before an icy drenching knocks him to his knees. He clings to the grab rope with both hands and tries not to show his terror. Another wave crashes across their bow, rocks them sideways, the craft tipped at 45 degrees before it slams back down. He wipes his eyes and hunches lower as the boat labours up the hills then thumps down into the rock-hard valleys below, slamming his lower jaw up into his top teeth, slicing a sliver off the side of his tongue. He spits blood. The rain is almost horizontal now, sleeting in, needle sharp.

He glances across at the only other volunteer, a chinless graphic designer called Roger with shit facial hair who is puking voluminously over the side, swathe of pasty bumcrack in the air. For the first time Andy wonders if he's been chosen because he's special, or for another reason. He shoots a searching glance at DI Barratt, hunched over the controls, tweaking the scanner for hits. The shaven head, the granite profile. Other cops have tugged Andy's sleeve, muttered darkly behind their hands about the things Barratt gets up to. The off-duty activities, the, ahem, manifest patriotism. We might *think* it, mate, but this guy actually *does* it. Word to the wise: wide berth. The roids don't help, whatever it is Barratt chucks down with his post-workout shake and thinks Andy hasn't seen. But Barratt has been good to him. Mentoring him, asking for him as detail on cases. He has. He has.

As if he can read Andy's mind, Freddie Barratt turns his head towards him, locks eyes amid the crashing tumult. A long stare down into dark tunnels. A shiver of fear in Andy's core. And then again the big wink and the paternal smile and he's warm inside again.

'Alright, kid?' he shouts.

'Fine, yeah.'

'Rough go your first time out.'

'No biggie.'

Barratt jerks his thumb in the general direction of the hapless Roger. 'You're doing better than that cunt, any road. He's not coming back.'

They laugh together and Andy feels special again, and then there's a ping. A ping on the scanner. Andy leans forward in excitement. Barratt checks the screen.

'Get your camera out.' No banter this time. No flexing. All business.

Andy pulls out his phone and begins to film, heart thudding in his chest. Barratt adjusts direction and rips the engine hard. They pick up speed.

OMAR

The world has broken apart. Everything is water. The sea boils and heaves like an overheated pot, thrashes like a chained animal, sucks and pulls and claws like an angry witch. Now it's foaming snow-capped mountains, chilly and cold and pitiless. Now huge teeth in a chomping jaw. Now landslides, giant plates that crash and collide. They are swirled and spun and tossed. Huge masses of water disappear below the tiny wooden boat and they are plunged into a deep well, surrounded on all sides by looming greenblack walls, then they're spat out and through the air until they crash down again onto the unyielding sea. The most terrifying thing is that when the huge waves rear up, they reveal the mind-bending immensity of the depths beneath. An impossible liquid chasm, like falling through wet space for ever.

Omar isn't scared until Abdi Bile tells him who to call back home if he doesn't make it. They've never discussed this, all throughout their journey. But Abdi insists now, makes him repeat the name. Then Omar gets scared. Then he makes Abdi memorize Asha's number. Makes him repeat it four times until Abdi snaps at him to go fuck himself, he's bringing them bad luck.

Now Omar is too exhausted for fear. The sea never stops. The waves come and come and come. They crash over them and push the boat down under the surface and he thinks it's over and they pop up and it starts all over again. He thinks of Asha and reaches for the plastic photo. It's still there, his good luck charm.

They are drenched and frozen to the bone. The engine is flooded and the little boat bobs hopelessly out of their control. Abdi mutters the *Dua* for protection over and over again. '*Bismillahil-ladhi la yadhurru ma'asmihi syai'un fil ardhi wa la fis-sama'i wa huwas-Sami'ul 'Aleem . . .*' He holds his soaked phone hopelessly in the air, standing on tiptoe, trying to get the map to reload.

Omar thinks, 'Whose dead fingers are those?' and it's his own hand, gripping the wood for dear life. He can't feel it and the fingers are yellow like old wax. He sends a signal to them to move and they don't and then they do, but he still can't feel them and they still look as though they belong to a corpse.

And then, over to the left, between the waves, he sees something. A sharp bright cone of light. Getting stronger.

Help. *Alhamdulillah*. Help is coming.

✺

JAKUBIAK

The sharp bright cone of the spotlight illuminates the threshing waters, waves lurching towards them like angry ghosts. Andy can't see anything beyond the looming waves but the scanner insists the illegals are straight ahead. The boat ploughs on. Barratt swings the cone of light from side to side. Maybe a noise, shouts? Andy cocks an ear, the thrill heightening his senses, but if there was anything it's been ripped away by the wind. And then they're right on top of the migrant craft.

Huddled, raddled shapes. Two crouched in front, three sat in the middle, two at the back. Drenched and freezing, blinking in the glare and waving their arms, despair turning to elation at the prospect of rescue. All at once these people are real and not a theory, and a powerful instinct to help them sweeps through Andy. He takes an automatic step forward and Barratt seizes his arm.

'Stay behind me,' he yells. 'Makes it look like there's more of 'em. Also my better side,' and a third wink, and despite their diminishing impact Andy remembers what he's there for. Capture the truth. The bigger picture. He takes a step back again and continues to film.

Barratt brings his loudhailer to his mouth: 'We are the Defenders of the Realm. We are authorized to deter illegal migration to the United Kingdom. You must turn back. I repeat: you MUST turn back.' Shouting and yelling from the illegals, but the wind whips the words away. The craft bucks, nearly chucks Barratt over the side.

He steadies himself, checks to see the camera is still on him, straightens his shoulders, deepens his voice. 'We are the Defenders of the Realm. You are being exploited for financial gain. You must turn back.' The other boat doesn't move. Barratt swings the cone of light round and shines it directly at them.

～❦～

OMAR

An explosion of light, like a punch in the face. Omar stumbles back, the sea clawing up at him, waves like uncaged sirens trying to drag him down. The black outlines of the others batting at the glare. A torrent of words none of them can understand. Squinting, ducking, they pile towards rescue, all the English they know tumbling out, Abdi Bile yelling, 'King! King! We love your King!' The boat tips terrifyingly on its side. A wave picks them up and throws them against the hard rubber craft, flimsy wood cracking on impact.

Abdi Bile puts one foot on their boat, one foot in the air reaching for the other. Wobbles for a moment in suspension, bottles it, dives back to their side. The three black silhouettes opposite don't move. Nobody reaches out a hand. They just stare. It's eerie. An eel of fear wriggles in Omar's guts.

Abdi tries again, a high-wire artist tiptoeing across the void. This time he makes it, clutching at the slippery rim of the other craft, legs dangling into the freezing sea. He hauls himself upright, reaches a hand out for help – and the biggest of the shadows kicks him unhesitatingly in the chest. Abdi flies through the air, lands hard back inside their boat. A shout of pain, a crack of ribs or wood.

They want them to go back. The rest are frozen in fear and bafflement, but Omar can see the truth. The angry silhouettes jerking their hands in dismissal. These men are not here to save them. They want them to go back. *They want them to drown.*

Omar thinks of the Greek fascists burning his tent, the Italian police baton that broke his front tooth. He thinks of his father's bony hands clawing at his, ripping the promise from him not to let his mother and sisters starve. The bloodstained sheets they carried him away in that same evening. He thinks of Asha waiting for him. He kicks for the finish line, the way his dad taught him.

He jumps into the other boat.

JAKUBIAK

Another one jumps! Tall skinny kid, broken tooth. He lands on Barratt. The two of them clutch one another in a crazy dance until Barratt throws him off. The kid wobbles but regains his footing. Andy's camera swings automatically over to him. Barratt launches into his spiel. 'We are the Defenders of the Realm. You must leave British waters.'

The kid snarls, sinks down, clutches a grab rope. Barratt's

waving an urgent hand at Andy to stop filming but Andy doesn't see it, caught up in the drama in front of him.

Barratt claws at the kid. 'Out. OFF. GET OFF.' He tears the kid's jacket but he wriggles down further.

'Fuck you. I stay, I stay.'

Andy sees something snap in Barratt. A twist of the face, a flare of the eyes. He wrenches the kid to his feet, drives him back feet kicking, hands scrabbling. He almost has him out but the kid hooks his ankles under the neoprene rim, his upper body lunging out over the water.

Barratt hesitates for a fraction of a second. The kid looking straight into his face, waves thrashing across them. The rapt eye of Andy's camera taking them both in.

⁂

OMAR

A tumble through infinite cold. The water no longer green but liquid black and freezing. The shock and the churning somersault force his mouth open and salt stings and rips at the back of his throat. He chokes and coughs and breathes the sea. He can't get head above feet, can't get a sense of where he is, the icy water batters and buffets him. *Where is the surface?* He looks for a glimmer of light, something that shows where to go, but there's nothing but infinite black. Pure panic seizes him. Omar thrashes and beats at the liquid prison. He opens his mouth to scream for help and more salt water floods in. *I'm going to die. I'm going to drown and Asha will never find me, never know that I'm gone, that I tried to find her, that I kept my promise.*

Calm. Stay calm. This is a race. It's like a race. Lungs exploding, no air, limbs seizing up. In a race you keep your form. You just have

14

to stay calm, in control. You don't panic. Omar knows how not to panic.

There. A spillage of light. Omar ignores the agony in his chest and swims towards it.

Chapter Two

CHERRY

The breathing of the sea wakes her up. The hiss and rush of pebbles being washed in and sucked out. A rhythmic stony soothing sound, as if there is no pain in the world and nothing to worry about. She lies there letting the sun warm her face, a green-gold glow seeping through her latched eyelids, spreading purples and reds across her field of vision, while she tries to remember who she is.

And then Cherry Bristow, senior ward matron, paragon of healthcare, rolls over and pukes her fucking guts up. Great racking yowls as if she's being turned inside out, as though she's trying to rip something more toxic than two thirds of a bottle of vodka out of her system. Which of course she is.

Liam.

Finally her stomach stops doing the triple salchow with back-flip, 9.95 from the Slovak judge, and air fills her lungs, tangy, delicious. She is alive. The downside is that she can now feel her hangover, which is roughly similar to being rhythmically belted in the back of the head with a two-by-four. Pulses of nausea crash through her skull in time with the sea. There's a clink of glass on stone and she seizes the cool bottle and presses it to her aching forehead.

Breathe in. Breathe out. Slow and calm. Put Liam, and all that he implies, back in the lead-lined box of her heart, to which only solitude and alcohol have the key.

Finally Cherry opens her eyes and sits up. It's a beautiful morning. The sun glows like a freshly cracked egg. The sea sparkles like a million pieces of polished glass. She reaches around for her phone. Not in anything resembling a pocket. No handbag, fuck knows where that's got to. What is that lump she's sitting on? She reaches a hand down cautiously. Her phone is stashed down her pants. Impressive planning from a woman who can't remember how she got here.

Seventeen missed calls and seven texts. Mostly Robert. A couple from Michael. One from Danielle, which is unusual. Must be Robert's doing. She can deal with all that later.

She hauls herself to her feet and looks for her shoes. One's a few feet away, but no sign of the other. She limps along the stony beach for a little while, hunching away from her clammy clothes. The storm last night may not have rinsed her soul clean or done much for the state of her uniform, but it has scoured the dry crust of the mundane off the world. The shallow water is a luminous turquoise, turning gorgeous dark emerald further out where the shelf drops off. Clumps of seaweed pulse bright green. All kinds of cool shells. The surgical clarity of the light. Everything is vital and alive and full of the promise of redemption.

And here's her other shoe! Magic. The heel is cracked but she can tape that up when she gets to work. Get a kit change from her locker, hot shower, bit of slap and she can face the world. Maybe get down to Phlebotomy with a bag of coffee beans, plug herself in, swap out a couple of pints of her tainted blood for a lovely dark roast infusion. Anything is possible this morning.

Even by their incredibly fucking irritating standards, the seagulls up ahead are making a racket. Cherry looks up. There is something else further along the beach. The gulls are pecking at it.

A mound of clothes.

17

JAKUBIAK

Breathe in. Breathe out. Slow and calm.

Andy Jakubiak raises and lowers the bench press bar, barely conscious of any physical exertion, so preoccupied is he with mastering his panic and fear. The gym has always been his safe space, the one place where he is in control. He got here at six this morning when it opened. First guy in.

Up. Down. Up. Down. Slow and calm. He has three 20kg plates on each end of the bar and is attracting admiring glances from other lifters for his ease of effort. Normally Andy notices that, *lives* for it in fact: the nods of male approval, the requests to work in, the respect, the sense of acceptance. But right now all he feels is utter terror, and all he wants is to make it go away.

It had all made such sense in the warm snug of the pub. DI Barratt with his hand on Andy's shoulder. Pints on the table. Low voices, urgent and intense. Barratt *listening* to him. Taking him seriously. The first man to understand Andy's alienation, frustration.

Some of the reading material was a bit full on. Anders Breivik on the dilution of whiteness. The manifesto of Brenton Tarrant, the guy who did Christchurch. Bit heavy in places, to be honest. Not totally Andy's cup of tea. The basic point is right though surely. Everyone else is getting a slice of the pie and we, the white indigenous, who've spilt our blood for this nation for generations, are getting fuck all. And so we have to do something.

But he didn't know Barratt was gonna do *that*. How could he?

In and out. Slow and calm.

But to be there. See it happen. And do *nothing* . . .

In a sudden spasm of self-loathing, Andy racks the bar and sits up. Nothing seems real. The cheesy EDM. The perky flirt at reception. The lifters in their wifebeaters and trackie bottoms. It's all plastic, it's all fake. Don't they *know*?

For the fifth time since he got here, Andy's hand reaches magnetically, guiltily into his pocket, like a smoker who just can't break the habit. He pulls out his phone, which he has on airplane mode because DI Barratt has already sent him three cheery matey texts this morning offering to take him out for breakfast, and that is the last person on earth Andy wants to talk to right now.

He starts the video again, the video he can't stop watching.

This is after.

Because the kid didn't drown.

There's nothing at first but blurs. Then suddenly the kid erupts from the sea like a sword from a stone. Gasping and choking, exhausted, grasping for a hold, and this time Andy does step forward, does extend a hand, there it is in the video, his other still automatically filming while he grasps the kid's hand and then BOOM! The flash of a huge boot into the side of the boy's head and the camera shakes slightly. A fraction of a second and another BOOM! and the size 13 boot of Detective Inspector Frederick John Barratt connects flush with the kid's face. A terrible crunch and the head snaps back at a horrific angle, and the kid is gone. And the dark turbulent waters are all that remain.

'Y'alright, mate?'

Andy looks over his shoulder and instinctively hides his phone. It's Neville, an occasional workout partner and similar devotee of heavy lifting. They've had good conversations about eccentric versus concentric phases. That's the only thing they've had conversations about, to be fair.

Now Neville is standing a little way back, with the twisted half-smile people wear when they don't quite get the joke. More precisely, when they aren't sure whether it is in fact a joke at all.

'Fine. Just, er, police stuff, y'know.'

'Right, yeah, sure.'

'Case I'm working on. Not really meant to talk about it.'

'Right, yeah. Course not.'

A painfully awkward pause.

'You done with the bench, mate?'

'All yours, mate. All yours.'

CHERRY

Stones crunch under Cherry's feet as she runs, her former track glories still evident in her loping stride, though there's no real point. She knows what it is before she gets there. Cherry was BFFs with Death for two full years, during a period everyone has collectively decided to obliterate from the memory banks but which is scarred across Cherry's soul like burns from a house fire.

Death leaning against the door frame in the ICU, a rueful indulgent smile on his face as he watched her flipping over those dying from Covid. Lounging across her back seat on the way home, feet on the headrests, humming softly as she sobbed uncontrollably into her steering wheel. For a little while she thought Death had left her for someone else, but then back he came, trailing the bean counters and the privatizers, chuckling as if to say, I knew I'd be back here soon, can't keep a good man down.

So she's not rattled or scared or even that interested when she gently turns over the mound of clothes, just to see if it's worth trying CPR. The floppiness of the body inside the clothes suggests there's no rigor mortis yet, so maybe there's hope. But the angle of the neck, which she sees next, the head lolling like a bruised flower on a broken stem, makes it clear that's wishful thinking. The hair, the clothes, the whole demeanour, they all look foreign. Which means it's probably one of the refugees.

In the last three or four years, a new sound has regularly swept low over the town. A persistent buzzing clattering, too loud for council hedge-trimmers or lawnmowers, not that the council can afford to do either any more. A helicopter hovering like a great metal raptor, scanning then pouncing, diving down towards its prey: little inflatable boats dragged here by the currents.

Cherry and her nurses have been called down to the harbour a few times to deal with hypothermia, dehydration, lacerations. By then the people from the little boats have been decanted onto ancient coaches, like the ones that used to take Cherry on school trips. Very strange that journeys through Africa and the Middle East and war zones and refugee camps should culminate here, among the worn brown and orange paisley seat covers, the driver chomping his Greggs pasty and listening to *Steve Wright in the Afternoon* while odours of seawater and blood and engine oil infiltrate the stale air.

So she feels a general but limited sadness. She can see the body is a young man and this is far too early and it's a waste, but there's been so much waste these past years, so much throwing away, that there's a limit to how much you can immerse yourself in it daily before you go a little numb.

And then she sees his face. And a shocking electric nausea bolts through her.

The dead boy is Liam. The same long elegant limbs, the same poise even in death. The body could be her son. He has a broken tooth, but otherwise he could be her flesh and blood. Instantly Cherry is back in her son's bedroom, the creaking of the twisted sheets under the heavy burden, reaching her arms up to turn the dangling load around, hoping and praying that somehow the face will belong to someone else. She staggers back and gasps, a rasping sucking sound entirely out of her control, and looks wildly around. Is this some kind of . . . ? Are there *cameras*? What *is* this?

Somehow she's on her arse. From this angle the boy is *looking* at her. Looking right in her eyes. Pleading for something. Instinctively she reaches out and grabs his hand and *oh Christ* it's still warm despite the sea. Not proper human warm, not like he's really there, but there is still a faint vestige of when this shell contained a living boy. She grips his hand harder, squeezing as if she can stop this tiny trace of residual life from slipping away. And now she can't see him because the view is misty and she's *pouring* salt down her face and she's howling and howling and howling and all the walls are falling down, all the barriers she put up between her and her heart are collapsing, and the sadness and regret and the rancid knot of guilt in the pit of her stomach are flooding out, and she howls and howls, and still she holds his hand.

JAKUBIAK

Safely back in the patrol car, the first thing Andy does is lock the doors. Neville's reaction has made the decision for him.

All night he was sat on the edge of his bed, weighing up whether to turn Barratt in. It's a tough one. Barratt is not loved at the station. Feared, yes. Respected, at a distance. But not loved. He tends to accidentally get missed out on the WhatsApp banter threads, the pub sesh invites. The Defenders of the Realm stuff is known and tolerated and even agreed with by many, that perspective on social integration being a key reason why they joined the police. But there aren't all that many who'd go to bat for the man himself.

But at the end of the day you cannot grass up a superior officer. That is the code. You do not dob in one of your own. Because who knows when you might be in his shoes, needing the ranks to close around you, to cover your arse? The first thing you have to do as a police officer is prove you can be trusted.

Andy knows if he mentions Barratt to anyone in authority, even on something like this, he'll be calling for backup and getting endless static, clambering up some piss-stained staircase in a dark estate full of knives all on his lonesome. Already nobody really wants to ride with him. It's always supposed to be two in a patrol car, but the last three weeks he's been out on his own. Cuts, the detective super said.

Still, he was gonna do it. March into the super's office, phone in hand. But the expression on Neville's face, of judgement and disgust, sets him straight. He can hear the questions now. 'And what exactly were *you* doing there, PC Jakubiak? What's *your* involvement in all this?' Who's more likely to be the fall guy: a DI twenty years in, or a street plod going nowhere?

He'll say nothing. That's the only choice, really. The dark, the rain, the howling storm: nobody can put faces to shapes. Maybe the kid survived. Got back on his boat. Even if he didn't, there's no trail. The only way there'd be a trail would be if Andy created one, by making a noise.

He starts the engine and feels his thudding heart ease. He's made his decision. He won't grass, but he needs to get away from DI Barratt. Ask the super to reassign him. Find a new gym. It'll all be fine. He sails past Costa and Waterstones and William Hill's, regular and plastic in the bland banal sunshine, and wills himself back to something like normality.

The radio crackles, asking for his location. He answers, gives it.

An incident at the beach. As the closest officer, would he please attend?

What kind of incident? The dispatcher doesn't know.

'What d'you mean, an "incident"?'

The dispatcher, gently puzzled, repeats: that's all she knows. Would he please—

He hangs up on her. The dread wells up out of his guts like a flooded storm drain. There's no way. No fucking way.

Andy ponders puncturing a tyre. Instead he turns towards the beach.

≈≈≈

CHERRY

She sits with the dead boy after she calls 999, still clutching his hand, keeping guard over him. There are a couple of morning joggers and she's not having anyone coming over for a look, rubbernecking, posting pics on social media. She's not having him robbed of any further dignity. People taking selfies. Police taking selfies. Police selfies with dead bodies, like they did to those poor sisters in London.

She didn't want to call 999 at all. She doesn't want to deal with the police one bit. There's no love lost between Cherry Bristow and Her Majesty's Constabulary, who go together like Wetherspoons and Wahhabite Islam. Far too many beer-soaked police 'socials' in rancid sticky-carpeted pubs, Robert invariably the only black man in the room, listening to boozy war stories and digs cloaked as 'banter', incredibly original stuff about dick size. The resentment of Robert building up underneath, wondering why he had to stay in the fucking police anyway.

She checks her watch. She'll be late. Again. She texts Jackie, her line manager. The response is . . . unsupportive. Is it actionable under HR protocols for your line manager to text you three bottle emojis and the purple aubergine? Thing is, Jackie's right. There's not a lot of patience among her colleagues right now for those who don't pull their weight. But Cherry is already full to the brim with

24

her own personal guilt, she doesn't have space for the professional variety too.

Something in the boy's other hand catches her eye.

It's clenched around some kind of crumpled plastic with glimmers of colour inside. She pulls tentatively at it. His fingers grip it so tight she can't pull it out, and she gives up. Minutes pass, still no sign of the twats in blue. An impulse seizes her, one she knows she shouldn't follow.

She peels the stiffening fingers away one by one and extracts a crumpled laminated photo. She flattens it out on her thigh. It's a girl, brown, early twenties, gorgeous ringlets cascading down her back, joyful smile. She looks happy and hopeful and in love with the future. Behind her is part of a London street sign: —son Street, NW10.

The fact that he was gripping this picture so hard, as if it was the last thing on earth he would willingly surrender . . . And then everything is misty again.

When did she last cry? She thought she'd lost the ability. Bone dry ducts at Liam's funeral, her family staring at her like she was betraying them. Trying to will herself into performing for them. Not possible. Nothing coming out. Cherry has never been able to do what is expected of her, only what she feels is right in her soul.

This boy is not Liam. Of course he bloody isn't. Don't be stupid. He is one more corpse in an endless line of them. But she looks into his eyes, and there is a plea there. There is a plea there and she can see it, plain as day. What makes him so special? She doesn't know, and it doesn't matter.

Maybe it's because he is alone. He is all alone, in a strange strange land, a cruel and unhappy land. And so she makes him a promise.

I will see you right. I will make sure you get a safe and decent place of rest. And I will try if I can, no idea how, to make sure this girl in the photo knows what happened to you.

A bulky uniformed figure is sloshing across the pebbles towards her. Finally. Not before effing time.

Cherry puts the crumpled photo in her pocket. For safekeeping. She'll give it to the guy later.

She brushes herself down and stands up.

Chapter Three

CHERRY

For a healthcare facility they have fucking fatal food. Deep frozen, deep fried, drowned in gloop. Facsimiles of vegetables. Nothing but fizzy drinks to wash it all down. Maybe it's part of some sinister plan to keep the punters in long term, but why subject the staff to it?

Maddison and Mackenzie, staff nurses and bezzy mates, wave at her from their usual spot in the canteen. Maddison is local, slim, bottle blonde down to her eyebrows and pretty under all the 'gold robot' contouring they go in for these days. Maddison's not a huge fan of bodily fluids ('icky') or members of the public actually coming into the hospital ('pushy'), both of which are a bit of an issue in a nurse. Her 'real dream', she's confided to Cherry, is to own her own salon.

Mackenzie is from Bolton, brunette and colossal, size 34 and rising. They have to order her special uniforms. Mackenzie is also possibly the most nakedly sexual person Cherry has ever come across, with a deceptively innocent heart-shaped face and complete conviction in her body. Mackenzie has left a trail of hard-ons, busted pacemakers and wrecked stationery cupboards she's shagged in all across the hospital. They had to reassign her from the stroke ward because the relapse rate was off the charts. Maddison has told

Cherry that Mackenzie's main income is from her Only Fans and she only keeps working at the hospital because of the free giant uniforms, which are an integral part of her routine. Cherry looked it up and her jaw is still sore from hitting the floor.

Mackenzie nods while ploughing through a pile of fries the size of a small Scout hut, and Maddison gestures to her to come over. They both like Cherry cos she takes no shit, look up to her as a bit of a role model. She likes both of them well enough too. They're a good laugh, down to earth, and not bad workers in their own ways. But right now, Cherry has her mind on other things. She's waiting for Michael. It's been a very strange morning.

Michael O'Rourke is Cherry's best mate. Six foot seven in his stocking feet and the calmest person she knows. A gentle giant whose most aggressive gesture is to slide his glasses back up his nose when stressed, Michael is above all a kind man, and as Cherry gets older and the world becomes more definitively and irrevocably run by cunts, that strikes her as a more and more precious quality.

Michael suits his work perfectly. He's the hospital's senior APT, anatomical pathology technician: he runs the mortuary. Not a place that particularly suits emotional volatility, or one in which witty banter is highly prized. She knows how she'll greet him, the same way she always does: 'You look like you've seen a ghost.' And he'll laugh indulgently like it's the very first time he's heard it. Michael doesn't believe in ghosts, which she imagines is the first thing they ask you at the interview for a job at the mortuary.

She needs some of his calmness. The police officer at the beach freaked her out. He wouldn't go within ten feet of the kid's body. Turned his back at one stage. Cherry had to virtually drag him over to the corpse and physically write her name in his notebook. Then he went mental, started yelling about who did she think she was and how he was in charge. Yet the second the ambulance turned up, he was gone. Didn't escort the body to the morgue, which surely he has to do by protocol. They normally do anyway.

Maybe that's why she didn't hand him the laminated photo. It rustles in her pocket, reminding her of her small deception.

Cherry rode in the back of the ambulance in the policeman's place, waiting til the paramedics' backs were turned then giving the dead boy's hand a squeeze. You'll be alright, I've got you. Dropped him off with Michael, made a lunch date to find out more about who he was. Michael has plenty of experience trying to ID 'wash-ins', beached corpses. Most of them he can identify – from fingerprints and DNA swabs if they've ever been nicked, dental records if they haven't, databases of the missing. Then it's a case of tracking down their families, arranging collections and burials. She's never asked what happens to an unidentified wash-in.

She hopes this'll be one of his success stories, anyway. Last year they had the most wonderfully moving funeral for a girl from France who'd run away from home. No trace of her on any of the UK systems, but Michael figured something out from her necklace and from listening to French radio, which you can get longwave down here. The gratitude in the faces of the girl's parents Cherry won't forget for a long, long time.

So she puts the boy to the back of her mind and tries to get on with her work, ducking Jackie's gimlet glare. But Liam's face. Opening store cupboards to a sudden glimpse of Liam's face. Snapshots of Liam's face on random patients. Liam's face in the mirror in the women's toilets – that one was the realest, to the extent that she was convinced he was behind her. Whirled around, made the girl coming in jump out of her skin. Liam's face and all the feelings that evokes. Failure. Guilt. A yawning abyss of pain. So she needs Michael, his soothing presence, his dry gentle mockery of her.

She checks her watch. Not much breaktime left. Checks her phone. Nothing.

And finally Michael is here, sliding into the seat opposite her, no food, not apologizing for being late which is very unlike him, his skin a greenish-grey pallor. He sits and stares at her plate.

Slides his glasses up and down his nose like a ski jumper building for take-off. There are cracks in the right lens that weren't there this morning.

Cherry stares at him. Finally she says, and for the first time she actually means it, 'You look like you've seen a ghost.'

'I've had a very strange morning,' says Michael.

～≈≈～

JAKUBIAK

The kid's face. Staring at him from that awful angle with an expression of . . . Reproach? Judgement? Is he even the one from the boat? It was dark. There's no reason he has to be. He looks just like the video though. A fizzing pyrotechnic explosion of rage at Barratt going off in Andy's chest.

The dread as he'd sloshed across the beach, the stones forming heavy drifts around his ankles. Of all the fucking punters to find the body. Not a tearful jogger, goose-fleshed in her Lycra, yearning for the consolations of authority, a hefty gym-built arm round her shoulders. Or a bumptious old boy, chest puffed out, mentally guest starring in *Line of Duty*. No. A fucking nurse. What was she even doing on the beach at 6.30 in the morning, in soggy uniform? Competent, in control, territorial even, taking his actual fucking notebook off him to write her name in capital letters so he wouldn't miss it.

CHERRY BRISTOW

He couldn't bring himself to ride with the body in the ambulance. Went back to his car to gather his composure before going to the mortuary. Keep it short and sweet: brief outline of the case to the

APT and then get out into the fresh air, leave it all behind. At least that was the plan.

It wasn't his fault. It was the place, the polished surfaces and pristine slabs and empty metal bowls and sharp scalpels. Freaky. And the freakiest thing was what wasn't there. The absent bodies, the missing dead. Andy could feel them concealed all around him. Chopped up and reconstructed, guts stuffed into cavities, limbs reattached, bagged up in plastic, locked into drawers, the blood sluiced away down the drain, the hard evidence of death replaced by the unconvincing alibis of antiseptic and floor cleaner.

And then the strip lights went. Buzzing like trapped metal flies, alternating light and dark and light and dark so the room was broken up into snapshots, juddering glitches of time. Making movement look static and nothingness look like movement. When the APT walked towards him he was three metres away and there was a flicker and he was right on top of him and Andy almost screamed out loud.

That is when Andy Jakubiak panicked. And made the wrong call.

❧

BARRATT

The Complete Guide to Anadrol Abuse, Addiction and Recovery
Abusing Anadrol can over time lead to improper levels of dopamine and serotonin, two important brain chemicals, making it harder for the brain to produce feelings of pleasure.

Yeah, yeah, yeah. I know all this.

This can lead to a host of unpleasant mental states such as:

- *Paranoid (extreme and unreasonable) jealousy*
- *Extreme irritability and aggression ('roid rage')*

Yeah, well, now you mention it . . .

• *Delusions – false beliefs and ideas*

I do not have delusions.

• *Impaired judgement*

I do not have impaired judgement. I am the king of good judgement. Fuck this.

Freddie Barratt abruptly flicks off the window on his phone and leans back on his settee. Dial back the dosage a tad, that's all. Nothing wrong with keeping himself in the requisite physical condition. Showing the world the outside – muscular, vigorous, tough – that reflects how he feels inside. If there's a price to pay for that, so be it. Bit more self-control would help though. Yeah.

He'd been relieved when Andy called him from the morgue. Was starting to worry a bit. About being ghosted. About who else Andy might be talking to. Picturing the scene: super behind his desk, Andy in front, his fucking phone between them. Freddie thought long and hard on the journey back about grabbing that phone and chucking it in the fucking sea, but you get more bees with honey. Wind him up, piss him off, you never know who he might go squawking to.

Andy is a good sort. Not the sharpest tool in the shed. Wouldn't make it through B&Q quality control, let's say. Sweet that he thinks he's being held back, though of course Freddie doesn't disabuse him of the notion. It's nice to have a protege. It gets lonely sometimes, being the only one who can see the truth.

The real problem is that you can find a lot of what Freddie Barratt believes, fervently and deeply and in his heart of hearts, in the papers now. Broadsheets, not tabloids. *Question Time*. It's almost trendy. There'll be fucking 'You Will Not Replace Us' T-shirts in

Asda next. Freddie doesn't trust any of it though. He knows when he's being played. Snide pricks seeking attention so they can flog scammy crypto. Posh boys cosplaying as radicals of race to get columns and votes. But none of them are true believers. None of them willing to put their necks on the line for the future of this country.

Over-confidence. Yeah. That was the problem. The relief at Andy's call. Swaggering into the morgue expecting the gangly APT to roll over like most civilians at phrases like 'national security implications', and to release the body into his custody. He has weights and ropes ready in the boot of the car. Off one of the local trawlermen, who comes on a mission now and again. Proper deep-water fishing stuff, big lumps of blackened iron and thick twisted matted fibres. And a body bag.

Barratt the postman. Return to sender. Addressee not known.

Then get Andy to delete the video and job done. Last night a glitch in the matrix, that's all. But a bit more self-control, Freddie, that's the ticket.

He scratches his balls. Definitely shouldn't have slammed the morgue twat against the wall, either.

CHERRY

'He did what?'

'I just told you.'

'Slammed you against a *wall*?'

'When I wouldn't give them the body.'

Michael rubs his nose as if he might wipe it off his face altogether. Cherry leans back in her chair.

'Well, that's assault.'

'It's not assault.'

'Michael, it's assault, and we're reporting it.'

'Yeah? Who to?'

'You have bruises? Well then. Show me.'

'There were two of them and one of me.'

'And?'

' "And?"! What d'you mean, "And?" *And*, they're the *police*.'

Their voices rise in intensity and lower in volume. Others look round, drawn by their conspiratorial hunching. People elbow each other. Are they *rowing*? Lovers' tiff? Lovers' tiff, them two?! You think . . . ? I bet she would, she'd do anything with a pulse, but *Michael*?! Bent as a nine-bob note, mate. Shh, don't say that, HR's on the next table.

Michael grabs his glasses from his face and puts them on the table with a definitive thunk.

'He has a broken neck.'

A vertiginous dizziness swims through Cherry's head, like when a roller coaster drops away and leaves your soul behind for a second.

'Clean snap between C2 and C3.'

She thinks back to the beach, the boy's head lolling at that horrific, unnatural angle.

'Also facial contusions. Three teeth loose.' Michael looks her in the eyes. 'How do you think he got all that at sea?'

A long silence as they look at each other.

'Who is he?'

'I've no idea. Nothing from fingerprint ID, or dental.'

'How did he die?'

'If they'd let me alone, I'd have checked for water in the lungs. But there aren't the usual signs of drowning, froth in the mouth and all that.'

She scans the room. Half the canteen is watching them. She looks back at her friend.

'What'll happen to him?'

'When?'

'If you don't identify the body.'

Michael blinks a couple of times, sits back. She presses him.

'If you can't find his family. Someone to take him. What happens?'

He looks at the wall. His tongue thickens his next words like flour in stew.

'The usual procedure for an unidentified corpse is a public health burial.'

'Which means?'

'Common plot. Cardboard coffin. No headstone. No mourners.'

'A pauper's grave?' The words leap unbidden out of her mouth. It's like something her gran would've said. The gut fear of an earlier generation, redolent of shame and failure, a final humiliation. Something from Dickens. She didn't know they still had them, paupers' graves.

Michael nods. 'The cheapest possible option. To "reduce the burden on the state".' He enunciates the last bit with the precise, pointed disdain of a disappointed cat.

'No. No no no no no.' Her head rocks violently from side to side. Sudden tears spill out from under her closed lashes, tears she can't rationally explain. Of all the deaths she's witnessed in the past few years, all the pain and loss, why is she attaching herself to this one? A death she didn't even see, a kid whose name she doesn't even know?

'I'm not having it.'

'Cherry . . .' His gentleness just upsets her further.

'I'm not having it. It's not right. It's not fair.'

'It happens.'

'He's come all this way, from God knows what, just to get dumped in a fucking pit? No name, no memory? It's not *right*.'

'It happens. To people closer to home too.'

'Yeah, well. It's not happening to him.'

She leans back, her arms folded across her chest. That's it. That is definitive. Her mind is made up and the world will just have to adjust and accommodate.

Michael can't help but laugh. At the thrust chin, the jaw set like concrete.

'What? What are you laughing at, you big lummox?'

'The chin on you. Tyson Fury couldn't get through that.'

Now they're both laughing.

'I'll keep trying,' offers Michael. 'But if there's nothing, there's nothing. I'm not a magician.'

Cherry scans the canteen, curves her body around the table as best she can, a protective shield to block prying eyes. From inside her coat she withdraws her crackling, rustling prize, the laminated photo. She smooths it out.

'But there's not nothing. There's this.'

Chapter Four

HODGES

There's a banging noise coming from the holding cell. The slamming of objects against the metal door. Some kind of chanting. The same phrase over and over.

Officer Danny Hodges of the Border Force Regional Intake Unit, the migrant processing centre for a major swathe of the south coast, looks up from his phone. Fucking animals. Dirty fucking coons. He's trying to watch the game.

It's the pricks from earlier, he'd stake his life on it. The six who came in that morning, led by the fat little Somali motherfucker who was shouting all kinds of shit. Livid, as if the British people hadn't literally fished his ragged arse from the jaws of death at our own expense and were now giving him free food and accommodation. The level of *entitlement* is just astounding. Some do-gooder obviously taught him the word 'lawyer' on his travels, and they were all yelling it in his face. Lawyer lawyer lawyer lawyer lawyer. Yes, you'll get your lawyer, in time. When possible. This is not a fucking charity. We are not here to give you handouts.

He goes back to the game. Chelsea are still leading 3–2. It's the fourth minute of added time. Come on Chels, come on the mighty Chels, hang on boys.

The volume from the cell is increasing. Shut up, you noisy pricks. It's the Champions fucking League.

Not his fault there were already fifty-eight men in the holding cell. Not his fault there's one toilet. And it's blocked. This is not a country of endless wealth. There is no magic money tree. We don't—

FOR FUCK'S SAKES CHELS YOU FUCKING USE-LESS CUNTS THAT IS A FREE MAN ON THE EDGE OF OUR FUCKING BOX WHAT THE FUCK ARE YOU DOING JAMES YOU SPASTIC PIECE OF SHIT I HOPE YOU DIE OF FUCKING CANCER

The ref blows his whistle and Chelsea have drawn 3–3 and lost top spot in the group. Fucking Reece James didn't track his man. This is why you don't play niggers.

CUUUUUUNNNNNTTTTTSSSS

The phone goes in the fucking corner. He swings to punch the wall but the last time he did that he was off for six weeks. He looks around for catharsis, an outlet for his rage. The noise from the holding cell is louder than ever.

Yes. Yeeess. Blow off a little steam. Main perk of the fucking job. No other reason to be here. Certainly not the wages.

He reaches for his baton and pepper spray. Reaches under the desk to switch off the CCTV in the holding cell. Can he be arsed to go get a Taser? Nah, let's go one on one. Mano a mano. Old school. He thinks about going in the break room and giving the rest a nudge, see if they fancy playing a little skull bongo, but better not to go in mob-handed. No need to get your stories straight. No one to rat you out.

Officer Danny Hodges steps lively down the corridor like a hungry man heading for his first square meal in days. A grin on his face, baton beating a tattoo against his outstretched hand. This'll be fun. Speed's the key. Snatch squad style. Crack the door, grab the nearest, spin him, arm up his back, back out into the corridor with the cell door slammed behind, head into the wall BOSH, down. Whole thing should take two, max three seconds. Fucker won't even know what hit him. And then, party time. Play them drums. Beat out a sad, sweet tune on a worthless black body to lift the heart and soul of Officer Danny Hodges. Let these cocksuckers know what country they're really in.

The noise as he approaches the door is deafening. Enormous crashes against the walls. Whatever they're throwing, it's heavy. Something hits the door so hard he sees it almost jump off its hinges, leap out of the frame. Hodges slows his stride, hesitates a moment. Is this really such a good idea, all on his lonesome? But now his blood is up, his dick is hard for ragepain, he wants some black meat to punish.

He steps up to the door and peers through the small Plexiglas window.

They're in some kind of order, some kind of nightmare phalanx. Dozens and dozens of red mouths open screaming, dozens of fists in the air, the beds smashed to pieces and turned into weapons, the toilet ripped from the floor and waved in the air, spurting faeces and filthy water. They see him through the window and a raging ululation goes through them. They surge forward, crashing against the door, faces distorted with fury and vengeance, screaming at him, wanting his blood.

Hodges stumbles away from the door. His back collides with the far wall. He trips himself and slides to the floor, the locked door the only thing protecting him from the screaming faces. He scrabbles away and as he looks back at the window, there's a horror vision of red tongues and white teeth and all their mouths open and screaming at him. And for the first time he can hear what they're shouting, the rhythmic chanting resolves itself into words, one word, repeated over and over and over again.

MURDER

MURDER MURDER MURDER MURDER MURDER
MURDER MURDER MURDER
He runs back down the corridor, the accusation in pursuit.

CHERRY

The door creaks open as quietly as she can manage and domesticity leaks out like carbon monoxide. The banal susurration of the telly. Pans clattering in the kitchen. A horrible stench of something burned or burning. A wave of panic runs through her, like her head's in a bag and she can't get enough air. Liam won't be there. And the next day he won't be there. And the next. But all the recriminations and the rages and the misunderstandings, they'll be there for the rest of fucking time. She has to grip the door frame to stop herself from running away.

The commonly cited statistic is that eighty per cent of marriages break up after the death of a child. This stat is a myth as far as Cherry can make out, and she has looked. All over the internet. Talked to a couple of psychologists at work. But the reason it's commonly cited is it feels absolutely true to life.

Cherry has not talked to Robert about Liam. She cannot talk to Robert about Liam. Every time she's tried he has something to do. Repaint the front room. Rip out all the kitchen units: units from a fitted kitchen mind you, fitted at considerable expense by a skilled carpenter paid to fit kitchens. Robert is not a skilled carpenter. He is an ex-policeman who thinks a plane is something you use to go on holiday. The kitchen units he is building from scratch look, frankly, fucking shit. This she can forgive.

His decision to repaint Liam's room and to take down all the pictures and photos of Liam throughout the house WITHOUT

ASKING HER? Far, far less. They screamed at each other for three hours, or she screamed at him and he took it and because he took it she screamed some more, and then she put all the photos back up and went out to buy vodka.

It's like there's a thick glass wall between them, of the kind you see in US prison visiting rooms on the telly. A lot of the time it's like she can't really hear him, certainly can't remember what he's said, but then she can't remember much of what she's said over the past months either. She can just see his lips moving and a desperate, bottomless sadness in his eyes that hurts her so much and yet enrages her in some deep unforgivable place because he won't *admit* it and instead hides behind terrible DIY, and so she resents him and then hates herself for resenting him and it's easier, so much easier, to go to work and then take a bottle to the beach. She's considered an affair, but it feels cheap and Cherry has never been cheap, and also it just sounds like so much fucking *work*.

She stands outside her house and takes a deep breath. This is her home. She lives here. She'll cook dinner, open the windows to banish the ghost of whatever shite they've ruined and make something fresh and fragrant, even though being there robs her of all appetite. She'll pick up into a light jog and close her eyes every time she passes the door of Liam's bedroom, the way she has for months and months. Find a way to apologize to Robert about last night, though there's nothing new to be said, nothing she can tell him that she didn't last time.

She creeps quietly in, hangs up her coat with a synthetic rustle, plasters on a fake grin, turns round and jumps out of her skin.

They're standing there, shoulder to shoulder. Side by side Danielle really is her father's daughter. They've moulded into one another even more over the past few months. They were always of one mind, inseparable, but now they're identical. They have the same posture. Same expressions on their same-shaped faces. Robert even at fifty has a beautiful face, but it's a man's face. Too blocky, too granite carved, too unyielding for a girl. But then if Danielle is anything, it's unyielding.

'Where've you been?' says Robert.

'Where've you been?' echoes Danielle. 'Mum? We asked you a question. Where have you been?'

⁂

JAKUBIAK

Nothing is said in the car for a good long while. Andy keeps expecting Barratt to tell him where they're going, but the older man is grimly focused on driving. Well within the speed limit, making all the signals. Not like him at all. Black bomber jacket, black jeans, black leather gloves. They're in a plain-clothes car Andy's never seen before. The back of Andy's neck begins to prickle and itch.

A soft thud in his lap. He looks down. For a fraction of a second a skinned face stares at him from vacant eye sockets. He jerks in revulsion before he realizes what it is.

'Put it on.'

Andy picks up the balaclava and turns in his seat to glare at Barratt.

'I've had a call,' says Barratt. Then silence.

Fucking spit it out then. Christ. Don't leave me fucking hanging.

'From a mate in Border Force.'

'Oh yeah?' says Andy Jakubiak patiently, in lieu of chinning his detective inspector.

'The others off that boat got picked up this morning.'

'What?'

'They're at the intake unit now. Danny's gonna keep 'em away from the lawyers as long as he can.'

'Lawyers? Why does he need to—'

'They've given a description of us, mate,' says Barratt casually.

The car seems to lurch and veer. The dread, the liquid nausea, bubbles wildly up again.

'They're shouting about us in the hallways.'

'What kind of description?'

'Pretty detailed. You and me are quite distinctive, I suppose you'd say.'

'But how can they, it was dark, it was—' Babbling as though he can dissuade reality from existing.

Barratt makes a hard right turn. 'It's cool. Shouldn't be a major problem.'

'Shouldn't be a major fucking—?!'

'He said she said. Their word against ours.'

Another right turn and with a sickening sense of inevitability Andy knows where they're going, probably has from the minute Barratt called him down to the car.

Barratt pulls into the darkened rear entrance of the hospital and parks in front of the delivery doors for the mortuary. He looks Andy full in the face.

'The point being, if there's no evidence, there's no case to answer. No body, no problem.'

Andy puts his hands on his head because that's what they do in films when something unbelievable happens. The sense of unreality that has dogged him all day is becoming stronger by the second.

'But the morgue guy, he'll—'

Barratt puts his hand on Andy's shoulder. With the calm definitiveness of a father telling his seven-year-old son that ghosts aren't real and to go to sleep now, he says, 'There won't be anybody here this time of night. No body, no problem. Trust me.'

43

CHERRY

'Dinner is served.'

The lump lands on Cherry's plate with a dull wet crash. It looks like a chunk of bathroom tiling after a house fire. There are several distinct layers of burned shit one on top of the next, making up an inch-thick glossy black shell like a pricey piece of Chinese lacquerware. Leaking out from the carbon carapace is a thick reddish oil with gristly lumps in it. Cherry bounces her knife off the crust. It creaks and moans like a haunted house in high winds. What did Danielle cut this with, a blowtorch?

'It looks lovely, darling. Thank you.'

'Want more?' asks Danielle, her malevolent grin more medieval torturer than dutiful daughter.

'I think we'll start with this, don't you, love?'

'There's loads more.'

'I'm sure there is.'

Robert gestures to her to sit down, and of course she does what Daddy tells her. The only sound for some time is the futile sawing of table knives where only a tungsten carbide-tipped drill bit will do.

'When did you start cooking, Dani?'

'When you stopped.'

'Danielle.' Robert, low.

'It's true though.'

'I've been working. To keep a roof over our heads.'

'We thought we'd try an experiment. Have some fun.' Robert the peacemaker.

'Right. Good idea.'

'You don't seem to be enjoying it, Mum. Eat up.'

Cherry scans the room. Everything is Liam. Things he used. Places he sat. The family photos Robert put away and she put up

44

again. The four of them round a campfire in a national park not far down the coast, Liam flexing his biceps comically, Danielle laughing as she holds a flaming branch aloft. Flying a kite on the same part of the beach where the dead boy washed up this morning. She thinks of him, the refugee kid, all alone on slab or shelf in Michael's morgue.

She lingers on her photo of Liam winning the county U18 800m, blown up and framed. It was taken from behind the finish line (which earned her a major bollocking from the marshals) as the runners are charging up the home straight. Liam is tearing through the field, his knees driving, his arms like pistons. You can see he's going to win from the quality of his form compared to the rest, whose heads are back, shoulders tight, arms thrashing sideways. He's smooth, calm, shoulders down, eyes fixed on the gun barrel of her camera. He always relied on his kick, his blazing finish. He started out as a 400m runner, like Cherry was when she was his age, and his last 200m was usually his fastest. Negative splits. The hardest way to win a race. She never had the stamina or the mental toughness to do that.

Liam hated the photo, always hustled his friends past it, thought they'd think it was his idea to blow it up so large, that it was him showing off. Robert once told her, back when this photo was a source of joy to Cherry and not of unbearable pain and regret, that Liam looks – in his determination, his focus, his grace – exactly like her.

Now she turns to him again, tries one more time if not to break through the glass wall then at least to tap on it, to get his attention, a smile, a flash of the old charm.

'Good day?'

'Mmmmm.' Robert's head is bent over his plate, poking his dinner cautiously like a bomb disposal expert confronting a hitherto unknown incendiary device. What feels like a geological age passes before she realizes this is all she's going to get. She switches her attention to her daughter, but even before the words are out of her mouth she knows it's a mistake.

'How about you, Dani?'

'Since when do you give a shit?'

'Language,' mutters Robert and then falls silent again, like some gnomic oracle forbidden by divine proscription from uttering more than one fucking word per century. A high-pitched whine starts up near Cherry's left ear. She thinks it's a mosquito, even slaps at it, but it rises in pitch and intensity and now it's in her right ear too and now inside her head, rising and rising, the physical sound of the ever-building tension in the room, an electric shriek battering against the inside of her skull trying to get out. Cherry grips the sides of the dining table hard with both hands and uses all her self-control not to scream along with it, not to scream and scream and scream. Her husband and daughter stare at her with surprise and concern and a tinge of genuine fear, as though a wild hawk has suddenly landed at their table.

And then her phone rings.

⌇⌇

MICHAEL

Michael sluices down the slab. He watches the different coloured bloods, the crimson venous, the scarlet arterial, dilute and mix and blend and disappear down the drain in a thin rose flush. The clots and lumps and other evidence of trauma vanishing with it.

The kid was dead more or less when he hit the water. Michael is sure of it now. There's almost nothing in the lungs. When someone drowns, most of the time their lungs are filled with whatever they drowned in, the body's desperate gasping for air aspirating only fluid. Then you have the physical damage to the respiratory system.

Lung distension. Alveolar oedema. Thick froth around the mouth and nostrils. Cerebral hypoxia, which is the actual cause of death.

There was none of that. There was just the clean snap between the C2 and C3 vertebrae of the spine. The contusions. The tooth damage. It's blunt force trauma all the way. But from what, he can't say.

There's no trace of the boy on any form of ID system. Nothing on dental, but if he'd never set foot on these shores there wouldn't be. Nothing on missing persons that jumps out. And so it's very likely to be a public health burial, with or without Cherry's picture. Which is sad, but at the end of the day, what else can he do?

It's late now, past dinner time, way past the end of his shift. He's been here since six a.m. and he's bone tired and starving, drooping with fatigue and low blood sugar. He has the lights on low to pretend there's no one here, because strictly speaking he's not meant to do that many hours in a row (though who's *not* doing that many hours in a row these days, in the NHS?) and the strain has made his eyes hurt. He did it for Cherry, her distress at lunch.

He's never seen her like that, especially over what is, at the end of the day, a random. But he has seen everything else: the ward deaths, her collapsing home life, the gaping never to be filled chasm that was the suicide of her favourite child. Her bottling everything up. There was very little Michael could do about any of those things. But he could do this.

And of course because of the police this morning, telling him to hand the body over, not to put it into the system. He wanted to prove to himself he wasn't scared of them. Isn't scared.

He'll register the body now. That's why he took so long over the autopsy, went back and checked and double-checked: so he could be absolutely certain, one hundred per cent sure of his findings. So he can put the body into the system and back his judgement all the way. To register it. Now. Yes. Put it into the system. Go ahead.

47

His fingers linger over the keyboard. He shifts his weight and feels the bruising along his ribs and spine from being slammed against the wall. He takes a breath and enters the first line.

There's a clattering at the locked rear double doors.

That's weird. Way past time for deliveries, cleaning agents and whatnot. There've been no calls about accidents, house fires. No new short-term tenants to be brought in.

The back doors rattle again, louder. And there's a thump, a kick. Muttering voices.

Michael freezes. He shuts down the computer. He sidles, very gently, over to the long back window. From the far end, if he squishes his neck up against the glass, he can see out and down at an angle to the rear entrance. There are two bulky figures down there in dark clothes. One turns slightly, and an ice-cold spear hits Michael in the chest.

It's the two policemen from this morning.

CHERRY

She jumps the red light and doesn't hear the horns. If she goes the wrong way up the one-way street, she can be at the hospital in three, maybe four minutes. The next light is orange turning red when she shuts her eyes, puts her foot down and ploughs through it. Cherry has no idea what she's going to do when she gets to the mortuary. She just knows she needs to get there.

She turns into the one-way street that leads uphill to (or from the point of view of the drivers that are supposed to be on it, down-hill from) the hospital. It's residential, parked cars on both sides, a thin rivulet of empty tarmac down the middle. There's someone making their way down. Bollocks.

It's an SUV. Of course it is. The preferred way for rich people to tell you their children are more important than you are. Barely scraping past the parked vehicles, literal microns between paint jobs, it barrels its way towards Cherry. She'll have to pull over and wait. Instead she drops a gear and puts her foot down. What are you doing? She's travelling now. No, again, hun, what the actual fuck are you doing? A peremptory bray from the SUV's horn.

They're closing on each other fast. Sixty metres, fifty, forty. A lunatic calm envelops Cherry, the kind of blissful mental clarity she's never got close to with meditation and scented oils. She knows she isn't going to move whatever happens. And therefore he must.

She's close enough now to see the driver. It's not a him, it's a her. Fucking hell, it's the hospital's new Chief Operating Officer. Samara something, universally despised as the Widowmaker. Hired from a London consultancy on a laughably huge salary, on the recommendation of a laughably expensive firm of headhunters she *part-owns*, the Widowmaker promptly laid off a third of the hospital workforce within three months of her arrival. By rights she ought to be known as the Widowermaker since ninety per cent of the people she fired were women, but it doesn't scan as well.

Cherry remembers friends of hers who were let go. She drops gear again and stomps the living fuck out of her accelerator. The car is flying now. The extended moan that emanates from the SUV's horn is part rage, part terror, all baffled incredulity that probably for the first time ever in the Widowmaker's gilded, cosseted Roedean/Oxford/Goldman existence, the world is not simply going to give way on her command. Thirty metres. Twenty. Ten. At the last second Cherry closes her eyes.

The shattering of metal and glass takes place not all around her as she expects, but behind. She opens her eyes and looks in her rearview mirror. The Widowmaker, as the powerful invariably do when confronted with resistance, has shat herself. Metaphorically. Though who knows at this point.

Cherry does not look back again. She swerves into a small, dark car park at the side of the hospital just in time to pick up Michael's millionth call.

'They're coming up the stairs. They've kicked in the back doors.'

'Get out. Get out, Michael, please. I don't want you to get hurt.'

'What are you going to do?'

She hangs up and punches her way in through the side entrance. She still has no idea what the answer to his question is.

JAKUBIAK

Barratt throws open the doors to the mortuary, with Andy right behind him. Nobody there. Well, nobody alive. The kid is stretched out on a slab, right in front of them. He's been cut open and stitched up again. Neat train tracks of black thread climb from navel to throat, a road to nowhere.

Jakubiak takes the body in with a hurried half-glance and turns quickly away to check the room. Someone was here very recently. Coat over a chair, papers next to a lukewarm cup of coffee, cutting tools slick. It must be the guy from this morning, just like Andy predicted. That's the end of Barratt's plan, surely. The guy'll know who it was. He'll remember them. You can't just *take* a body.

'Come on.'

He turns. Barratt has his hands under the shoulders of the dead boy, causing the head to loll and bounce sickeningly. Andy glances sharply away.

'Get his feet, mate.'

'What about the guy?'

'What about him?'

'He's round here somewhere.'

'And?'

'Maybe he's gone to get help.'

There's a sound from the corridor outside. Barratt's head snaps round like a raptor. He lets go of the kid.

'Wait here.'

'Fine.'

'And cuff yourself to him.'

'*What?*'

'Handcuff yourself to the body. Just in case the cunt gets by me.'

'I'm not *handcuffing* myself to—'

A jerk and a snap and a cold metal ring clasps his wrist.

'Just in case.' Barratt winks. The effect of the wink is rapidly wearing thin on Andy. 'Back in a jiff. Make yourself comfy.'

DI Barratt has handcuffed him to a corpse.

Andy shouts after him. 'Detective Inspector? Detective Inspector Barratt?'

Retreating footsteps echo down the corridor.

CHERRY

This way to the mortuary passes the dispensary. Cherry's one of the few senior enough to hold keys. She opens the door, seeking inspiration. Cleaning things are stashed in a corner, but a woman wielding a mop and purple Cillit Bang does not automatically strike fear into the hearts of men. There's all sorts of tablets and pills, but what's she supposed to do with those? Insert them as suppositories and hide til they take effect?

Largactil. Now we're talking.

Long ago, back when Y2K and Netscape Navigator and political alternatives to vicious fraudulent kleptocracy were real things, Cherry worked in the infirmary at Wandsworth Prison. To 'make things better'. She quickly realized you can't make prison better, because prison is precision engineered to make things worse for everybody. She also realized there are no sick people in a prison hospital, at least not in a conventional sense, because a prison hospital is a dumping ground for the mentally ill and the deeply disturbed. And so her number one tool was Largactil. Largactil is an anti-psychotic, cutting edge in its time but now out of date, whose primary benefit from a stressed practitioner POV is that it knocks people the fuck out. The inmates called it the Liquid Cosh.

She sneaks along the corridor, the slap of her shoes on the washed lino sounding in her ears like the tread of an elephant, loaded syringes of Liquid Cosh in her pocket. The plan has been refined. She'll try to talk them into leaving, but if push comes to shove she'll knock the older one out. She knows vaguely who he is, remembers Robert talking about him in most disparaging terms. He's the problem. The young one will listen. She's feeling almost confident as she edges into the mortuary.

What she sees makes her more so. It's only the young one there, perched awkwardly on the edge of the slab, peering down into the dead boy's face with the pained intensity of the carved marble *pietà* she saw on a city break in Rome. Searching for some kind of enlightenment. His gaze is so intent he doesn't notice her when she walks in.

'Don't shout.'

He looks up, eyes glazed as if trying to place her face from a dream, then his mouth jerks open.

'You can't. We know. So just go.'

His mouth snaps shut again. He lifts his right arm to chest height, almost involuntarily. The body on the slab spasms roughly towards him.

The two of them are shackled together with handcuffs.

Right. That, erm . . . That could be an issue.

The two of them stare at one another for a long, long second. Then he bellows. 'DI Barratt!'

'Don't—'

'DI BARRATT!'

He lunges towards Cherry like a crocodile erupting from the shallows, on her before she can move, knocking kidney pans and cutters into the air, scattering bagging tags and bone saws around them. His bulk crushes the air out of her, compounded by the horrid weight of the corpse he's dragging behind him, whose free arm flops obscenely over his shoulder like a drunk mate at the pub.

She screams. He reaches his free hand towards her mouth and turns to shout again for his mentor. He's halfway through Barratt's name one more time when she sinks the needle into the side of his neck and shoves down the plunger. No more than a few seconds after, his eyes roll back and vanish into his head as the Liquid Cosh does its work.

Well that's not very professional, Cherry. You're supposed to inject Largactil into the muscle body rather than directly into the bloodstream. Just as well there's no assessors around. In related news, she's trapped under not just one but two heavy, immobile bodies.

And there are footsteps in the corridor.

She wriggles helplessly. The footsteps come closer, louder. A fractional pause, and then he's in the room. For the very first time in her life Cherry Bristow thinks she might die.

It's Michael. His jaw hangs at approximately the level of his breastbone. 'I heard you scream.'

They crash through the side entrance and into the darkened car park. Michael, who has remarkable strength for his slender frame, is doing most of the heavy lifting, dragging the heads and shoulders. Cherry shoves the feet along. Where's a hospital wheelchair when you need one? Michael's mouth is wide open and a steady stream of noise is emanating from it, presumably some kind of commentary on what he's seen and what they're doing, but she can't really take any of it in.

There's no way back. She hasn't burned her bridges so much as nuked the fucking Golden Gate. How can she possibly explain any of this? Where would she start? And in that second, she realizes she doesn't want to. She doesn't want to be here, this place, this job, this life, any more.

This is something she can *do* for somebody, not just fester uselessly, swirl round the drain amid guilt and regret. She can make sure his death doesn't go unnoticed and unacknowledged and unmourned. And by God she is going to do it.

She throws open the side door of her car. 'Shove 'em in.'

Michael goggles at her.

'SHOVE 'EM FUCKING IN.'

'You're not actually serious.'

'It's a hatchback. They have a very small boot, OK?'

'Cherry, what the FUCK—'

She explodes into the prone bodies propped against her car like overstuffed bags of shopping, shoving them with both hands. They shift a few inches towards the open door. She does it again.

'Alright alright *alright*. Fuck's sakes.'

Michael bundles the two bodies into the back seat of her car. They flop perversely against one another like drunken lovers clawing for flesh, holding each other upright. She throws an old grey blanket over them.

Cherry jumps into the front seat. This is her last chance. To stop at the border to madness. To stay within the confines of the normal world.

'Michael?'

He bends down to her window. She opens her mouth and hopes something sane and reasonable will emerge.

'Will you come with me?'

The expression on his face suggests that request is neither sane nor reasonable.

The side entrance flies open. A pumped-up, shaven-headed silhouette fills the frame. Michael slams an urgent hand against her door.

'Go.'

She screeches away as Michael lopes through the car park leylandii and beyond.

By the time Detective Inspector Freddie Barratt reaches the spot, all that's left are tyre tracks.

Chapter Five

CHERRY

The vinyl crackles like a fire in the night.

Lush strings, body and mind floating. Then the piano riff starts, taking her to a higher plane. She's where she belongs. She's happy and free. She's never wanted to be anywhere else as much as here. And this is her favourite tune.

She pushes through the lairy, sweaty crowd and into the main room just as the tune breaks, the kick drum kicks in, the bass rumbles through her guts, and a deep, authoritative voice opines that:

THE RHYTHM IS HOT

And the place goes mental. Unhinged, uninhibited ecstasy. The silhouettes around her, moving the same way she is, echo her, reinforce her, make her feel part of something bigger and joyous and true. She remembers her older sister's horror stories of clubbing in the Eighties: stood stock-still all night in case you messed up your three foot hairdo that was as stiff as the assigned gender roles, groped and pawed at, pint glasses smashing. This is not that. This is the magic of a jerry-built industrial warehouse transformed into a thumping fairy cave of lights and wonders and heart-in-the-mouth expectations. This is huge grins and hands waving in complex patterns. This is the embracing stench of Vicks VapoRub, pill farts and sweaty hugs, offers of water and friendship and acceptance. The tingly shock of cold water down her back, water she knows in the far-off rational part of her brain is sweat dripping from the ceiling but which she embraces because it's her immersion in the crazy chaos of this place. 'Easy, geezer.' 'Sorted.' 'Safe.' Nothing is small or mean or selfish here. Anybody can be anything they want.

I'M COMING, I'M I'M I'M COMING, I'M COMING HARDCORE

The year is 1992. Cherry is in her final year at school, but the rave is all she lives for. She still runs hard too, second in the county champs senior 400m last month, and because she's eighteen she can tear up the gaff all Friday night, with or without pharmacological enhancement, and still make it to 10.30 a.m. Saturday training and lead her fair share of the reps, though she'd have won counties easy if her blood type wasn't MDMA two to three nights a week. But who gives a fuck about any of that? Rave is her sole earthly purpose. The world has possibilities and she has Mitsubishis.

LET ME HEAR YOU SAY YEAH!

The tune fades. Cherry opens her eyes, she hadn't even realized they were closed, and in front of her is the most beautiful boy she's ever seen. His body is sleek and compact, his eyes gleam even in the darkness, his cheekbones appear to be carved out of granite. He's offering her a bottle of water with a smile on his face.

'Robert,' he mouths.

Cherry smiles back. She takes the water, has a swig, feels it rush all the way down her insides and redouble the rush of the pill she dropped an hour ago. She goes to return the bottle and say something smart back to him, but suddenly she's crying. Why is she crying? That's not what happened. Tears run in impossible torrents down her face and fill her smiling mouth with salt.

That's not what happened. What is this?

Robert's eyes begin, literally, to smoulder. The gleams transform to burning embers and his face catches fire. Blue flames crawl like hungry insects across the skin around his eyes, blackened bones shoving through. His cheeks shrink and wrinkle and ignite. His lips twist into incinerated fibres. His hair flames and burns away in a sudden rush, trailing umber wisps and flickers of orange. He shows no pain or even awareness of any of this. His scorched and carbonized skull is still talking to her.

In terror, Cherry tries to spit the salt water that floods her mouth onto him, to quench the flames. But she can't. She only manages to choke and gag. She can't breathe. She's going to drown in her own tears, and Robert is going to burn alive because she can't help him. His torched face leans closer, shedding scraps of scorched skin, eye sockets two pits of dark crackling flame.

Cherry jerks awake. She's sweating hard.

The campfire is out of control. The wood she laid to one side has also caught, and now the whole conflagration is roaring at her.

Across the flames, the mute accusatory glare of the policeman she's kidnapped meets her eyes.

It's a cold night. She'd let him crawl part way out of the car to get nearer to the fire, anchored by the dead body he's still attached to. She'd gagged him with her tights while he was unconscious and tied his ankles together with the backup cardie she keeps in the boot (or Cardi B as she calls it, giving herself a little mental pat on the back for keeping up with pop culture. She unwisely said this out loud to Danielle once, and she actually growled). That should be enough. No need to make him suffer in the cold. But also no need to be stupid.

The flames reach higher. She kicks out in a panic, sending burning logs cartwheeling into the night in showers of sparks. A couple land on the policeman. He grunts and slaps them away with his free hand, but one is stuck between his shins. A muffled scream as his jeans start to smoulder. Cherry instinctively rushes over, paws it out. Big mistake.

He grabs her ankle and yanks her to the ground. She hits her head on hard timber and momentarily a blackness washes through her. He drags her towards him, his hand clawing up her leg to her thigh. She stamps with her free foot on his outstretched arm, his face. He grunts and turns his head. She kicks again and somehow he traps her foot under his upper torso, his free hand up to her stomach, his eyes relentlessly on hers, the gag still in his mouth, the stony silence of the attack making it all the more frightening.

She digs into her pocket and pulls out the loaded syringe of Largactil. There's a micro pause as each combatant weighs up the other, as he decides whether the humiliation of being tied up by a woman outweighs the discomfort of being knocked out by an anachronistic mental health drug for the second time in a few hours, which is more frequent than the recommended dosage even at Wandsworth Prison hospital. Then he lunges.

Less than a minute later, as the unconscious policeman lies face down on the ground, drool starting to seep through what were actually quite pricey tights, Cherry wriggles her legs out from under his heavy form and checks her pocket.

Only one vial left.

ROBERT

Robert hangs up as Cherry's voicemail message kicks in for the twentieth time. He stares at the wall. He doesn't know how long he stares at the wall for.

His gaze strays accidentally onto the photo of Liam and he wrenches it away in a panic. He *can't* look at his son's photos. Why doesn't she fucking understand that? It's not that he doesn't *want* to. It's that he physically cannot or he will crumble into dust. He will fall down and he does not have the strength to get up again. He's not like Cherry. Days and days she spent, poring over every drawing, every school report, every medal. Fucking *wallowing*. Like she was hogging him all to herself, making a show of her grief. It made him almost physically sick and too angry to talk to her.

He put the pictures away so that he could stay in the house. Why is that not obvious? Why should he have to spell it out? Every photo is a stiletto-sharp memory, through the eyeball and into the brain. A glimpse over the edge into an abyss of pain and loss so huge it takes his breath away, and he doesn't know how to begin to deal with it.

He meant it. He absolutely meant what he said to her. 'If you leave now, don't bother coming back.'

The words charged out of his mouth like guard dogs whose chains had snapped, snarling, biting, to defend their master's wounded heart. He'd felt such relief, almost a rush, at finally letting out the words he'd been reining in. But she left anyway. At a dead sprint, without even closing the door, and she hasn't come back hours later, and her phone is off. Something about the hospital, and a boy's body, but there is always something at the fucking hospital, and there are always bodies, and there was one boy who mattered more than all the rest and he did not get what he deserved, from her or from a lot of people or of course from Robert, and so why should anyone else?

He's been feeling this way ever since Liam died. Bitter and twisted, resentful at love between other people and their children. Scowling at mums in the street when they buy their kids a lolly, or adult sons when they hug their dad goodbye. People stare at him strangely and he realizes what he must look like, full of more irrational hate for random members of the public than a Murdoch newspaper, but he doesn't care.

But now all Robert feels, as he gets the voicemail knockback yet again, is bereft.

Danielle stomps down the stairs with a large cardboard box. She's glaring at him. Robert realizes he's been staring out of the window into the night like a dog pining for its master. He jerks back swiftly and looks quizzically at the box.

'What's all this?'

'Her shit.'

His daughter charges back up the stairs.

He looks in the box. All of Cherry's make-up is piled up as if an earthquake has hit the perfume section at Debenham's, the part he could never walk through without physically choking like someone in a First World War poem. Gas, gas, sick boys. Lipsticks, foundations, eyeshadows bob around in a sea of creams, sprays, perfumes and other stuff he can't name and Danielle hasn't put the tops on, which is leaking together into a pungent, highly expensive gloop.

The array of colours is mesmerizing. They remind him of a childhood painting set he treasured so much he refused to use it, just stared endlessly at the vivid blobs of colour and their bewitching names. Turquoise, emerald, Prussian blue, burnt sienna, rose madder, ruby, topaz, amber, cadmium yellow. He has never seen any of these colours on Cherry's actual *face*, but he supposes that is the skill, the dark alchemic art of make-up.

He looks up as Danielle reaches the landing with another box, out of which Cherry's most expensive cashmere jumper is dangling an arm, waving for help.

'What d'you think you're doing?'

'Collecting for charity.'

'Those are Mum's things.'

'She's gone, Dad.'

'You can't just decide that.'

'I didn't. She did. You told her. And she fucked off.'

'You are way, way out of line, Danielle.'

'She made her decision, and now we're getting on with it.'

A not insignificant part of Robert's soul thrills at the angry defiance of his daughter, and at her implicit defence of him. But obviously he can't tell her that.

'Put it back.'

'She's gone. You told her to go, and she went.'

'Put it all back. Now. You have no right to mess around in other people's—'

'I am looking after YOU!'

The box of clothes skitters across the landing and the contents hit the wall with a soft whump.

'You won't do it for yourself, so I have to. I have to be the fucking adult in this house cos the actual adults are behaving like fucking children, so I'm doing it, and the least I expect from you is some fucking thanks for looking after you EVEN THOUGH NONE OF YOU EVER LOOK AFTER ME.' The last sentence is delivered at ear-splitting pitch and punctuated with the crash of her door.

He's about to go up after her when there's a knock. Even though he knows it's not Cherry, because why would Cherry knock at the door of her own home, Robert nauseates himself at the speed with which he rushes to open it.

It's not Cherry. It's her friend Michael.

Robert doesn't like Michael. He doesn't like Michael because he knows how much he and Cherry share including *lots* of shit about him, whereas he can't even remember Michael's surname. And the fact that Michael is gay irks him. He's no more homophobic than the average middle-aged straight dude (less, he hopes, just cos of hearing so much grim stuff in police canteens over the years) but he's seen plenty of men hanging round Cherry in hopes of one thing, and the fact that Michael has no interest in that one thing means he only wants to be around her because he *likes* her which, Robert realizes in that moment, makes him much more jealous than some random dickhead wanting a shag.

Michael knows Robert isn't a fan, which accounts for his strange posture on the doorstep, one foot already turned back to flee. He's in scrubs and sweating like he's run a half-marathon. Robert stares.

'Hi, Robert. It's Michael. Cherry's colleague?'

Stares.

'Something's happened.'

CHERRY

She stares over the campfire and the unconscious man, into the night and into the past. From out of the darkness looms the face of her son, eleven or twelve years old, lit up beautiful and bright and laughing as he tries to stop the gooey mess from sliding off the end of his stick. She'd never heard of 'toasting marshmallows', some American thing Liam picked up from Netflix. It doesn't seem that hard but he's incinerated three so far and Danielle is ripping the piss out of him. He fails again and there's a brief blazing comet of artificial additives, and Liam giggles and shrugs an apology, and Cherry hands him another marshmallow from the big rustly packet.

This is where they always came. For long weekends and short escapes. For summer holidays when money was tight, which was often. It was Liam's favourite place, at least until he became moody and distant and that turned into his bedroom. It's in the photo she nailed back onto their living room wall. A campsite in a national park not too far down the coast, hidden in a lee of the South Downs. Surprisingly few people know about this side of the national park and almost nobody knows about the campsite, which isn't marked and is at a dead end down a muddy gravel track.

It's rudimentary at best. No cooking facilities, no showers, just a basic wooden hut you can hide from the rain in and a couple of moss-obscured signs detailing the local wildlife. But there's a beautiful little river that slows to a wide shallow bend, with reeds and kingfishers and a sandy bottom for paddling. And on the other side, across a series of slippery stepping stones, long sloping hills stretch up from a stand of glorious wide-limbed oaks that crackle electric green in spring and burn garnet and honey and bronze in the autumn. One of the biggest oaks offers down a friendly series of low branches like a ladder, almost designed for an active eleven-year-old boy to scramble up. Bats swoop at dusk. One of the things she and Robert always agreed on was the importance of nature.

She had no idea she was even driving here until she looked up, and there was the old hut right in her headlights. You never know where things will take you, do you? Never guess at the time that something that brings such joy would become a place of pain.

Suddenly she's overwhelmed by loss and loneliness. What the fuck is she doing? What is this insanity? Out here in the cold in the middle of the night in the middle of nowhere with an unconscious policeman and a dead body? Nowhere to go and no inkling of a plan. What the fuck was she thinking, or not thinking?

She'll go back. She has to go back. There must be a way to fix this.

Robert will know. Robert knows so many things. Christ, the things she's said to him . . .

She scrabbles around in her pockets and does the thing she's steadfastly refused to do ever since she left the hospital car park because she didn't want to hear from anyone, she didn't want to think or answer or 'talk about it', she just wanted to drive into the darkness for ever.

She turns on her phone. Literally dozens of rapidly escalating texts from Jackie, from senior HR, from the Widowmaker herself, pile up unread. She deletes a few, ignores the rest. Already they seem ancient, archaeological, remnants not just of a former life but of a former civilization.

Instead she calls Robert.

～≈≈

BARRATT

The silver box, the size of a small suitcase, sits on the passenger seat, a laptop open beside it. It's an IMSI-catcher, more commonly known as a Stingray. Every mobile phone has an International Mobile Subscriber Identity, like an ID number. It's how they communicate with the system's base stations, phone masts and such. The phone has to acknowledge the base but the base doesn't have to acknowledge the phone, which is platform capitalism in miniature, and here's where the door is open to the Stingray.

The Stingray pretends to be a phone mast, sending out stronger signals than regular masts to entice phones to connect to it, and then downloading personal data, hacking messages, eavesdropping on calls. It allows the police to harvest large volumes of data on attendees at demonstrations and protests, to use and abuse in profoundly anti-democratic fashion at their leisure.

Freddie Barratt bought two for the department. From the 'special projects/terrorism' budget line, which was basically free money for a good long while there.

The other use of the Stingray is in locating and tracking:

65

determining the strength of signal from a given mobile, and therefore the distance away. In the centre of the map on Freddie Barratt's laptop screen is a single glowing point of reference, unmoving, growing stronger all the time.

Andy Jakubiak's mobile phone.

And as he looks, Barratt sees another dot suddenly appear on the screen, on top of Andy's, redoubling the strength of the glow, pulling him in like a pub fire in winter.

Barratt grins, punches the top of his steering wheel and speeds up.

He doesn't notice it, but as he does so, he passes a sign that welcomes him to a national park.

※※※

ROBERT

Robert stares incredulously around him. This cannot be happening. He's sitting at his kitchen table. Everything is still exactly the same. The wallpaper. The boxes of cereal lined up like a shelf of well-read books. The fucking shit kitchen units he's been trying to install from a combination of Ikea pentagrams and instructions in Swedish put through Google Translate, to predictably disastrous results. And yet his wife has absconded with the corpse of a refugee as well as the police officer who is *handcuffed to it*, and he's on the phone to her giving her advice.

Her mate is leaning self-consciously against the wall. Danielle is sitting on the bottom step with her eyes bulging like she's done enough Colombian flake to stun a whale. He blinks twice, but the two of them are still there, this is still real, and he's still on the phone to Cherry.

'You have to get rid of the phones. His and yours.'

'OK.'

'Pull out the SIMs, crush them with a rock. You have to assume Barratt is tracking his mate's phone.'

'OK. And then?' she asks, a note of quiet desperation in her voice that only somebody who knows and loves Cherry Bristow, despite everything, would pick up.

He takes a deep breath and looks around the room. His eyes light once again on the picture of Liam winning the race. He looks – in his determination, his focus, his grace – exactly like Cherry. Like she still does now, to him.

'Bring them back here.'

Danielle explodes off the step and begins roaring. Robert gestures angrily to Michael to take her upstairs and turns his back on them.

'Bring them here. We'll talk to the young lad. I don't know him personally but Barratt's done this for years. Found little proteges to do his dirty work and take the fall for him. Nothing half as mad as this, but . . .'

There's a pause. He wonders if she even heard him. 'Cherry?'

'Yeah?'

'You get that?'

'Yeah. OK.' Another pause. 'Thank you.'

Now neither of them know what to say.

'Get rid of his phone. And come back here.'

'Will do.'

≈

CHERRY

She searches the policeman's jeans, back and front. Nothing. She goes through his bomber jacket and pulls out an expensive smart-phone, studded with apps that dazzle like digital diamonds.

It requires a passcode. Six digits. For a giggle she tries 999 999 but no joy. Zero sense of humour, the police. This phone surely has fingerprint tech though. She heaves up the bulky right arm, uncoils the sausagey index finger and presses it firmly against the touch button. The screen blinks to life.

The last thing the cop was looking at is a video. The still is a grey blur of waves. She presses the white arrow. At once she shrieks and puts her hand over her mouth. It's her kid. The kid on her back seat, gasping for air and struggling to get into a boat. To see him alive, even on film, shocks her to the point of dizziness. He's real. Not a body, not a moral obligation, but a real living boy.

Cherry gasps again in disbelief as a huge boot comes in twice, first into the side of the kid's head and then thunderously full into his face. His head snaps back horrifically. And then the boy is gone.

She sits back on her haunches, stunned. So much now makes sense. The weirdness of the young cop on the beach that morning, for whom the corpse wasn't a random discovery but a re-acquaintance. The aggression of the policemen towards Michael. Their obsession with getting the body back. Her insides chill as she realizes what this is really about. The stakes for which the bald cop is playing.

She goes to prise the SIM out of the cop's phone, then realizes she must keep the video. It's their main bargaining chip. Send it to someone she trusts before chucking it. Hurriedly she punches in Michael's number and presses Send. The coverage out here is shit. The blue bar of progress crawls like commuter traffic.

In the back of her mind she hears the crunch of tyres on gravel but it sounds too suburban, too far away to be part of this reality. It doesn't register until she looks down the muddy gravel path to her dead end campsite, and sees the twin headlights of an approaching car.

She panics. She grabs for her car door but there's no way past on the narrow lane. She bolts for the shelter of the old wooden hut, to lie low in the shadows, but what if the cop looks around for her? She has nothing to fight with. Into the hills. Cross the stepping stones and run through the oaks and up into the hills. She can outrun most men still. It'll be a long cold night, but at least she'll be alive.

She takes a step, two steps towards the river. And then she feels a hot angry force at her back, rumbling up like a new volcano hissing from the sea.

The young cop is standing behind her.

⚬

JAKUBIAK

The horrible sensation of the knockout shot lingers. Like sliding down a ramp into an oily slimy blue-green sea, gyring and tumbling in suspended animation, greasy sludge in his mouth and nostrils. It's like a horrible dream he can't shake the feeling of because he's not entirely awake.

He shoves the driver's seat vengefully back as far as it'll go. These tiny hatchbacks are such shit. A muffled howl of pain and fear from the nurse in the back. He'd shoved her in next to the body, the body he remembers with a horrified clammy shiver waking up pressed against, rough blanket over their head like lovers snuggling under the duvet. To pay her back, he's lashed her arms and feet together and shoved that filthy disgusting gag deep into her gullet. She'll complain, but he doubts anyone will pay her much mind when they get her back to the station.

He starts the engine. Barratt is still staring into the fire. Andy sounds the horn. Nothing. Andy leans on it hard. He's putting in for a new DI the minute they get back.

Barratt turns and stares at him. In the firelight he looks demonic.

His eyes are hooded into deep caverns, his nose a broken promontory, and shadows like horns flicker and play across the broad expanse of his bald skull. The runes and guts of the fire snap and snarl behind him like a leashed beast, spitting crimson and orange sparks. He holds out his hand.

'Notebook.'

What's he talking about? Andy rubs his wrist. It's swollen and bleeding where the handcuff bit deep and he wants to get some surgical spirit on it sharpish. Who knows where those fucking handcuffs have been? Barratt did that to him. Didn't even apologize when he unlocked the cuffs. Smirked as he shoved them back into his pocket.

'We need to get on, Detective Inspector. Get her back and charge her.'

Barratt still holds out his hand.

'Give me your notebook.'

Again the flame of rage ignites in Andy's chest. Barratt is the one. It was the nurse who humiliated him, but none of this fucking nightmare would've happened if Barratt hadn't . . . groomed him, he realizes with a sudden shock. Drawn him in and used him. For the first time he wonders if he can take his mentor. He's younger, fitter, better max on bench and squat. But Barratt would gouge him in the eye, then bite through his windpipe. Andy wouldn't do that. And that's the difference between them.

He levers himself out of the impossibly annoying midget car, whose designer clearly never did a dumbbell fly in his life, and slouches over to his boss to see what he's talking about.

'Why do you want my notebook?'

'Sir.'

Fucking hell, I will test your chin in a minute.

'Why do you want my notebook, *sir*?'

'Couple of details I wanna check.'

A beat, then Jakubiak sullenly pulls out his notebook. Barratt

70

leafs slowly through it. He stops at the entry Andy made at the beach. He reads the nurse's name where she wrote it in capital letters at the top of a page, then looks across at her.

CHERRY BRISTOW

Phone numbers underneath. Mobile, work. Home address. A thorough person. Unlikely to forget things.

'I know her.'

'And?'

'Robert Bristow's missis.'

'Who?'

'Black guy, ex-Met. Before your time. Transferred down here, couldn't take the banter. By the book type, straight arrow.'

'So?'

'So, *Constable*, that means she will also know who I am.'

Barratt and Cherry lock eyes for a long moment. Some kind of twisted understanding passes between them. Then he rips out the page with her name on it and chucks it into the fire. For a moment it clings on, miraculously intact in the heart of the blaze, then vanishes in a curl of smoke. In the back seat of the car Cherry spasms and kicks. She can see where this is going before Andy can.

'Get the bags.'

'What bags?'

'From my boot.'

Mystified, Jakubiak moves to the rear of Barratt's car. In the boot, along with the weights and ropes, are two sturdy black plastic body bags.

Two.

He gawps for a second, then slams the lid shut. 'No fucking way.'

'We've got no choice.'

'What d'you mean, we've got no choice?! We've got every fucking choice!'

'A police officer, Andy, is held to a higher standard. We are subject to suspensions, disciplinary action, whispers and accusations. We are persecuted. And so we must protect ourselves.'

'What's it matter what she says about us? She nicked a corpse!'

'There will be slurs against us. There will be agendas.'

'You have mates in the force. We can get backed up—'

'You're thinking, mate, and it's exactly how I used to think, you're thinking as though this country is *fair*. You know the attitude of elites to the police. They are *looking* to make an example of men like us to prove how fucking woke they are. They'll crucify us in the papers before this ever gets near a disciplinary.'

A big bit of wood explodes in the blaze, a rat-a-tat-tat of air pockets like gunfire. Andy jumps. Barratt continues.

'People go missing all the time, Andy. They disappear.'

'Yeah, but *I don't make them*.'

'Think of all the little fingernail shots in the missing persons database. Row after row after row.'

'No.'

'That's all she'll be, just another little fingernail.'

'*No.*'

Barratt reaches for his closer. He puts his big, heavy, paternal hand on Andy's shoulder.

'Trust me. I've got you. Trust me.'

And despite it all, despite the multiple ways Barratt has already fucked him, the weakness in Andy Jakubiak flares up again. The overwhelming longing that sometimes dulls but never goes away, the grinding ache for a father, for a big reassuring presence that smells of aftershave and musky warmth and cares for him, tousles his hair and takes him for a kickabout, rouses in his breast.

'She was driving too fast. Lost the plot. With what she's done, people will buy that.'

'Please.'

'She went over the cliff edge and into the sea. Won't be hard to do.'

Jakubiak shies and stamps like a frightened horse but doesn't refuse. 'Please, sir.'

Begging is weakness. Barratt knows he's got him. Crocodile grin.

'The tin can goes over the edge. The two of 'em go way out. What's the crash scene tec got to go on? Nothing. Maybe the tide took the bodies away. Or maybe she faked it, started a new life in fucking . . . Argentina. Not our problem, at that point.'

Andy drops his head. Barratt takes it as affirmation. He leans in close, forever over confident, and whispers in his ear.

'Top boy, you are, Andy. Fucking tip top. Now go get the bags.'

Chapter Six

ABDI BILE

Abdi Bile shifts from foot to angry foot. There is one payphone for the entire unit. He's been in the queue for four and a half hours. There are still two men ahead of him. And the prick currently on the phone has been talking for eighteen minutes. It's lockdown at five p.m., then it all starts from scratch again tomorrow, and the guards hold him back at unlock til the phone line has formed to fuck him up.

He got the phone card off an illiterate Yemeni, in return for helping him fill out the seemingly endless number of forms needed to prove your 'right to remain'. In Somalia, when they lock you up and beat the shit out of you, at least they don't also make you fill out forms afterwards. Perhaps this is what makes Britain a developed country.

07972 274398.

The guards hate him because of the revolt. The boys had held the cell for a full night and most of the next day. They couldn't get the door down or they'd have blown the whole joint up, smashed it apart, burned it to the ground. But power had shifted nonetheless. The inmates were in charge, no doubt about that. The guards eventually withdrew altogether and a strange echoing silence pervaded the intake unit, punctuated by the occasional shriek of triumph.

They'd got as far as drawing up a list of demands (the right to apply before you come top of the list) when the storm troopers burst in. These were professionals, not fractious disorderly slobs like the guards but a coherent unit. Big men in helmets and body armour, driving forward with shields outstretched like a Roman phalanx, crushing inmates against the walls, mercilessly beating and stomping the fallen with truncheons and heavy boots, wreaking vengeance for the humiliation of their colleagues.

But Abdi had seen armoured men like this before. He's seen most things before, at the ripe old age of nineteen, and he was not afraid.

He runs his hand along his swollen jaw and grins at the memory of the night they held the cell. It was worth it. He'd take every kick and punch twice over for that feeling of power, the electric buzz of having control, of shouting down the corridors in dozens of languages and dialects and idioms that FUCK YOU, we are the kings here, we will take no more shit, we are not afraid of you.

That's the lesson Abdi Bile has learned from his odyssey: you are stronger than the monsters.

07972 274398.

The prick on the phone makes a full fifteen seconds of fucking kissy-kissy noises before hanging up. Unless he's very intimate indeed with his lawyer, he is taking the piss. This is a line to call for help. This is a line to get them out of this shithole. Anything else is keeping other men in captivity. The next guy gets on. Hurry the fuck up.

07972 274398.

Abdi Bile shoulders the phone prick as he comes back down the corridor, not hard, just enough to let him know he was taking liberties. Big gangly slack-jawed slow-eyed Maghrebi motherfucker, Algerian or Tunisian. There are massive geographical, religious and cultural divides in here. Ties that bind and hatreds that separate, loyalties and enmities you can't transcend, certainly not when all you have in common is a jail cell. He owes this particular dick-head no loyalty at all.

The phone prick hits the far wall, sees who popped him and drops his fists in a hurry. Abdi Bile has garnered something of a reputation around the facility. Ripping out a toilet and waving it over your head on your first night will do that. He doesn't mind playing up to expectations. You get a better night of sleep here if people are afraid of you.

The big blond guard spots the infringement. Easily enough to send Abdi back to the cell. He bounds over eagerly like a dim dog towards its food bowl – until the brutal black and red swelling around Abdi Bile's jawline gives him pause. Abdi glares back with a mixture of boredom and truculence, a prizefighter tolerating a bout beneath his level.

Danny Hodges stares at that battered face and considers. There is an art to inflicting authority. It relies not so much on pain as the suggestion of it. The implication of violence more than the act itself. The terrors of the imagination are infinite. The anticipation is what hurts. The slash, the gut shot, the electric shock, are limited by comparison. Almost, sometimes, a weird relief. And therefore authority is often reduced by violence, not augmented by it.

Danny Hodges's semi-reptile brain does not attain these para-bolic loops of abstraction. But he does know that if he smacks a staunch little hard nut like Abdi Bile and the guy laughs in his face, he's the one who looks like a cunt.

'Problem?'

Abdi stares. Where would he begin? 'No problem,' he says in English.

A long beat, then the big blond twat moves away. The guy on the phone gets off, and the guy in front of Abdi gets on. He's next.

07972 274398. 07972 274839. 07972 274833. No, wait . . .

A bolt of blind terror shoots through him. He's been repeating the number like a *Dua* ever since the night of the crossing. It's the one solid thing he has. The night the white men murdered Omar and left their tiny wooden craft to buck amidst the huge waves, before the lifeboat reared suddenly out of the darkness and saved their lives, the phone number was the only thing that kept Abdi Bile sane. His duty to keep his promise. To remember the number Omar had entrusted to him, and to call Asha.

She can let Omar's family know what happened to him. Make sure he is mourned properly, acknowledged, remembered. Maybe she can even find his body somehow. Asha has been in this country for a little while, maybe she has connections, knows how shit works.

And, he wants her to get him out. Asha is his only contact in this country, his only link however tenuous to the future. Without her help, he could be stuck here for who knows how long? Certainly til he can raise the bribe money, and where would he get that, and who knows if the authorities here are honest enough to take bribes? It doesn't feel like it, at least not from the likes of him.

Reading the newspapers, it seems you have to be rich in the UK to be allowed to bribe someone, and then it's encouraged, even mandatory. Bribery should be open to all like it is back home, it's the only fair system. Abdi Bile's initial impressions of Britain are not altogether positive, though he's trying to sit on them temporarily until he reaches a more supportive environment.

So when he speaks to Asha, he's gonna say he can't tell her what happened except in person. Then when she gets down here, he'll play on her sympathies and see what she can do for him. Abdi feels a little bit bad about this. He knows how exploitative it is, how much it'll churn her up. But he is on his fucking own out here, in a big wide ocean. He needs every bit of help he can get to keep afloat.

He grabs for his wrist, where he'd scratched the numbers in ballpoint, but of course yesterday they finally got their first shower. Just a smudge left. He takes a deep breath. It's in there. Come the

77

fuck on. The number is in there. It's in his brain. He just has to calm down and let it come to him.

07972 427398. No, 274. 07972 274398. That's it. That is definitely it.

He shoots a look at the clock on the wall. Four and a half minutes left. He considers one more time the option of the mobile which a group of Afghans have smuggled into the holding cell, but he's sure the top guy is an informer, plus who knows what price he'll charge?

He puts a heavy hand on the shoulder of the man on the phone, Kerim, a warm-hearted if more than slightly dim Kurd.

'*Habibi.*'

This is a major violation of phone protocol. Kerim flashes a look of irritation and goes back to his call.

'*HABIBI.*'

Now Kerim is angry. He opens his mouth.

'It's for Omar.'

They've all heard the story. And even though many of them have stories of their own not too dissimilar, that one sticks in their collective craw. They didn't exactly expect the red carpet when they rolled up to the UK. But nor did they expect to be murdered by the police.

Kerim thinks, nods, utters a few words of explanation into the phone and hangs up. Abdi Bile squeezes his shoulder and thanks him with his eyes.

He picks up the receiver, the handle slick with other men's sweat and the mouthpiece rank with other men's breath, holds it slightly away from his face, and begins to dial the number.

PART TWO

The Second Burial

Chapter Seven

CHERRY

Five steps. Anyone can do five steps.

One. Two. By the third, pain is shooting through her shoulder. On the fourth step, she slips in blood and nearly falls. She staggers into a fifth step and squats, hamstrings burning, holding his dead weight upright with both hands. If she drops him, she'll never be able to pick him up again.

The rasping in her lungs recedes. She girds herself. Another five steps. One. Two . . .

MATT

The bell clangs and the door crashes open, the gust sending faded flyers for an air show cancelled years back after the pilot crashed into the spectators looping and plummeting. The clock reads 3.43 a.m. The A27 emits an occasional mournful distant whine, like an abandoned dog.

Matt, tall, thin, long stringy hair, black-framed glasses, shoots his head up from his book. Nobody checks in at this hour. Nobody checks in at any hour, not since they cancelled the air show.

A middle-aged blonde woman, really hot in her way (Matt tries to restrict Googling 'MILF' to three times a week cos it's ageist and doesn't really accord with his feminist principles), is holding up a hench, much younger guy. They stagger unevenly towards him. She props the guy on her shoulder with a slight wince, nods at the unbroken row of lumpy wooden numbers with keys attached and smiles at Matt without showing her teeth.

'Twin room, please.'

He doesn't move, stunned by the sudden intrusion of strangeness.

'If you have one.'

They stare at one another till she acknowledges that some clarification is probably required.

'Big night.'

'Yeah?'

'Birthday boy here overdid it. You know the way.'

Matt isn't looking at her. He's staring at the stream of dark blood advancing across the lino towards him, a thin red dog eagerly sniffing out new territory. She follows the line of his gaze. The blood begins to pool at the edge of the check-in desk. They both watch it gather. The bleeding man mumbles incomprehensibly.

Matt chews his hair as if split ends are a magical *khat* that'll give him enlightenment. He looks at the hot MILF. He should probably call the police. Instead, he reaches over his shoulder and pulls down one of the many unused keys.

'Twin room, yes?' He taps the ancient desktop into life.

She shows her teeth this time. Nice teeth. 'Yes, please.'

'Names?'

'Huh?'

'What are your names?'

The woman doesn't reply. She looks around. Behind Matt is a

shelf of dusty household products, emergency supplies for ill-prepared travellers. TCP. Heinz ketchup. Colman's mustard.

'Brandon Pickle.'

Matt's fingers freeze on the keyboard and his eyebrows are lost in the shaggy undergrowth of his hair. His voice rises a half-octave despite himself.

'Brandon Pickle?'

'Correct.'

'Right.' The fingers clatter briefly, sceptically. 'And you are?'

Her gaze runs along the shelf again, alighting on the disinfecting tablets. 'Mrs Milton. Like the poet.'

⚞⚟

CHERRY

The police officer is laid out on the bed, boots off, several towels underneath him to soak up the blood. She undoes his shirt, belt and trousers with swift practised efficiency and casts them aside. Checks his head. There are tears and loose flaps of skin but the skull is intact. She moves down.

The stab wound, which is more of a slash wound, begins just under the ribs and sweeps down in a long ragged crescent across the stomach and into the quad. The good thing is it looks relatively superficial and appears not to have nicked the femoral artery on the way out, or they'd really be fucked.

She examines the point of entry, pulling the flaps of the wound aside, sweeping the blood away with a hand. It spatters across the wall in an elegant parabola. Something for the cleaners to chat about in the morning. Assuming this place has cleaners, for which there is minimal evidence.

She's right. No visible puncture marks in the internal organs.

In fact she can barely see them. The knife has gone through the cloudy off-white layer of subcutaneous fat and lodged in the overdeveloped musculature. He'll struggle with sit-ups and if he has marathon aspirations they'll require a rethink, but he doesn't need the hospital. *If* they can ward off infection. And that's where her problem starts.

Though shallow, the wound gapes wide and will be very hard to close. The muscles on these pumped-up guys are so close to the surface that they stretch the skin out, so when it's sliced it rolls up on itself like a cheap window blind. Nightmare on a Saturday night. Takes minimum two nurses to stitch up one glassed gym bunny, depending on how much creatine and protein powder they've been chucking down their necks.

Cherry looks around. She's gonna need a needle driver, tissue forceps, some form of anaesthetic . . . and some help.

Only one place to go.

～☙～

MATT

'Got any spirits?'

The hot MILF is back. Matt looks up hastily from his phone before slamming it face down on the desk. He's definitely used up one – OK, all – of his three searches.

'Um, what would you like?'

The nice teeth are back again. 'What've you got?'

Matt goes in the back, rummages around for a while, comes back with a large mixed handful of cobwebby miniatures. He waves them at her with a shy grin of triumph.

'Perfect.' She winks at him. 'Wanna come up then?'

The sudden and total evaporation of moisture from Matt's mouth should be studied by flood defence engineers worldwide.

84

'If you can handle both of us, that is.'

Matt slaps an ear as though it might be deceiving him. His throat is drier than the American West. Eventually he hacks up a desiccated cough of agreement, more nod than word.

'Brilliant. I just need one or two more things.'

'Any—' Matt chokes his voice down to its regular frequency with some effort. 'Anything.'

'A heavy needle and thread, like a sailmaker's needle if you have a kit. Also some tweezers. And a pair of pliers. Needle nose, ideally.'

'What?'

Her eyes light up like she's just seen the love of her life walk through the doors of a fancy restaurant holding a bouquet of flowers.

'And this.'

She reaches over the desk and picks up his oversized stapler, slamming the top part hard into the wood to test it and nodding with deep satisfaction. She looks up at the utterly bemused clerk.

'There's a kettle in the room, right?'

'Errrrr, yes?'

'Come on then. Oh, one more thing: how are you with blood?'

<hr />

Not too good, it turns out. Matt twists his head nauseously away from the gaping wound. This is not how he imagined the evening might pan out. For starters, it's the man's groin he's bent over. The fit yet in retrospect *obviously* insane woman is uncapping the miniatures purposefully. The items she requested are soaking in boiling water in the sink. She hands him several open tiny Bailey's.

'Get one of them down you.'

Matt is only too happy to comply.

'Then feed him the rest.'

She returns his quizzical stare with one of bafflement.

'Can't be putting Bailey's in an open wound, are you mad? Dairy.'

Matt can't argue with that on many levels. He helps himself to a second, sucking it bone dry, before funnelling a third into the hench dude's drooling mouth. The guy starts to choke and spit it back out.

The hot terrifying woman looks at him as though he's a complete halfwit. She's decanting mini Jack Daniel's into a large mug.

'Pinch his nose.'

'Eh?'

'Pinch his nose shut,' she says, with the impatient air of someone explaining a card trick to a particularly dim-witted dog for the hundredth time. 'That'll make him swallow.'

Matt does, and the guy does.

'Couple more,' says the hot terrifying woman. 'It's the closest we have to anaesthetic.'

Matt looks up at her, already knowing yet dreading the answer. 'What, um, what exactly are we doing?'

'I'm gonna stitch him up,' she says forthrightly, back to Matt, hands in the sink. She turns round. In her hands are the needle and thread, the pliers and the tweezers. 'You washed your hands, yeah?'

Matt nods. She chucks him the tweezers.

'This is how it works. You hold the wound closed with those. Keep the two edges nice and level, as best you can. I drive the needle in one side, bam, and as far through the other as I can manage. Now it's likely gonna get stuck halfway, flesh being quite dense, so then I grab the sharp end with these,' she waggles the pliers jauntily, 'and yank it through. Tie the thread off, Bob's your uncle. We call that "the first throw". Rinse and repeat all the way to the end. Pretty simple really, though a bottle of Lidocaine and a suture kit would make all our lives easier. Any questions?'

The ball of bile lodged firmly in the back of Matt's throat precludes further verbal communication, but his gaze swings towards the massive stapler sitting ominously on the bedside table. The hot terrifying woman shrugs her shoulders slightly, as though he's made a good point in rebuttal.

'Yeah, well. That's where we have to get a bit unorthodox.'

Oh, *that's* where things get unorthodox. Good to know.

'Cut's got too wide. Wound's started to roll back on itself. See where the flaps are caught under?'

Matt does see, and very much wishes he hadn't. The towel underneath the guy's hips is a sodden morass. Red tentacles creep along the edges of the mattress and down to the floor.

'There's no way you can keep the wound shut without tissue forceps. So what we're gonna do first is, you're gonna shove the edges together by hand and I'm gonna staple them in place—'

She politely waits until Matt has finished gagging and has wiped his mouth, then continues.

'It's fine. Well, it's not ideal, but there's not a lot of other options. If I do a good job, we should be able to pick 'em out afterwards. I'll let you do that, if you're a good boy.'

She grins. For a lunatic, she really does have very nice teeth.

'Before we start all that, you have one other job. Probably the most important.'

Matt can't bring himself to ask. She carries on.

'Hold him down. Hard.'

And with that, she takes the mug of Jack Daniel's and pours it into the length of the open wound.

JAKUBIAK

The dawn chorus awakens him from uneasy dreams. Strange dark visions of black tides, leavened then ended by the high sweet song of birds. The primrose sun of early morn flowers through the window.

He doesn't know where he is. A small grubby room, smears of blood and dirt profaning the gorgeous light. Pain pulsates through him. He doesn't remember falling asleep.

The nurse is leaning against the wall, arms folded. Something about her demeanour suggests she's been watching him for some time. They lock eyes through a sunbeam. Eventually she speaks.

'Morning.'

Andy says nothing.

'We should probably try a formal introduction this time. I'm Cherry.'

He tries to sit up to investigate the pulsing in his abdomen. An electric spasm makes him drop his head sharply back, which causes a throbbing ache in his skull. He moans and tries to find a position that doesn't antagonize either too much.

'You're probably gonna need something of a refresher on last night, Andy,' she says. 'Sorry, I took a look through your wallet. Is it Jake-oobeeawk? That's a cool name. Where's that from?'

He glares up at her from his curled comma of pain. She grasps the bedsheet she's draped across his torso. Instinctively, vulnerably, he flinches. She gently pulls the sheet aside.

'Take a look. Careful now.'

He uncoils slowly, warily, a hermit crab from its shell. A beautifully neat ladder of stitches extends from his ribcage down past his groin to the middle of his thigh.

'I did that,' she says with quiet pride. 'With a little help.'

Finally he speaks, his voice a rusty hinge. 'I tied you up.'

'Just as well you're shit at knots then, isn't it?'

'I'm good at knots.'

'The evidence suggests otherwise.'

'Is that a *staple*?'

'Oh, charming. "Thank you, Cherry, for all your hard work."

Admittedly that is a staple, yes. We did get most of 'em out. Matt found some industrial disinfectant under the sink in the end, so it should be clean at least.'

She levers herself off the wall and straightens up.

'Right. Having sat through a lot of agonizingly dull NHS presentations which I wouldn't wish on anyone except the Health Secretary, I've learned to cut to the topline, which is that I saved your life. Second bullet point is you also saved my life, which potentially gives us something of a basis to work from. Few things to clear up first though. Any questions so far?'

'Where the fuck are we?'

'Motel off the A27. Remarkably shit.'

'What happened?'

'What's the last thing you remember?'

'Knocking Barratt out.'

'Yeah, not so much. He was gonna kill me, wasn't he? That's what you two were rowing about?' Andy nods slightly and regrets it. 'Well, that makes two of us. After you sucker-punched him—'

'I didn't "sucker-punch" him.'

'He turned away, you clouted him. Classic sucker-punch. No judgement. He'd have bitten through your fucking windpipe if you'd done anything else.'

Andy stares. How does she know things like that?

'I don't know what you were gonna do after that. Drive me back to the station, I think. I'd got the rope off by then and I was trying to work out whether to make a run for it when he smashed you in the head with a rock.'

Andy's fingers reach for the back of his skull.

'I fixed that up as well, don't worry.'

He finds a short ladder, though no snake.

'He carries a big knife, doesn't he?'

'A *kukri*.'

'A what now?'

'Japanese fighting knife. He orders them special. From Japan.'

'Well, that would be the obvious place to order a Japanese fighting knife from. You did well. You got up and got in between him and the car. I think you were trying to protect me. Some credit in the bank there, Andy. So he pulled his big Japanese knife out of his sock and went after you with it. Is he totally insane?'

'Roids.'

'How has he still got a job?'

'He's a good officer.'

'That says so much more than you think it does.'

'You hit him? Before he . . .' He mimes a stabbing gesture.

'Not so much before as during. Sorry. Had to go get the rock first.'

He reaches a hand down to his abdomen and takes in what she's just told him. The closeness of his brush with death. The full nature and extent of Barratt's betrayal. The flame of resentment inside him builds to an inferno.

His fingers caress her stitches. Sharp electric pulses of pain with every touch, yet also soothing in their regularity, their neat precision, their embodiment of care.

'Thank you.'

'You are welcome.'

A beat. He offers something. 'It's Jack-ubeeak. It's Polish.'

She nods thoughtfully. 'Interesting. Good to know. So, Andy Jakubiak. Next question.' Her face darkens suddenly. 'What the fuck was that video?'

BARRATT

Freddie Barratt straightens up slowly from investigating the tyre tracks, his limbs stiff and cracking like the embers of the fire before him. He woke cold and grey as ashes, and between the chill in his body and the thunderous ache in his skull he's moving a tad more gingerly than normal. But he's fitting it all together piece by piece, the urgent bloodlust for vengeance simmering beneath the skin.

The smashed phones don't tell him anything, other than someone has wised up. The blood trail round the tyre tracks is somewhat more instructive. From the direction the car drove off, there's no blood on the driver's side and substantial bloodstains on the passenger side. Which means a) she's driving and b) he hurt Andy, though hard to say how badly, and no way to tell if he's gone with her by choice or under duress.

He remembers pulling his knife on a fellow officer. Whatever passes for shame in Frederick Barratt's soul colours his cheeks. Fucking hell, Freddie. There are limits. He'll chuck the Anadrol in the bin when he gets home, promise.

But the question before then is, where does she go?

Back to her husband, most obviously. But with the corpse? And an injured police officer? Husband won't be having that, surely. Not straight arrow Bob. To the hospital then, her mate the morgue twat. But he's a coward, he's not gonna let her put him in any more shit. And she must know those are the first two places Freddie will look.

So where does she go? He could start doing the rounds of hotels in a given radius, but maybe she has friends nearby. No point going off on a wild goose chase. What's the smart play here, Freddie? What does the smartest guy in the room do in this situation?

Freddie Barratt stares into the ruined detritus of last night's logs. He thinks it through until he has his answer.

The smart guy heads back to the station. He takes charge. He gets ahead of what is coming.

There are strict protocols when a police officer does not report for duty. It's a stressful job, and it's got no less taxing lately from Freddie's point of view. The cuts, the kit that's falling apart, the frozen wages, the colleagues who get the chop and the added duties on top. The rates of suicide in the police are so high that if an officer doesn't turn up for work, the first assumption is a suicide attempt.

It's a safe bet that Andy Jakubiak will not be at work this morning. And if Andy doesn't show up, then the alert will go out. Calls to his phone. Calls on the radio. When there's no response, in-person calls to his home. If no one answers the door, they will break it down, like they did too late with poor Nigel Clayborn after his wife left him. And they will find Andy missing, and they will kick off a search.

And who will, naturally, be in the forefront of that search, taking charge with quiet composure yet implacable resolve, with all the accumulated resources of His Majesty's Constabulary at his disposal? Who but Andy Jakubiak's loyal partner and mentor, Freddie Barratt. And that, Freddie, is why you're the smartest guy in the room.

Barratt digs his keys out of his pocket and gets into his car, nodding respectfully at his own genius.

⪼⪻

JAKUBIAK

He tries to front ignorance but one look at her face says it's a waste of time. He struggles, writhes, tries to think of a way to put himself in a better light. He gives up, flops back onto the bed.

'It's a deterrence mission.' He's looking at the ceiling, not her.

'Fuck off.'

'It's only supposed to send them back.'

'Fuck *off*.'

'It's never meant to end like *that*. I didn't know he was gonna do that. I swear.'

'What did you think would happen? They'd shake your fucking hand and go back? Are you mental?'

'I didn't think.'

'No shit.'

'Just they'd be scared off maybe.'

'They've met a lot worse than you, sunshine. Who gave you the right to decide what happens to another human being? Who put you in charge of someone else's life?'

'It's my country too.'

She snorts and spits disbelieving contempt through pursed lips.

'No it isn't. No it fucking is not. It's not your country and it's not my country either, and one major reason is mingy little pricks like you keep getting their strings pulled.'

'I just . . .'

'You just what?'

'I just wanted to . . . I wanted to do something. I wanted a say. Over what happens in my land.'

'How many "deterrence missions" have you been on, Andy, as a matter of interest?'

A beat, then his shoulders slump and he sighs heavily. 'That was my first one.'

She laughs. 'Your first one. Right. Ever feel like you've been had, fella?'

He looks at the elegant curve of his blood on the wall, a kind of strange handwritten confession, and says nothing.

'Well, it's just as well you were there, as it goes. Because that video is what's gonna put him in jail.'

Instantly he shoots up onto both elbows, wincing. 'You have it?'

She's looking out of the window, face illuminated by a bright light from inside as well as out. 'Of course I have it.'

'Where?'

'Never you mind. Somewhere safe. With someone reliable.'

A wave of panic washes through him. If that video gets out, goes viral somehow, he'll be in the same boat as Barratt. He tries to push himself off the mattress. The nurse shoves him back down. Then she sits at the base of the bed and crosses her legs with a certain definitiveness.

'The way I see it, Andy, having had some time to think while you were catching up on your beauty sleep, is we have two choices. Option One is I knock you out with this.'

She pulls the final vial of Largactil from her pocket and twirls it between her fingers. Greasy grey-green acid sludge swirls through his brain. He flinches.

'Don't make that face, mate. Could be worse. Have you seen *Misery*? The Kathy Bates film?'

The expression on his face and the way he wriggles back and instinctively curls his feet away from her suggest he has.

'I didn't know he was gonna do it, I *swear*.'

She rubs the back of her neck casually and looks away. 'We had a cat once we called "Catty Bates" cos she'd scratch us every time we tried to leave the house. Very possessive. Count yourself lucky to get the knockout shot, I'd say.'

A beat. She looks at him and smiles. The prospect of drastic pedal alteration recedes slightly.

'Anyway. Option One would give me five, six hours' head start. But I don't want to do that. Do you know why I don't want to do that?'

He doesn't answer.

'I don't wanna do that because you'll catch me. You know my car, you know my name, you have ways of tracking people I don't know about. You'll catch me. So that brings us on to Option Two.'

She pulls out the crackling laminated photo and displays it for him.

'I'm going to take that boy out there to this girl here. I'm going to make sure that child gets what he needs, which is a proper burial among his people. That is what I need to do, and I'm gonna do it so help me God.'

The passion in her voice could melt steel.

'And you're gonna help me. You know the tricks of the trade. Where the cameras are or whatever. You're gonna help me get there.'

'Why would I do that?'

'To make up for what you've done. Because I think you're a decent person, underneath.'

' "Underneath"? Thanks a lot.'

'And because I can tell them what really happened. How none of this is your fault. You were dragged into it. It's all down to that bald cunt, excuse my French.'

'He is a bald cunt.'

'Get me to the girl, and I will get you off the hook. Your word and mine against his. But fuck me over and you'll be in the frame for manslaughter, at a minimum.'

All the air rushes suddenly out of his body and he slumps back against the mattress, staring again at the spirals of agglomerated dirt and cobwebs that decorate the ceiling.

'Think about it,' she says brightly. 'Your choice. But don't take too long. I'm starving.'

Chapter Eight

ASHA

'Sit down.'

Khadija stands in front of her, face baked into the hard rills of her usual scowl, the two of them inches apart in the thin space between their narrow little beds. Asha is more than a little afraid of Khadija. Khadija is tall, angular, spiky with disenchantment. The men in the kitchen call her Sharp Tooth, though not to her face. In all the months they have unblocked toilets together, scraped grime and grease from ovens and plates next to one another, slept a metre apart, Asha has never seen her smile. There are rumours about how Khadija earned the money to pay for her passage, rumours which Asha finds hard to credit unless men enjoy being terrified and which she has no intention of trying to confirm from Sharp Tooth herself, preferring her face in its current shape.

'Sit *down*,' says Khadija again, ominously.

Asha sits, nearly bumping knees with the tall girl and apologizing faintly. Khadija does not sit. She stares down at Asha for a long moment.

'I told Zelalem,' she says finally.

'Khadi, no!' Asha struggles to rise but Khadija pushes her firmly back down. 'You promised!'

Khadija had caught her the night before, sobbing on her bed.

The stress of constantly checking her phone for days, the gnawing tension in her stomach building and building as time went on and still nothing from Omar – and then finally the call out of the blue from some guy she'd never met, in some scary-sounding place with crashing metal gates and shouting male voices, telling her he had news but could only give it to her in person and she had to come to the scary-sounding place which is somewhere she doesn't know, far away. It was all too much.

For a person living illegally thousands of miles from home, Asha has limited experience of life. She is only seventeen. Until the previous year her father had kept her on a tight leash, segregated from boys and largely confined to the house, her dalliance with Omar conducted under conditions of strictest surreptitiousness and secrecy. He was a delivery boy to her father's house, bringing fresh bread and curds. Soon he was there even on days when there was no bread to deliver, his bag plumped out with a pillow to get past the man on the gate. They met in the back stairwell, hardly touching, hearts aflame.

Then Asha's elder brother died, and with him went the money he sent unwillingly to Asha's father, the tribute of the conquered to the conqueror, and suddenly everything changed. Asha was bundled onto a plane with a fake passport and a real student visa. Her father is a bureaucrat somewhere deep in the bowels of government, so he has access to such things. 'The British will sell anything to anybody, everybody knows this,' he reassured her when she asked him if the scheme would work. 'You will be fine. Besides, they are always on strike there now, nobody will ask you questions.'

Asha was so excited on the plane she could hardly stay in her seat. The home of Harry Potter and the Queen (RIP)! Sure enough, when she arrived the border staff were too swamped and resentful to check her paperwork properly. Zelalem, the owner of the restaurant where she was to work, fat and greasy with wandering paws, met her on the other side.

Despite the long hours and sharing literally a cupboard with

Khadija and the fact that everything she earns goes straight to her father, she is still excited. She loves the novelties, the idiosyncrasies: the squawk and bounce of how London girls talk, the slouching swagger of how London boys dress, little nuances of English like how 'shit' and 'sheet' are similar but so different, yet 'I'll see what I can do' and 'It's possible' both mean 'No'.

It's all such a rush compared to her stultifying former life. Sharp Tooth growls at Asha's naivety and mutters dark warnings about how she won't feel the same when she's been here for years and years, but Khadija will never know the suffocation of her father's house and anyway Omar is coming and they can be properly together and it's all part of some incredible adventure.

But Omar has not come, and instead this strange boy has called. 'Abdi Bile'. It can't be good news. Nobody withholds good news. Dread churns through her insides, and horror at what might've happened to Omar, and resentment that the boy in prison is stringing out her suffering. At least it sounds like a prison, this 'intake unit', far out of London on the southern coast.

How can she even get there? She has no money. She has the fake passport but the visa has expired. She's barely ever left the small tangle of back streets where she lives and works. Zelalem won't allow it. He says it raises the chance of an immigration raid, where the government comes in the night and disappears you into administrative darkness where no one will find you. And he definitely won't allow her time off, he never does.

She unwisely confessed all this to Sharp Tooth in a tearful overwhelmed gush and extracted a promise in return that she wouldn't tell the boss. And now Khadija has betrayed her.

'He'll tell my father!'

'He won't tell your father.'

'How do you know?'

'Because I told him if he told your father, I would cut off his penis with a chopping knife and shove it up one of his nostrils. It's small enough to fit,' says Khadija, with the toneless inflection of a woman confirming she's sent the email ordering new stationery.

'*Why?!* Why did you tell him?' Asha is so caught up in her own story that she misses entirely what Khadija is trying to tell her between the lines.

'Because otherwise he wouldn't have given you the time off.'

'What? He's . . . But—'

'Look,' says Khadija grumpily and roots around in the pouch of her apron, withdrawing a substantial handful of crumpled notes and tarnished coins. 'We had a collection. Enough to get you down there.'

Asha looks at the money and then tentatively back up, scarcely daring to believe her good fortune.

'The guys did this voluntarily?'

'I made them do it voluntarily.'

'Oh, Khadi,' says Asha, and heedless of the potentially violent consequences, buries her face in her friend's middle and holds her close for some time.

Anyone who does not know Sharp Tooth Khadija would swear that what flickers then across her razor lips is a smile.

ROBERT

The crack of dawn and her colleague is here again. What does he want now? Robert's already stressed out enough. It's been hours since he spoke to Cherry, there's no sign of her and every time he calls it goes straight to voicemail. The last thing he wants is to talk to Michael.

Robert looks down on Michael from the landing window as he hops from foot to foot like a lizard on hot sand. Pressing the doorbell, putting his ear to it, looking around with arms raised as if appealing to an invisible ref, pressing the bell again. There's something spectacularly irritating about this guy. Robert got sick of interviewing weirdos while on the beat, pen patiently poised for the pointless point as they blathered on. The public were one of the main reasons Robert quit the police. That and the institutional racism. If you want to hate the public, take a job in public service.

And yet Robert was always able to get on with it, whatever life threw and continues to throw at him. So why do people like this fella apparently get out of bed every morning completely bamboozled by basic social interactions, like the Guy Pearce character from *Memento*? That was a great film. They don't make films like that any more in Robert's opinion, though he hasn't been to the cinema for well over three years. Lockdown, not his fault. How the hell did what's-his-face go from that to *Interstellar*, three hours of a man travelling across multiple universes and time planes to end up behind his own bookcase?

Robert's cinematic musings are interrupted as Danielle shoulders him aside on her way downstairs.

'Answer the fucking doorbell.'

'Don't talk to me like that, please.'

'Then answer the fucking doorbell. I feel like I've got tinnitus.'

'I don't want to answer the . . . Danielle, I said don't . . . *Leave* it.'

Danielle opens the door.

'What?' she growls.

'It's your mum,' says Michael awkwardly, holding his phone out in front of him, combined peace offering and protective amulet.

'What about her?' says Danielle, in the tone of a hostage taker deciding which surplus hostage to shoot first.

'She's sent me this video.'

～⌒～

BARRATT

Freddie Barratt kicks in the door of Andy Jakubiak's studio flat. He's never actually been inside. Neat, self-contained, orderly, with virtually no distinguishing features. Not unlike Andy himself. Come on now, that's harsh. He showed some balls, Andy, to be fair to him. He also overstepped the mark, and that is why he must be punished.

Classic rental. Featureless, designed to leave as little trace of its rolling cast of temporary inhabitants as possible. Magnolia walls, taupe carpet, grey sofa that folds out into a single bed. He had Andy down as a futon kind of guy, dunno why. Freddie hates futons. Like sleeping on padded cobblestones. Deliberately uncomfortable. Fucking hippy shit. He's livid at futons and the owners of futons for a second or two, til he reminds himself there isn't actually one in the room.

Rows of Andy McNab paperbacks arranged in alphabetical order in an Ikea bookcase. McNab can fuck right off. Money for old rope. Freddie could do way better if he put his mind to it. He's often pondered a police procedural with a hard, possibly bald hero with radical views unacceptable to chickenshit liberal society, whom nobody understands but who does his fucking job nonetheless. McNab did write a book on successful psychopaths which Freddie quite enjoyed, to be fair, til it started to feel a little close to home.

'No body here at least.'

He points towards the kitchen. 'Check in there. I'll take the bathroom. It's more likely he's hung himself in the shower than put his head in the oven. Statistically.' Freddie's quite enjoying this.

Lisa Bailey, the policing equivalent of Andy's taste in interior decorating, a mousy, instantly forgettable woman who'd bleed beige if you cut her, nods nervously and takes a cautious step into the kitchen. Freddie asked for her specially because she'd be least likely to ask awkward questions. He sticks his head into the bathroom for effect and winks at himself in the mirror. All going to plan.

'Detective Inspector.'

Lisa is calling him. When he enters the kitchen she's holding up Jakubiak's police radio with a concerned expression. It squawks disconsolately with the disembodied voice of the dispatcher.

Freddie looks around. Scattered plates on the table, half-eaten food, a glass of protein shake which has separated into soggy mealy powder and water and has a dead fly floating in it. He'd called Andy from outside the flat with no warning.

'Any sign of his phone?'

Lisa shakes her head.

'What d'you think?'

The policewoman looks surprised. Freddie Barratt is not exactly renowned for asking opinions of others, especially females.

'Looks like something urgent.'

'Mmmm. Now what do we think that might be?'

'I don't know, sir.'

'A call, maybe.'

She shrugs. It's obvious to both of them that Barratt is sketching out his preferred version of events, so what's the point of dragging it out?

'Yeah. Perhaps someone he was hoping to hear from.'

ROBERT

'I say she sent it. It was from a number I don't recognize. But it must be from her.'

Michael props the phone on the dinner table and presses the white arrow. The sounds of rain and wind and waves suddenly enter the stifling quietude of the house, washing oddly against the fitted carpets. All of a sudden Robert is plunged into a world he hasn't been in for some time, a world of fear and action and uncertainty, and he realizes he's missed it, badly. Danielle comes up behind him, curious, and as it starts the two of them recoil in unison. Their gasp sucks the air out of the room.

The dead boy looks just like Liam. Same face shape, bone structure, inherent grace of movement. So when the huge boot slams into the side of the boy's head, then when the second time it crushes his face and his neck snaps back and he disappears, it's like watching Liam die.

None of them were here when he hanged himself in his bedroom. That's why he could. That's what all three of them have been running through in their minds, over and over, in their own individual hells of regret. What if I'd come back early? If I'd not gone for that beer? If I'd forgotten something? An unexpected return, a charge up the stairs, arms around Liam's legs, holding him up, rescue . . . Fantasies of salvation. The many tortured iterations of 'if only'.

But none of them saw him die. In fact neither Robert nor Danielle even saw his body until much later, when the spark of truth, of unmistakable life, was no longer in him. And so to watch this living boy who could be their flesh and blood be murdered in front of them isn't just a shock, it's a landslide, an avalanche that buries the heart. For a moment Robert loses all his senses, like he's drowning in air, surrounded only by his monstrous breathing and a tinny buzzing in his ears. His hands flap by his sides, the wings of a broken bird. He hears a gasp and the thunder of feet and a door slam and a howl of pain from Danielle's bedroom, and he remembers who and where he is.

He lowers his forehead onto the wooden table, appreciating the smooth cool grain against his forehead, and breathes in a couple of times. A tentative hand on his shoulder.

'I'm sorry.'

He gets it together, sits up.

'I thought you'd better see it,' says Michael. They both listen to Danielle sobbing her heart out.

'They were very close.'

'I know.'

'She's not got over it. Not even started really.' Robert exhales again, the weight of it all too much to carry alone suddenly. 'She blames her mum.'

'Why?' Michael has heard Cherry's side of this at length, but never from the other angle.

'She and Liam argued a lot. She thought he was malingering. Which compared to her patients you can see why she thought that, but . . .' Robert takes another breath. 'Depression. We didn't really understand it, you know? In a kid like that. Big strapping boy, good at everything, everything in front of him. Hard to . . . Hard to accept it's real. Not just in his head. Though not for her.' He points upstairs. 'She always knew.'

Danielle continues to howl.

'How about you?'

'Do I blame her mum?! What kind of a question is that?'

'Have you got over it?'

There's a gentleness and a generosity in the man's voice that cuts Robert to the quick, opens him up and angers him at the same time. He's not used to being listened to, his feelings being sought. He changes the subject so he doesn't have to answer.

'That's the lad? The body they took from the morgue?'

'It is, yeah.'

This explains a hell of a lot.

'Have you heard from her?' Michael asks, without much hope.

Robert shakes his head. 'Not since you were here before. I've tried her phone any amount of times but it's always straight to voicemail.'

'Me too.'

'When did you get this?'

'Last night. It must've come through while I was asleep.'

'Did you call the number it came from?'

'I did. Also voicemail. It's a guy called Andy. I wouldn't swear to it, but he sounds a lot like one of the cops who came to the mortuary. The young one.'

This is bad. This is very bad.

'She's in bother, isn't she?'

'She is. Yes.'

✦

CHERRY

The first stage of human decomposition is called autolysis, or self-digestion. It begins about four minutes after you die. The blood stops circulating and waste products, mainly carbon dioxide, build up in cells, turning them acidic. The acid ruptures the cell membranes, releasing enzymes which begin to eat the cells from the inside. Muscles stiffen. Little fluid blisters appear on the skin, eventually bursting to give a characteristic sheen.

Cherry touches Omar's arm. It's stiff and the sheen is obvious. And the skin is coming loose too, which is bad. That's the next phase. The skin loosens and the body begins to bloat and swell with the gases and waste products of decay. That's when things start, literally, to get messy.

So that gives her, what? Less than twenty-four hours to get him to his girl in a state she can present him in. The good news is London isn't far away. It's a small country. There's just the minor issue of actually finding her.

She drags the rough blanket back over the top of the body

where it's lying on the back seat, but it doesn't entirely cover the dead boy. She tries to shove Omar a little further out of view, but the rigor mortis makes it difficult. Omar's legs have stiffened where they're dangling off the seat and the ankles have hooked under it and won't come out. She fumbles with the dead feet for a while, but they won't shift, locked into place, and she can't move the body without help.

She gestures at Jakubiak and he takes an involuntary step back, shaking his head vigorously, mingled disgust and disbelief on his face. Suddenly she's blindsided by self-doubt.

Is this remotely respectful to this poor dead child, dragging his slowly decaying corpse hither and yon on some wild goose chase? She remembers the gross obscenity of the Queen's body being schlepped all over the nation like a misplaced Ocado delivery, amid weeks of painfully crude propaganda that would've embarrassed the North Koreans. The darkly hilarious line of companies tripping over themselves to 'pay tribute': Delta Force Paintball. Peperami. The British Kebab Association. Joking with colleagues in low voices at the flagrancy of it all, at the transparent weakness of the regime.

But is she any better? Now it's her turn? Is she too not just using a death for her own ends?

She backs away from the car and bumps into Matt. He leans unmistakably into the contact. She steps back. Matt grins and waves something long and hard at her. Number plates.

'You'll need different plates.' Clearly he's been thinking this through on her behalf, or just watches a lot of *CSI*. 'They'll track you down in no time with yours on.'

He tries to peer into the back seat of the car. Cherry blocks him. She's told him they're 'on the run', which visibly increased his ardour. She hasn't told him why, or who else might be on the journey.

'Where'd you get those from?'

'My boss's car.'

'Obviously.'

'Switched 'em with yours.'

'And he won't notice?'

'Pissed out of his head most of the time. Shagging the day recep-
tionist in the Aspire suite as we speak. It's not really a suite, truth
be told. More of a large bedroom with bath and shower space
attached. I wouldn't recommend it, not for the price.'

Cherry thinks again of Liam. He's her lodestone in all this. The
way she feels about him is the one thing she knows she can
trust. She knows she failed him, and she must do something to
make up for it. And she knows most of all if she hadn't had his
body to wish goodbye to, his grave to visit whenever she needs,
that she would be irretrievably broken, even more than she is
today. And so she must give this boy and his family the same thing.
She must.

Matt waves a screwdriver suggestively at her. 'Shall I screw them
in then?'

'You do that.'

He squats down to do the front and squints back up at her.
'D'you know *Thelma & Louise*? That old film?'

Cherry was seventeen when 'that old film' came out. She went
with Abbie Parkin and Samantha Morris, and they *screamed* when
Louise shot the rapist. Jumped up on the folding seats, punched the
air, dropkicked their popcorn into the neighbouring rows. Used 'I
apologize', 'I apologize also' in a drawn-out Southern drawl as a
secret code between the three of them for *everything*. Didn't bring
in homework for the others to copy? Crashed and burned chatting
up a hot boy? Borrowed an item of clothing to go out in and forgot
to bring it back the next day? 'I apologize.' 'I apologize also.' She
also rubbed herself raw over a then unknown Brad Pitt, but who
didn't? That lingered only so long.

The feeling of watching the film and thinking that she too would soon be free like that, free from all the orders and the systems and the officious busybody dickheads, an open road of endless human possibility stretching out in front of her, stayed with her for years. It sits inside her still, somewhere. Did she ever find that open road? Is there maybe still time?

They don't make films like that any more. Or do they? Cherry doesn't really know. She hasn't been to the cinema for about four years (lost the habit in lockdown, not her fault) but it seems like it's all superhero shite. Talk about a giveaway that your society is irredeemably fucked: the only way it can imagine someone having any basic agency, let alone triumphing over evil, is to have them bitten by a giant radioactive spider or whatever.

But it was the time too, what it meant at the time. Maybe no movie can mean the same to her at 48, a fair few laps into her journey round the block with no obvious purpose to it, as it did at seventeen, when everything is bright and untainted and shining with infinite possibility and she knew where she was going and why. Things *meant* something then. Songs and films lodged in your heart and became part of who you were. Now things just *are*, and there are far too many of them.

She walked past a bunch of kids sprawled on top of each other on the grass the other day, just hanging out, and imagined what it must be like to be them. The thrill of possibilities, the novelty of your body and mind rubbing up against someone else's, maybe for the first time out of the control of schools and parents and structures. The truth and joy of just being alive, outside of all the bullshit. She realizes she wants that back badly, that thrilling sense of everyday life meaning something.

'You remind me of her,' says Matt, who has finished the plates.

That's sweet. 'Which one?'

'Um, the hot one?' Good, she'll take that.

'I mean, they're both hot. The old one?'

Cherry strokes his face gently before Matt can screw this up any further. 'You take care now. Thank you for your help.'

Matt watches them depart, the groin area of his jeans in serious danger of immediate rupture. The MILF quota is getting rinsed to fuck today, and he does not care.

Chapter Nine

CHERRY

Not a well-known part of the country this, Hastings/Bexhill way. Shitty transport links have saved it from the terrible fate of most of south-east England, becoming hollowed out dormitories for middle management commuters and freelance IT consultants. The villages are Tory, though not as obnoxious as Surrey or as racist as Kent, but the towns got an overflow of bombed out East End factory workers after the war and still have that old school sense of community. Leftish in that genial, lackadaisical, talkative way that was common in our big cities, before gentrification destroyed working class communities and precarity swallowed working people's free time. Idiosyncratic. Fond of a drink, fond of a dabble in minor crime, not especially fond of working shit jobs to fill someone else's bank account, and isn't that what life is all about really? A pint and fish and chips on the beach and if you pay me in cash mate we can skip the VAT. People are carpenters and photographers. They do P&D and they paint canvases.

It all reminds Cherry of the South London in which she grew up, which is now lost and gone for ever. It's why they came down here; that and it was where they could afford. The older men remind her of her dad, a mechanic who in his spare time made the most extra-ordinarily delicate and inventive sculptures out of worn-out and discarded car parts. He never showed them to anyone apart from her. Said they weren't made for showing. Once, when she pressed him after a few drinks, he said what did he know really, he wasn't a 'proper' sculptor. But he'd taken her to every sculpture exhibition the Royal Academy ever had, still in his oil-stained overalls if work had overrun but no shame amidst the sniggering well-upholstered regulars. Captivated, his head tipped to one side, peering like an inquisitive Modigliani at the stone and wood and bronze.

A grievous pang of longing runs through Cherry Bristow. She wishes she could talk to her father one more time. He would know what to do. He would know, instinctively and without asking, why she was doing it. And he would be proud.

'Take that,' says Andy Jakubiak, pointing at a little slip road. She does, then looks at him. He's peering back in deep discomfort at the shrouded figure looming in the back seat and sniffing the air. And it's true, there is definitely what might charitably be described as a tang. Cherry rolls down her window. Jakubiak turns to her.

'ANPR.'

'Which is?'

'Automatic Number Plate Recognition system. There are cameras on all major roads. The streams go to a central database and they're kept on record. If we don't wanna be tracked, we need to stay on the country lanes.'

She's pleased at his use of 'we'. 'Even though we've changed plates?'

'Maybe that weird skinny lad's boss isn't as pissed as he thinks. The minute they have our plates, they can find us.'

Cherry smiles brightly.

'See, that's what I keep you round for.'

They drive on through lanes overhung with oak and ash and hornbeam: holloways, ancient roads curved in on top of themselves with time and age. High banks like green cathedrals, trees pressed together above their heads like hands in prayer. Below them a path that was trodden into being like grapes into wine by centuries of peregrinations and transportations, millions of feet and hooves and cartwheels slowly wearing down the resistant earth. Nobody knows that these days, of course. They just think it's the B road to Sedlescombe.

Then suddenly the silent green cloisters disappear and they pop out into fields of livestock and stands of coppiced chestnut. Low post and rail fences, frontages of pleasant houses, semis more than detached, or low bungalows in small private grounds. Little glimpses of hidden worlds, the secret lives of fellow citizens Cherry will never meet.

They pass a field full of llamas, then another. When did that become a thing? What do they use them for? It must be the fur, you can't eat llama surely. Can you shave them to get the fur, or do you have to kill them? Is there a massive market for llama products in a visibly collapsing state? The basic economics of this country grow daily more impenetrable to the naked eye.

'How long have you been in the police, Andy?'

Andy's head hurts, he can't find a comfortable position to sit in and the smell in the car is getting worse by the minute.

'What is this, a blind date? Yeah, I'll have fifteen wings please mate, extra hot, and a large Peroni. She'll have the lemon and herb.'

'I would never have the lemon and herb. Is that because I'm a girl?'

'You're not a girl.'

'Tell me about it.'

But she does feel like a girl. Youthful and energetic, stripped of the soul-sucking burdensome accretions of adulthood: the council taxes and the parents' evenings, the parking fines and the Zoom meetings. Most of all, she feels like *herself* again. For the last two days she's been the Cherry she remembers, or at least thinks she remembers, being as a young woman: decisive, clear-headed, capable, *funny*. She hasn't felt like this, been this Cherry for years. Since long before Liam died.

Where did the real Cherry go? How did she lose her? She makes herself a promise not to let her go again. She realizes with a shock that she's not just doing this for the kid, she's doing it for herself.

She spots a little roadside café half hidden in the woods, cheery red 'OPEN!' sign propped in the whitewashed window frame, and pulls into the small empty car park beside it.

'What are you doing?'

'Eating.'

'With him on our tail? And *him* in the back?'

'I've always said never let a man of any kind get between a woman and her food, though admittedly this is pushing it. Aren't you hungry? I'm *starving*.'

'You don't know Barratt like I do,' mutters Andy darkly.

'He's not fucking . . . *Minority Report*, is he? He's just a bald racist twat with a computer,' retorts Cherry. 'We've switched the plates, that's gotta buy us some time. There's no one else here. Come on. My treat.'

☙❧

BARRATT

Freddie Barratt finishes deleting the last of the CCTV footage from the hospital car park.

Pleasing meeting with the detective super and a couple of regional top brass earlier. Freddie thinks he acquitted himself pretty fucking well, all things considered.

'If you don't mind, sir, I'd prefer not to involve too many others at this stage. I'd like to take care of it myself. I do know him best. And I don't want any stain on his record, you know, a big operation that's held against him afterwards. I don't think there's anything to be concerned about if I'm totally honest, boss. Let's just get him back and keep it to ourselves.'

Barratt the kindly uncle. Grizzled heads nod in unison. Definitely a shared preference for discretion. Who wants to admit they've lost a police officer down the back of the settee? A chance for Freddie to 'take control of the narrative', as they say in the PR training sessions.

It can't be a cop kidnapping. That would mean total chaos. A MISPER (missing persons) designation for Jakubiak, the National Crime Agency called in, an emergency 'red room' set up, a high-ranking Senior Investigative Officer called down from London to take charge of it. The works. No expense would be spared for a missing police officer. It'd be national news type shit.

That situation would get completely out of Freddie's control. Very quickly there would be questions he could do without, such as who's that distinctive-looking hairless chap in the background of this footage in which we also find the missing constable. Or at least that would be a question, had said footage not seemingly been auto-deleted by the hospital surveillance system.

The story he's planting instead is an unlikely *amour fou*. Freddie doesn't use the words *amour fou*, obviously, he's a little more graphic. 'Thinking with his dick, sir, if you don't mind me saying.'

They don't. We are cops. We talk like men. When we're fucking allowed to.

'Rush of blood to the head. The real head, if you know what I mean.'

'Who is she, DI Barratt?'

'A witness he met the previous day, sir. A lot older than him. He acted very strange around her, made some excuse to clock off early. He's kind of a lonely kid. Easily led. You might've seen I've been making an effort to take him under my wing. Duty of care and all that. We find her, I'm pretty sure we'll find him.'

Barratt the concerned mentor. More nods. A clap on the back from the super on the way out.

That puts him in a good spot. Couple of days' grace at least. No one looking over his shoulder. Plenty of time to do the necessary.

Right then. Let's see what she's about. There is a little glimmer in Freddie's amygdala that respects Cherry Bristow for getting away from him, and is excited by the chase.

He puts Cherry's plate number into the automated system.

CHERRY

Inside, the café is warm and cosy with lovely red-and-white chequered tablecloths, the waitress is smiley and welcoming and the only other occupants are a cheerful, quite deaf old man called Bob who genuinely tips his cap to her and his adorable English sheepdog, which lies at his feet gazing up at him besottedly and snapping up frequent treats. Her name, Cherry soon ascertains, because Bob tells her loudly about four times, is Leila.

She orders pancakes smothered in butter and maple syrup for her and bacon and eggs for Jakubiak, who has gone to the loo. He takes so long over it that the food is on the table by the time he comes back. In the meantime she fusses over Leila and casts half an eye on the TV in the far corner, which is tuned at low volume to one of those twenty-four-hour rolling channels full of news so constantly depressing that there's no way anyone can actually watch it for more than forty-five minutes tops. War. Famine. Pestilence. Inflation. The four horsemen of the fuckoffalypse.

There's a piece about a crisis in one of the public services, but Cherry can't hear which one. Does it really matter though? She's thought for a long while that it'd be easier to start the news by listing which public services *aren't* in terminal collapse, which would save time for more transphobia and attacks on refugees and charities. The problem with the 'managed decline' of British society isn't only the decline part. It's that it's managed by Sam fucking Allardyce, sticking the big man up front and lumping it into the mixer in a desperate attempt to scrape a draw and avoid relegation.

Suddenly there's a brief image of somewhere Cherry knows very well: the main road about four streets over from where she was born. Then another image of people shouting furiously. She's on the verge of getting up to see what it's all about, but at that moment Jakubiak returns and takes an irritated seat.

'You alright? Thought you might've gone full Elvis on me.'

'Couldn't, could I?'

'Couldn't what? Eat so many deep-fried squirrels you have a heart attack on the bog?'

'Couldn't *go*. Nothing's working.' He shoots an accusing glare at her as though somehow she's worked some surgical witchcraft on him, but she's too busy ploughing through her breakfast to care. What with Danielle's carcinogenic efforts last night (how was that only *last night*?!), and the weird lunch with Michael, and waking up on the beach the morning before, not to mention all that's happened in between, she realizes she hasn't had a proper meal for over thirty-six hours. Jakubiak too is plainly famished and for some time the only sound is the clatter of forks on plates. When they're finished, they feel mutually better disposed. Nothing promotes companionship like eating together.

Jakubiak pushes his empty plate away, having virtually scraped the top layer of glaze off it as well as every scrap of food. Cherry goes to pay and comes back. Cash, obviously, untraceable. Not everywhere still takes cash these days, which is utterly mental, but this place does.

'So what's the plan?' enquires Andy, somewhat sceptically.

'I told you,' she says, carefully bringing out the laminated photo so as not to draw attention to it. 'Find her.'

'Yeah. I'm still waiting for the "How" part.'

Cherry taps the road sign with a fingernail. 'Go to this address.'

'—son Street, NW 10 is not an "address".'

'It's part of an address.'

'Brilliant. Just fucking drive around the whole of London till we find it, yeah?'

'Not the whole of London,' she says reasonably. 'Just that bit.'

'Right. And what then? We stand around on the street corner with a corpse in the back, asking if anyone's seen this girl? Who's almost certainly illegal herself and will be way undercover.'

'Got a better idea?'

Andy exhales loudly and drops his head onto the table with a thump that makes the forks leap. 'Seven years,' he mumbles with his face in the nice tablecloth.

'Seven years what?'

'Seven years is how long I've been in the police. You wouldn't fucking believe it, would you?'

'What d'you mean?'

He sits up. 'Look at me.'

'You look fine. Bit bruised.'

He ticks them off on his fingers. 'Groomed by a madman. Kidnapped by a witness. Absconded with a corpse. Yeah, it's all gonna look fucking awesome on the CV.'

'When you put it like that . . .'

'Detective Inspector here we fucking come.'

'What made you join?'

'Why?'

'My husband was in the force.'

'So I heard.'

'I could never understand what made him do it.'

Andy thinks for a moment. 'The sense of order, I suppose.'

'Rearrange your CDs alphabetically if you want a sense of order.'

'Who has CDs?'

'Usually no one accidentally shoots a black kid four times in the head doing that.'

'I wanted a place to belong. A place to fit in.'

'How's that working out for you?' She regrets being sarky when she sees the look on his face.

'It's hard out here, you know? It's like there's so many different ways you could go it's impossible to choose, but then you can't get to any of them and nobody helps you and when you can't get there you're made to feel like it's all your fault.'

A strange doleful bell clangs in Cherry Bristow's insides. She's had this conversation before.

'You sound like my son.'

'Yeah?'

'He said the same. Couldn't work out where to go. Couldn't find a place to fit.'

'Yeah? What did he do?' Andy is genuinely interested. The way he looks at her *so* reminds her of Liam: the same desperate intensity of need, the same vulnerable uncertainty. Except suddenly she can't see him because her eyes are prickling and sparking. She wrenches her head away. She takes a couple of deep breaths, controls herself. In the distance she can hear a dog barking. She turns back.

'He killed himself,' she says calmly.

Andy is squirming in his seat and staring fixedly down at the tablecloth.

'I'm sorry. I didn't mean . . .' he says, without raising his eyes.

'No, it's fine. Not your fault.'

'I didn't—'

'Really, it's—'

'I've *got* to piss,' he says, tries to levitate from the table, howls with agony as he yanks his stitches and hobbles painfully away.

Perhaps the squirming was more than just embarrassment. Poor kid.

The barking is louder and more urgent. Cherry looks across the room. Bob and Leila are gone. She looks into the car park. The sheepdog is standing on her hind legs with her front paws pressed against the side of Cherry's car, barking furiously. Bob is peering into the back seat to see what could be causing such a ruckus.

Cherry stands up urgently, knocking over a coffee mug. And that is when she sees, parked right next to the entrance to the café, a police car.

⁂

BARRATT

Almost instantly Freddie registers a hit. A tangle of country lanes off the A27. Well-known dogging spot, as it goes. Which means they have CCTV in the vicinity, though not so much for law enforcement as for the free amateur pornography. Freddie can neither confirm nor deny that he might have availed himself of the facilities at some juncture, though the cameras were mysteriously off on those evenings.

He's almost disappointed in her. Thought she'd put up more of a fight. Shagging *now*? Of all times? The weakness of the flesh. And he was right about Jakubiak too. He's never really wrong about people. Perhaps that's why he hates so many of them, because he can predict them so easily.

He reaches for his phone and his car keys and zooms in on the plate hit. The image resolves itself slowly. He leans forward. Then he leans back.

It's not her car. It's an Audi A4.

Right, so Andy got her to switch plates. But why keep the plates and change the *car*? Something is fucked up. He zooms closer. A man's head appears. Bristly toothbrush moustache, slicked-back hair, general unfortunate resemblance to Ned Flanders. OK, so maybe she's moved on, found a better mark, though Freddie knows he's stretching it now. Then another movement and a woman sits up, scraping her hair back from her face and breathing heavily.

Right. So unless the nurse is a fucking master of disguise and has lost twenty years, gained four stone and become fucking *Asian*, it's not her. Freddie slams a furious fist onto his desktop.

It's fine. It's fine. We move on to plan B, that's all.

～≫≪～

ROBERT

Robert picks up the phone. He was never very popular at the station down here. It's kind of a provincial place and he was always too urban, too experienced, honestly perhaps a little too possessed of melanin to make them feel comfortable. Plus by then he was already half checked out, already doubting his commitment to the profession. But there are still people he can call.

'Lisa speaking.'

Lisa Bailey might seem lacking in confidence, but these days most of that is a facade designed to get men to underestimate her. When Robert got there though, it was absolutely true. Without really meaning to he took her under his wing, taught her to trust her insights, not to apologize for having opinions, to keep plugging away when she was knocked back or patronized or overlooked. It's not something she'll soon forget.

'Hi, Lisa, it's Robert Bristow here.'

'Robert! So lovely to hear from you. How've you been?'

They make small talk for a while, catch up.

'Look, Lisa, can I ask you something? Apropos of bugger all.'

'Of course.'

'What's Freddie Barratt been up to lately?'

A beat or two. 'How do you know about that?'

'How do I know about what?'

☙❧

CHERRY

She sits back down as casually as she can manage and watches the two officers get out of the car. A lanky middle-aged string bean with grey hair and a tiny petite blonde half his age who nonetheless looks weirdly like him. Perhaps they're related. There must be a sitcom somewhere in the world about a lovable father/daughter cop combo and the many endearing scrapes they get themselves into. Robert and she used to watch the police procedurals that are almost the only thing on our screens now that don't feature the royal family, mainly so Robert could point out all the mistakes and technical errors. Danielle HATED it. She called it 'Copaganda Night at the Bristows'.'

Neither of the cops looks, thank God, over their shoulders at the wildly excited dog and the inquisitive older gentleman. Instead they walk hungrily into the café and look around. Cherry's blood briefly freezes solid in her veins, but they catch sight of the waitress and break into easy conversation. So they're locals. Not looking for her. How fucking long is Jakubiak going to be in the toilet?

She's not the only one who's noticed the arrival of the police either. Bob is attempting to come back in, making a Sisyphean effort to haul a deranged Leila away from Cherry's car, straining at the leash, advancing inch by inch. Cherry panics, thinks of diving through the door of the gents, but it's in full view of the whole room. Instead she remembers seeing that the toilets are a kind of outhouse, built as an extension onto the main café and hopefully with some kind of window or ventilation in the back.

᷐᷐

JAKUBIAK

Andy Jakubiak can finally, gloriously, urinate. All the stress, the weirdness, the pain from the impromptu surgery, had combined to gum up the works, no matter how insistent the demand. It had taken two visits to the loo and a relentless mental focus on a film he once saw about Niagara Falls (so awesome, he's never been to America, he must go), but at last he's flowing freely and copiously. He takes a deep, satisfied breath and looks upwards.

The nurse is staring down at him through the dirty rectangle of mesh above his head. He shrieks and instantly desiccates again.

'WHAT THE FUCK—'

'SHHHH. It's nothing I've not seen before.'

'I was *unconscious* then, it was different.'

Her eyes flicker downwards for the briefest moment. 'Not particularly.'

'Will you fuc—'

'The police are here.'

'What?'

'And the old man has found the body.'

If it was possible for the human body to retract urine, Andy Jakubiak would be doing it right now.

'Finish up, walk *very* casually outside without making eye contact with anyone, and meet me at the car. Now.'

Chapter Ten

BARRATT

Plan B is telematics.

In the old days, the target switching plates would've been a big problem. But in our modern mass surveillance age, there's always something else the authorities can use, and in this case it's telematics, the 'black box recorder' of the road.

There is a powerful little computer stashed away in the guts of lorries and cars, monitoring speed, fuel consumption, tyre pressure, all sorts. It's the norm now in commercial fleets, but insurance companies sometimes insist on them being installed in domestic cars too, to give them more excuses to turn down claims. Most modern cars will have one, unless you insist they take it out.

From Freddie's point of view, the great thing about telematics is that the computer also contains a SIM card, for constant informational transfer, which means the car can be tracked by GPS. So assuming the nurse's car is new enough, which it is; that they haven't changed vehicles, which seems unlikely cos where would they get a new one, and why would they have bothered switching the plates on the old one if they had; and finally that Andy Jakubiak was either too junior to know about telematics or too busy looking up chest workouts on his phone when they did the briefing, which seems inevitable, then Freddie should be back in the saddle.

He fires up the GPS system. Sure enough, it pings up a hit.

∽≈∾

ASHA

Asha gets off the train. It's been a strange journey. She was taken aback not so much by how crowded it was, standing room only but still not as bad as at home, as by the abject misery of the people. Beaten down, dispirited, silent. They didn't even talk, bar mumbled rages into phones, and never to each other. At home shared discomfort is an excuse for shared conversation, but here everyone remains locked in their own private despair. The views out of the window are no better: packed motorways, concrete flyovers, high-fenced yards piled with twisted shards of broken metal, glum tracts of housing stolid and unremarkable in the sheeting rain. Tangles of tracks like clogged iron guts. Perhaps the rich parts of Britain are somewhere else.

Khadija had warned her there would be cameras everywhere. Not honest ones that look like real cameras but little bulging bug-eyed dark orbs that burst out of stanchions and roofs like mushrooms after rain, the fruiting bodies of a society's moral decay. She tries to avoid them as best as possible, having heard dread rumours from the men in the kitchen about something called the Home Office, but the little sneak cameras are hard to see and harder to avoid. And the more she makes a special effort not to be noticed, the more noticeable she feels. She shivers. This is a different, more scrutinized sense of menace than she is used to.

The town she finds herself in does nothing to raise her spirits. Grey, sullen, simmering with the furious anonymity of a guilty man entering court with a baseball cap pulled down over his face. Not many people in the streets compared to London, and they're largely old and white and seem to be in terrible health, shuffling and cough-ing through their daily routine. Many of the shops are boarded up. Even the Cash Converters, where Asha bought her phone in London, is closed here.

Eventually she thinks she finds the 'intake unit'. It looks like the picture she found of it online: same banal cheap manufacture in raw livid brick, same underlying sense of exploitation. Lots of young people, many of them Chinese, some who look like her, a strong contrast with the surrounding town. There's not as many barbed wire fences as in the picture though, and the kids come in and out of the building very easily for what is supposed to be a prison. Where are the guards?

Asha lingers outside for a while, unsure what to do. Eventually she plucks up the courage to approach a charismatic hijabi girl with a raucous cackle who is laughing and joking with friends in Arabic, a language Asha learned from her mother, and shyly ask her a question.

'*Habibti*, is this the "intake unit"?'

The girl smiles politely but in bafflement. Perhaps she doesn't call it that, or know the English term. Asha translates what she thinks it means into Arabic.

'A prison for young people who aren't supposed to be here.'

The group creases up and breaks apart, howling with laughter. Asha can feel her face crimsoning with the hot blood of shame. She starts to pull away when the hijabi girl puts a firm hand on her arm and scolds the rest into silence.

'Shut up! Shut up! Stop making her feel bad!'

She turns to Asha.

'I'm sorry, *habibti*, it's only funny if you know what this place is. It's student accommodation.'

BARRATT

The bitch's car is visible on Freddie's screen plain as day, thirty miles or so north-east of here, making steady progress through the country lanes in the general direction of London. Freddie's good mates with Lee Jenkins, the station commander round that way. They're both part of a WhatsApp group that shares, let's call it an uncompromising perspective on social issues. Barratt pulls his phone out.

'Lee? Freddie. How are ya? You check that link I sent you? Fucking rapists mate, that's what they are. Fucking child rapists. How many more times? Course the government won't do fuck all to 'em cos they're brown. State of this country. Anyhoo, it's something a little closer to home.

'We've got a runner, pal. One of ours. That young lad I've been mentoring? Yeah, I thought so too. Not sure, but there's a woman involved. Thinking with his dick as per, correctimundo. Personally I wouldn't do her with yours, but there we have it. Each to their own.

'Look, Lee, I don't wanna ruin this kid's future. If it goes MISPER, he's fucked. Out on his ear. Let's just do this on the downlow. I've got their car on GPS, I'll send you the coordinates. Get a unit to pull 'em over and keep 'em til I get there. No drama. Brilliant, mate.'

⁓⁓

Brian Hamilton, the tall grey police sergeant, has *finally* managed to get rid of the annoying old man and the barking dog and is midway through his full English when his radio goes. Brian listens to his station commander in stony silence, chewing steadily on a piece of eggy toast.

'You are having a laugh.'

'What d'you mean?'

'You are having a fucking laugh, Lee.'

'I don't get you, Brian, sorry.'

'They were *here*.'

'Excuse me?'

'A middle-aged blonde woman and a bulky younger guy?'

'Correct.'

'They were *here*, in the caff. They drove off like ten minutes ago.'

'Then it won't take long to catch up to 'em, will it?'

'I am halfway through my full English,' says Brian the sergeant, with the outraged disbelief of a nun pulled out of the queue for an audience with the Pope. He receives predictably short shrift for his breakfast-based alibi, hangs up and turns to his colleague.

'I'm afraid we'll have to go, love.'

'That's alright, Dad . . . Sergeant. I'm finished anyway.'

'I told you! I TOLD YOU!' shouts Bob gleefully as Brian and his daughter leave the café, both studiously ignoring him. Leila barks deliriously. The police car pulls out into the lane like an alligator sliding into the river from a muddy bank.

ROBERT

The three of them sit round the table with much-needed glasses of wine, even though it's ten a.m. Danielle finishes hers in one go and holds it out again, raising what's left of her recently self-threaded eyebrows (which frankly look like the part of the Amazon the Bolsonaro government gave away to soya conglomerates, not that Robert would *ever* have the balls to say this to her face) when a refill is not immediately forthcoming. The ghosts of tears track down the side of her face. Robert gives her a long slow stare and fills her glass part way up again.

'So let's reprise,' says Robert.

' "Reprise",' snorts Danielle.

Robert slides the glass of wine away from his daughter. She slides it back.

'She finds the body on the shoreline, which she then escorts to you,' he starts.

'Correct,' says Michael.

'That's where she meets this younger officer. Andy. Do we think there's something between them?' He says this in such an uninflected, dispassionate tone that Danielle shoots him a glance of genuine concern from underneath her scorched stumps, a look Robert doesn't see.

'I don't think so,' says Michael. 'I never got that impression. Also she knocked him out with an industrial strength sedative, which isn't normally the hallmark of a functioning relationship.' Michael can be dry when he wants to be.

'But he's working with her.'

'We don't know that at all.'

'He's not answering his phone. He's not been in contact with his superiors, which is an absolute no-no.'

'We know that because?'

'Because Barratt is looking for him. Lisa says he's managed to keep it all under wraps so far, taken it all on himself. A one-man search operation.'

'Lisa?' says Danielle.

'Ex-colleague.'

Danielle manages to convey scepticism, intrigue and titillation in one grunt. She downs her wine for the second time. Robert takes her glass away.

'Why would he be working with her?' puzzles Michael. Robert shrugs.

'Any number of reasons. Personal. Sexual. Financial.'

'Financial? Where's the money in this?'

'Well, if he's not working with her, and he's not in contact with the police, that means she's got him under some kind of constraint, or coercion. He's a big man by all accounts. Do we think she's capable of that?'

A pause as all three of them think of Cherry, and independently conclude she is very much capable of that.

'So that puts her with at least one and potentially two heavy, quite distinctive burdens.'

'In a small car.'

'She's gonna have to keep out of sight, take her time, side roads. Where do we think she's going?'

'It's got to be London,' says Michael.

'Why?'

'Because of the photo.'

Robert looks quizzically at him.

'She found a photo on the body. She showed me at lunch. Young girl, big smile, taken in London.'

'OK. And you could tell that because?'

'Road sign behind her. NW 10.'

'Cherry didn't hand this picture in? With the corpse?'

'Didn't trust the cops with it, she said.'

'Fairs,' says Danielle. 'I wouldn't. Cops are cunts, end of.'

Robert bristles, which of course is the exact reaction Danielle is looking for. They've been through this any number of times and somehow he always falls for it, always lunges right into her trap.

'She seemed to think the girl was connected to the boy, maybe family or a girlfriend, and could be traced somehow,' adds Michael.

'Who is she? What's her name?'

'I have no idea. I don't think Cherry does either.'

' "Traced"? Traced in what way?'

'I don't know. I'd have thought that was more your department.'

'You don't know *anything* about her? Nothing at all?'

Michael shakes his head. Robert leans forward in mounting disbelief.

'You think she's taking a dead body to London, possibly in tandem with either a captive or a cooperating police officer, to look for a girl she doesn't know anything about, whose name she doesn't even know, based on a photograph she found on the corpse?'

'I do,' says Michael. 'I think that's about the size of it, yeah.'

Robert massages his temples hard, then presses his hands against his face. He blows out air between his flattened palms like a surfacing whale through its blowhole.

The thing is, this is why he loves her.

'Do you think you can draw a picture?' says Robert.

'Of what?'

'Of the photo Cherry showed you.'

'I only got a look at it for a few seconds.'

'It's important, Michael.'

'I do have a half-decent memory, though,' murmurs modest Michael, a man so gifted with detailed recollective powers that he could challenge the average photocopier.

'It could make all the difference. Everything in it. The girl, the sign, the background. Whatever you can remember.'

'I've actually been taking night classes. In life drawing,' says Michael with a shy smile.

CHERRY

As they get further from the coast and into the blast zone of the London commuter belt, the houses get bigger and the atmosphere gets colder. Thick laurel hedges and high wooden gates with digital keypads block sight of all but sprawling gables and tall chimney stacks. Glimpses of manicured gravel drives. The space between the homes expands markedly. The only people on view are servants of the modern type: tree surgeons and gardeners, cleaners and Ocado drivers. But no sign of the inhabitants. Discretion is what they pay for here, the right not to have anyone overlook their gardens and more importantly the bank accounts that paid for them. The primary purpose of getting rich in Britain is to tell everyone else to go fuck themselves through the medium of bricks and mortar.

These are not the *real* rich though. Those live in town, when they're in the country and not in Dubai or Florida or until recently Russia. These people are their fluffers and pimps, their fellators and facilitators, their pinstriped enforcers. These are the houses of investment advisors and structured finance specialists, tax manipulators and setters-up of offshore holding companies. Of expeditors of corporate monopolies and promulgators of shareholder dividends, of consultants to oligarchs and hedge funds and members of the House of Lords seeking lucrative government contracts for essential services they don't even pretend to provide, at vast ruinous expense to everyone except their school and college friends in government. The very worst people in Britain, basically. *Times* columnists and George Osborne notwithstanding.

Cherry glances at her watch. They're making good time. Two, three hours to north-west London, depending on the route they choose. She even allows herself, if not an outright whistle, then a small hum.

And then, in the rear-view mirror, seventy or eighty metres away, the police car appears.

No sirens, no lights, but a purposeful pace, the intent lope of the predator. It gains on them, the wolf closing inexorably on the deer. It's one of the greatest achievements of Cherry's life not to hit the accelerator. Stay calm. Don't give anything away. Perhaps it's not after them after all. But it closes. And closes. Panic rises in her throat. The driver is on his radio.

It's the grey string bean from the café. Beside him is the tiny blonde. Cherry fucking floors it.

Without realizing it, she's hit the gas going around a blind bend and chicanes straight through another, giving them a good lead before the police can respond. Sixty metres, seventy. Her foot is jamming the accelerator down so hard she can feel the jackhammer vibrations of the chassis up into her thigh. Screaming and shouting from Jakubiak. She scans desperately from side to side. No turn-offs, no side lanes, no places to hide. The road straightening and giving them away. The shitty tinny car that was all she could afford betraying her, her pursuers growing large in the mirror again, lights flashing this time, siren still off.

She sees a small side road and cuts for it at a sudden dead angle, rear fishtailing out, scree of grit and chippings in her wake like in *The Dukes of Hazzard*, Saturday afternoon childhood treat TV. How fucking cool is this, thinks Cherry Bristow, for a long, strange moment observing herself dispassionately as though perched on her own shoulder. I was never cool, I never looked like Daisy Duke, and I *definitely* couldn't drive like her. Until now. The things we can do when we're freed from care. When I'm in prison, I will hold these memories tight and rock myself to sleep with them.

Another sudden side lane, this one even smaller, not been paved for ages, the tinny car leaping and bucking amid the potholes like a can being kicked down the road. The police bump along behind but she's gained distance again via her manoeuvres. It leads along the rear of some sprawling pile no doubt acquired by nefarious and malevolent means, thickets of rhododendron obscuring the wages of sin. It occurs to Cherry that this is likely a domestic track, leading to their thoroughbred stables or some shit. A dead end. Run to ground. A strange peace spreads through her at the thought, that the burden will be lifted off her, the decision taken out of her hands.

But it's not a dead end. A sudden lunge left and the trail pops back out onto a proper road, a road moreover that forks just ahead. The chance to confuse her pursuers revives Cherry's fighting spirit. Foot to the floor again, she picks the left-hand fork. If in doubt, always choose the left.

Except in this instance, her instincts may have led her astray. Two quick curves and she rounds the second to a dead end, the wide sweep of a gravelled cul-de-sac in front of an enormous house. They're right on top of a slim dark-haired woman who's closing a massive set of spike-topped metal gates with a keypad. Cherry swerves to miss her, unavoidably screeches to a halt, all momentum gone, the police surely moments away. The dark-haired woman bunches up her face and opens her mouth in fury.

Then she looks in the back of the car, and screams.

Chapter Eleven

CHERRY

'They'll go in a minute,' says the dark-haired woman. 'When they don't get an answer.'

The three of them cluster round the entryphone screen, watching the cops hammer the buzzer over and over. Nobody moves. They breathe shallowly. The concerto for buzzer in E minor ends in a long coda of sonic irritation before the tall one throws his arms in the air and they drive away. A long collective exhale fills the room.

'Won't they be back?' asks Cherry.

'I doubt it,' says the woman. 'They didn't see you come in. There are other houses, other roads they must check. Now, who would like maybe a cup of tea?'

'Kill for one,' says Cherry. 'Three sugars, please.'

They're in a kitchen so big the sound of their conversation echoes back to them, which only increases the sense of unreality. When the dark-haired woman opened the metal gates and urgently waved them inside and down into a huge subterranean garage, they were too baffled and grateful to ask her why. She's still given absolutely no indication as to why she's helping them out.

The woman futzes around for a bit and then puts mugs down in front of both of them. The thunks on the mahogany table resonate loudly round the huge room, vibrations coming from the empty acres of polished metal fixtures and delicately veined marble flooring. From the pristine state of the eight-ring gas stovetop, it doesn't look like it gets used all that often.

'Three sugars,' says the woman to Cherry archly, more judgemental over her nutritional choices than her sudden arrival with body in tow.

'Not my fault. Years of night shifts,' says Cherry defensively.

'Sugar is horrendous for regulating your glucose levels,' says Andy.

'So is being punched in the face.'

'No it isn't.'

'Wanna find out?'

'That doesn't even make any sense.'

'What was your name again, darling?' The woman has an earthy voice and an endearingly broken nose which means her excellent bone structure isn't too annoying.

'Cherry.'

'Sweet. Like the French?'

'Like the Coke,' says Cherry, who's been through this exchange before. Who names their child after a fruit? she has asked her mother many times. What else made the shortlist? Pomegranate? Guanabana? Guanabana Bristow has a ring to it, to be fair. She's missed a trick with Danielle there.

'I am Radka.'

'Andy Jakubiak,' says Andy Jakubiak.

'Pleased to meet you, Andy.'

'Cheers for taking us in.'

'My pleasure.'

'Can I ask why?' he enquires, eyebrows raised. But something more urgent is on Cherry's mind.

'They must be following us, right? That can't be a coincidence, the same cops. How?'

'Do you have phones?' asks Radka.

'Ditched 'em.'

'Then it must be the GPS in your car.'

'There's GPS in our car?'

A vague guilty memory of a briefing he wasn't really listening to cos he was reading about new techniques for the Romanian Deadlift washes through Andy's mind. He decides not to mention it.

'I assume so. Most new cars have it. I only know this because Alasdair – that's the owner of the house – is absolutely paranoid about being traced or listened to. He has some kind of a blocker over the whole area. About half a mile in any direction. So they won't be able to follow you here.'

'Alasdair sounds very normal.'

'He is not normal.'

'Sorry, that was that English thing where you say the opposite of what you think.'

'No, I understand. In the Czech Republic we also have this, what would you call it? Acid irony. It's quite strong in our literature. Have you read Hrabal?'

'Who?'

'Bohumil Hrabal. One of our classic novelists.'

'Not heard of him, sorry.'

'I would recommend *Closely Observed Trains*.'

'I'll take that on board,' says Cherry. She sips her tea. It's excellent. 'What does this Alasdair do to earn a crust then?'

'He is an oil trader.'

'Right. Honest day's graft.'

'No, in fact it's much worse than you think,' says Radka, blowing a steady stream of smoke from her roll-up. 'He's a speculator. That's why energy is so expensive, not some fucking war bullshit. The propaganda in this country is so funny. Growing up under end-stage Communism is great for understanding British society, you know? So many similarities: the powerlessness of the people, the corruption of the leaders. The transport system here is vastly inferior to the old Czechoslovakia. Also, we only pretended to work. You really do.'

She breathes out smoke again, and just a little fire.

'Alasdair puts oil into these huge floating tankers and sails them around the world in endless loops so they can drive the prices up more and more and more. This is his job. Denying people heat and light. So he is directly responsible for many deaths.

'All for this place,' she circles her hand above her head as if waving an invisible lasso, 'where he hardly ever is. He's a very nice man, of course. A bit weak. Bad chin. I ask him why he does this and he tells me if he doesn't do it, then someone else will.'

'And where is Alasdair now?' asks Jakubiak.

'I believe Uzbekistan.'

'Handy. For oil anyway,' says Cherry.

'They boil their dissidents in it, so I am told. I don't know if that's before or after they sell it to Alasdair.'

'So it's just you here?' asks Jakubiak, tiring of hydrocarbon politics.

'Fiona is in the Maldives. She's an unhappy lady. Oscar is at film school in London. The tree guys will be here soon to cut the hedges. But otherwise yes, just me. Cleaning an empty house.'

'How long've you been here?'

'About five years,' says Radka. 'I mean, not in the building. I go home at night. I'm not Rapunzel.'

'You seem very educated.'

'For a cleaner, you mean.'

'No, I—'

'I don't accept this. That stupid people do the manual jobs and smart people do the email jobs. In my experience it's hundred per cent the other way round.'

Cherry thinks of the hospital porters' wit and surreal hilarity on crushingly long night shifts, compares them to the bovine conformity of the managerial class above her, their vicious panicky resentment of any form of challenge, and regrets what she said. She's been asked to cross the picket line in her head and become management any number of times. She'd rather be an Uzbek dissident.

'I am educated,' shrugs Radka. 'I have a degree in organic chemistry. For a while I worked in a lab not far from here. But you know, the usual bullshit: rota squabbles, people stealing your lunch from the fridge, ugly men trying to fuck you. Same as the Czech Republic. My boyfriend is Alasdair's accountant. This job came up, so I took it. I have a lot of time for reading.'

'So *that's* why you let us in,' says Jakubiak.

'What do you mean?'

'Cos you wanted some company.'

Radka looks puzzled. 'I'm not lonely, if that's what you mean. When I say I have a lot of time for reading, I mean I have a lot of time for reading. I *like* reading. No, I thought it was obvious why I let you in.'

'Not to me.'

Radka leans forward and stubs out her rollie.

'Don't you know what you have in the back of your car?'

BARRATT

'Disappeared? What the F U C K do you mean, disappeared? How can they just fucking *disappear*?'

The rest of Barratt's peroration reaches a pitch of outrage high enough to concuss passing birds and ends in an almighty crash.

Lisa Bailey knocks politely on the door to his office, stifling a giggle as she does so. Dickheads like Barratt are the biggest threat to her bland facade, her cult of no personality. They don't half make it hard not to laugh at them. No answer, so she knocks again. A raging grunt of acknowledgement.

She opens the door to find Freddie standing over the smashed remnants of his phone, ruminating on the detritus like a Greek oracle sifting through the burned intestines of a sheep, searching for signs, hidden meanings. Or possibly just his SIM card. Shards of glass from the touch screen are embedded in the wall next to him.

'Anything I can do for you, sir?' asks Lisa, with as straight a face as possible.

'You can get me a new fucking phone,' says Barratt, without looking at her.

꧁꧂

CHERRY

'I'm a witch,' says Radka with calm unshowy conviction, the way another woman might say she's good at interior decorating.

The three of them are back in the enormous underground garage where they skidded to a halt in chaotic exhilaration at their escape from the police. The cavernous space could stand in for one of Alasdair's oil tankers in a pinch, but contains just Radka's Mazda, a pink soft-top convertible that sits expectantly like a pair of pouting glossy lips ('Fiona's little runabout,' says Radka dismissively), and Cherry's hatchback. They are staring into the back seat of the latter. Radka is also holding a black bin bag with several lumpy items jostling in it, which she retrieved from the bowels of the kitchen. There is unmistakable fear on Jakubiak's face.

'A witch?' he asks nervously. Andy is not a horror devotee. He

139

has never even made it through the first episode of *Stranger Things*.

'Sure,' says Radka. 'Also housekeeper and organic chemist.'

'And literature buff,' adds Cherry.

'This too.'

'The diverse skillset of the modern woman. Is it an A level, witchcraft, or more of an NVQ-type vocational qualification?'

'Don't make fun.'

'Sorry, I . . . It's not every day you hear . . .'

'It's not pointy hats and riding on brooms. It's more . . . normal than that. Like if somebody widened the TV screen of life a little bit and you can see beyond the frame of what others can sense. I've always been able to see and hear things. Ancestors. Spirits. For a long time I was afraid of it. Then I realized it is something much older than me. Witches are women who have been cursed and persecuted and locked away because they knew things powerful men did not want them to know. And so it's resistance, forming connections with other human beings and with the forces beyond us. There are many more witches out there these days, now everything has gone to shit. It's a form of love, really. Love in a time of despair.'

'Well, I quite like the sound of that,' says Cherry.

'So, can you, like, talk to him?' queries Andy, glimpsing the potential positive dimension to the dark side. 'Find out who he is, and where to take him?'

The withering look Radka gives him could eliminate more crops than climate change and genetic modification combined.

'It's not spiritual FaceTime.'

'No, I know that—'

'It's not fucking . . . Yodel from beyond the grave. I can't ring up the dead for a chat and a set of delivery instructions. "Please leave corpse behind shed if not in." '

'I'm sorry,' says Andy, abashed. 'Then what can you, you know, see?'

'I can see his spirit,' says Radka, pointing.

⚞⚟

OMAR

A refugee camp on one of the Greek islands. A space hacked into the dying olive groves for three thousand people which now holds twenty thousand or more. The olive trees are dying from climate change, the relentless heat and the lack of water, but it's winter now and temperatures at night are well below zero. The UNHCR tents are raised off the ground on wooden pallets. The shabby tarps and lean-tos further out in the groves have no such luxury. People freeze to death regularly on the cold bare earth. There are gangs of feral dogs.

Omar keeps to himself. There's hardly ever electricity and at night the darkness feels engulfing, like it's sending out tentacles to drag down and swallow unwary travellers. The dark here is a monster from ancient legend, a modern Scylla and Charybdis. This journey is constantly testing you, setting out obstacles and digging pit traps, seeing if you have the practical and moral wherewithal to get by. You cannot survive this odyssey without both luck and courage. If there was ever a chosen people on this earth, it is those who make it through this trial by fire and water and bureaucrat. If we had the courage they do, we would write them into our songs and stories.

Out in the shadows of the camp, behind the mounds of rubbish piled higher than a tall man can reach and the waves of rats that pulse from them like nightmare living tides, there are men with knives. The rage, the boredom, the frustration, the poverty. All

141

night long young men and teenage boys stagger into the tents of the volunteer medics with stab wounds. Women wear children's nappies during the hours of night, which chafe and rub them raw. They piss and shit themselves rather than risk going out into the darkness where the toilets are. On the first of each month, when the residents receive their tiny allowances, the supermarket beside the camp runs out of wine and brawls puncture the air all night long. Just because people share a common source of misery does not make them allies, or well behaved.

Omar had a tentmate who paid him a little money for the berth, a likeable Syrian who caught some kind of brain fever (the notorious 'camp flu': virulent meningitis, according to the medics) and was shipped to a hospital. They say the Syrian was sent to Athens, escaped from the hospital by tying his bedsheets together and climbing out of a third-floor window, and now he has a good job as a waiter. Or he dressed up as a hospital orderly to get away and is now working as a mechanic, or as a construction worker. It all depends on who's telling the story. But in all of the versions, he is sending good money home to his family.

Others say that when they treat you in hospital in the big cities they have to process your application to stay, or best of all your application to move on to the richer countries of Europe: Germany, France, England. This is something the local authorities here flatly refuse to do. For a while Omar went round getting people with camp flu to breathe on him, but he never caught it.

He had another tentmate, a skinny Yemeni who said he was twenty but looked no more than fourteen, but he had screaming fits in his sleep. Eyes wide open, limbs absolutely rigid, a howling sound as if from the guts of hell. The worst thing was the kid always said he slept through the night, didn't remember a thing. He even claimed Omar was making it up to charge him more. He was very upset when Omar kicked him out of the tent.

So now Omar keeps to himself. He moves around the camp a lot, avoids the shifting allegiances and changing loyalties as different groups rise and fall in power, wax and wane in number. He does occasional jobs for a local farmer, hauling rocks and cutting wood. The farmer is a nice guy. Taught Omar a few words of Greek. '*Malaka*' is the most common one. What does it mean? asks another migrant worker, a tall angular Sudanese. 'It means a man who . . .' says the withered old Greek in his battered felt hat, and vigorously jerks his hand in front of his crotch to general hilarity. *Malaka* also appears to be a term of endearment, in fact a term for pretty much everything. They sprinkle it on their speech like salt on food.

The bleat of the goats in the yard is soothing. It reminds Omar of home. He doesn't intend to stay long though. His plan is always to move on. To find Asha.

❧

ASHA

The hijabi, whose name is Marwa, leads Asha through a tangle of suburban streets. The houses remind her of the people on the train: crowded together in forced proximity, yet absurdly trying to pretend nobody else is there. Eyes rigidly out front, holding their shoulders millimetres away from each other as though if they don't touch they can maintain the pretence that this is the life they always wanted. Cheap wooden fencing between them. Mean little strips of grass in front, often paved over with concrete or tarmac. This is not the world a migrant expects to see, the world of the mundane and the crude. These are not the promises which put them into the boat or under the lorry or, in Asha's relatively privileged case, onto the plane. The banality and the unhappiness disturb her far more than the lack of wealth.

She asks Marwa why the people have paved over their tiny areas

143

of grass instead of growing flowers or fruit, and her new friend says, in a voice reserved for dim children and libertarians, that it's so they can park their cars. Asha can see this, but she can also see there is plenty of parking in the streets. She speculates that it's a matter of control. Something to stamp on, to be master of, even if it's just grass.

Marwa is a loud person. She's from Hull ('a place in the north, quite shit') but her family is from Egypt, which explains the Arabic. She's studying IT and computer science. 'It's fucking boring wank mate, to be honest with you, but it's where the jobs are, know what I mean?' Marwa has long polished red fake nails and a dissident laugh that sounds like a flock of birds squabbling and she likes an adventure. Asha keeps trying to dissuade her from taking her to the intake unit, she can just show her the way on the phone, but Marwa won't have it.

The houses scatter, replaced by the peripheral detritus of the English provincial town. Run-down garden centres. Shabby garages with oil-stained forecourts. Industrial barns of crinkled metal in garish colours, lapped by lakes of tarmac siloed off into white-lined boxes, the British obsession with fake privacy again. Large white letters on their sides: B&Q. Sainsbury's. Poundland. Asha doesn't know what these buildings contain but they obviously exert a great pull on the local people, who trudge in and out of these prefabbed temples in supplication.

Eventually these too fade away and the intake unit comes into view, glowering even more sullenly than in the pictures, surrounded by nothingness, scrub land dotted with bushes and torn plastic bags. The barbed-wire fences loom higher and thicker than she imagined, topped in places with shredded clothing, institutional sweatshirts which flap noisily in the wind like the remnants of some flawed and ruined flag. Otherwise a striking silence. Barred windows with heavy glass between the bars. Nobody comes in or out of the large steel gates. The only movement is a tangle of crows brawling over a discarded box of chicken bones. Asha shivers.

For the first time, Marwa's smile fades. She turns to her new friend. '*Habibti*, what exactly do you want here?'

⁓⁓

CHERRY

'His spirit won't leave his body,' says the suburban housekeeper-witch.

Cherry is not what she would call a spiritual person. Never got far with the guided meditations and scented oils and whale music, the imprecations to 'open your mind'. In the weeks after Liam died, a surprisingly large number of people sidled up to her and nudgingly asked if she believed in life after death. Sent her links to mediums, or the emails of friends who'd used some kind of spiritual lifehack 'and it really helped'. It made her fucking *furious*. The cowardice. The refusal to face hard reality. She might be coping with that reality by getting fucked out of her head several nights a week and slowly torching all her key relationships, but at least she's never taken consolation in lying feelgood bullshit, in which so many people seem to be immersing themselves these days.

But she believes Radka. Straight away and unquestioningly, she believes her.

'When I saw you drive like an imbecile, I was going to give you shit.'

'Thanks.'

'I certainly wasn't going to hide you. But then I saw his spirit. And I have to help that.'

'Why can't he? Leave?'

'I don't know. It's different in different cultures. The spirit is unhappy for some reason. It's turbulent, can't find peace.'

'Because of the way he died?'

'Possibly. The most common reason is because it needs a proper burial.'

Cherry spins towards Jakubiak, validated, strangely exultant.

'I told you! I told you he needs a proper burial!' He stares back at her, glassy-eyed.

'But there is something he needs even more, at least right now,' says Radka. 'Speaking with my organic chemist hat on. Not to mention a functioning sense of smell.'

She inverts the bin bag. Out fall several large boxes of Maldon sea salt.

ROBERT

Robert is packing a bag. He is a man prone to over-preparation. Five pairs of underpants or six? How many shirts? Should he bring an extra jumper? Shaving kit as well as toothbrush? He only means to be away for a day or two. Definitely not shoe trees, that's a step too far.

He sighs. It's been a long time since he was on the road, working a case, tracking down suspects, the thrill of the hunt. A long time since he was out of the house overnight, to be honest. The idea that he should be back in the saddle at long last, but that the suspect is *Cherry* . . .

He drops in a family-sized bottle of mouthwash, then relents and takes it out again. The bedroom door flies open and Danielle stands there stocky and unrelenting.

'Right. There are microwave dinners in the freezer—'

'No.'

'It's just a day, two max. Mrs Hilton will pick you up if—'

'No.'

'I have to find her, Danielle. Whatever you may think of your mother, she is in big big trouble and I'm not going to let her—'

She swings a backpack off her shoulder and onto the floor with a thump.

'I'm coming with you.'

Now it's Robert's turn to refuse.

'No. No chance. I don't have time to babysit—'

'Babysitting? Who's babysitting who? You're lucky to have me.'

'All due respect, you don't know anything about—'

'I understand her better than you do, Dad.'

'No, you don't.'

'Yes, I do. I know the way she thinks. I've always known the way she thinks. And there's no fucking way I'm letting you do this on your own.'

❧

JAKUBIAK

'It's a really good point,' nods Cherry. 'Should've thought of it myself earlier.'

'What is?' asks Andy suspiciously.

'Bit mad to do it with Maldon though.'

'About fifty pounds' worth there,' laughs Radka. 'Dishwasher salt would work better, but we don't have any. They are never here to use the dishwasher.'

'To do *what*?' snarls Jakubiak. He can tell something unpleasant is coming, and they're taking the piss out of him about it.

'A basic method for preservation of organic lab samples is immersion in saline environment. Osmotic withdrawal of cellular water slows the process of decomposition.'

'Speak. Fucking. English.'

'We're rubbing salt into his skin, Andy. To stop him from rotting,' says Cherry pleasantly.

'We are *not* doing that.'

'We don't have a lot of choice, really. He's bloating now. You noticed the smell. Hard to miss. Like the lady says, this is the best thing we can do for him. Given the circumstances.'

'It's very effective, actually. Also inhibits microbial growth,' chips in a grinning Radka, lab tech *manquée*, grievous loss to science.

'No. No no no no no no. Fuck that.'

'Driving round London with that stench coming out of the car is probably not the smartest plan. And it'll be a nicer trip for both of us. All of us, really.'

'What the fuck is *wrong* with you?'

'A question I've been asked so many times and still don't have a good answer for, mate.' She leans forward, sombre all of a sudden. 'I'm not bringing him to his people in a state they cannot be proud of. In a state they can't bury. Maybe they do open casket in his culture. Maybe they don't. Either way I want him looking his best.'

'His fucking *best*?! Oh yeah, Tinder money shot there.'

'It's fine, Andy. Really. You go back to the kitchen and have another cup of tea. Radka and I will take care of it.'

Andy Jakubiak picks up one of the large boxes of salt and in a towering rage hurls it against the wall. It explodes in a shower of glittering saline snowflakes, creating a sudden and unseasonal Christmas snow globe effect around the three of them.

'STOP TREATING ME LIKE A FUCKING *CHILD!*' he screams.

The fury and hurt in his voice echo off the walls of the cavernous garage, drifting through the air among the white crystals. The women fall silent.

'Do you think I'm only doing this because you threatened me? Do you think that's all I'm about? I wouldn't fucking be here if that's all it was. Your son killed himself, you're in horrible pain, you think this is something you can do to make up for it or whatever, I get that. It's fucking nuts, but I get it. So how come it hasn't once crossed your self-absorbed little mind that maybe, just maybe, I need to do something too?!'

When Cherry raises her eyes from the floor, she sees there are tears in Andy Jakubiak's eyes. She coughs gently.

'I'm sorry, Andy. I am. I've been selfish. I apologize.'

'I apologize also,' says Radka in a small voice.

'If we're going to do this, then let's fucking do this.' He shoulders roughly past them to the car. He takes a deep breath, wrenches the car door open, wrestles the stiff corpse out of the back seat, places it on the ground with surprising gentleness, and pulls off the blanket.

All three of them gasp. They can't help it.

For a start there is the sudden waft of decay, the repulsive stench of putrefaction that chokes the back of the throat. But then there is what has happened to Omar since they last saw him. Amid the bloating the skin is also loosening, puckering and withering like old leather. The sheen on it is more obvious now, the dark internal leachings of degradation. The stiffness in the limbs means they no longer look like they belong to a person. They remind Andy of old tree roots he saw on his father's land as a young boy, one of the few times he was ever allowed to visit him. Washed down from the mountains decades before, relics of ancient forests and antique floods. Hardened and weathered, still tormented somehow long after their demise, twisted and entangled around each other.

And yet in his nakedness, his total openness, the dead boy has never looked more vulnerable, and therefore more human.

Andy rips open one of the boxes of salt, grabs two big handfuls and begins to rub it forcefully in. Almost instantly he retches. The sensation of the boy's skin is even more horrifying than the smell. Disgustingly gelatinous to the touch, squidgy and squashy and shifting with every motion, a horrid sensation like small live jelly-fish causing little ripples under the leathered skin. He gestures, still furious, to the women to join him at his work, and they do.

'It will work better,' opines Radka tentatively after some moments, 'if we also put it inside. Into the body cavities.'

'Whatever it fucking takes,' spits Andy Jakubiak.

⤜⤛

OMAR

The greatest dangers in the camp, even more than violence and violation, are boredom, frustration and the steady loss of hope, like the slow puncturing of a tyre. Queueing for food, queueing for washing facilities, queueing for medical attention. The lassi-tude of waiting withers people away. They join the ranks of the inert, the passive, the despairing, sitting in the mouths of their tents all day heads down, without the energy to go and hassle the NGOs or the asylum people but without the balls to pack up and move on, 'because you never know, it might happen tomorrow'.

Omar will never be one of those people. He guards his hope as by far the most valuable of his meagre possessions. And so the night the fascists and the police burn down the camp, he is ready.

The police are supposed to be there to guard the 'protected' sec-tion, an encampment of the vulnerable, but what they mainly do is gouge bribes from people and fuck the women who will take their money and stare with metallic hostility through the chain-link fence which separates their compound from the rest of the camp.

In recent weeks, though, they've had visitors. Better-fed, better-dressed men, sleek and menacing as bullet casings in their bomber jackets and heavy boots. The bullet men prowl the fence with

150

binoculars, pointing, making notes. They are the tip of a long chain, a chain of contempt and dereliction and disavowal.

The rest of Europe won't take the refugees from Greece, because they think it will encourage more to come. The rest of Greece won't take them from the island, because they think it will encourage more to come. The local residents begin to tire of their island becoming a prison, of being involuntary wardens of an unending humanitarian crisis. And the beneficiaries, of course, as always, are the fascists. In weeks to come, six Afghans will be charged with what occurs tonight, but everybody knows that's bullshit.

The fires start small. They emerge one at a time like stars at dusk, twinkling across the firmament of the camp, beautiful like diamonds in the night. Cooking fires are officially illegal but they happen all the time, so nobody notices. But Omar's prey senses are so alert that it only takes the tiniest touch to trigger them. There aren't normally so many, he thinks. There aren't usually so many people cooking at the same time.

Then the little blazes begin to expand and join up, reaching tendrils of sparks and flame to one another. The fires hold hands and skip forward like happy children. Omar is on his feet, shouting FIRE FIRE FIRE in any language he can think of, pulling people out of tents, pushing and shoving people who stumble and cry out for their children and drop the armfuls of random possessions they've grabbed in seconds of panic. Irreplaceable documents and cracked pots mingle in the mud and are trampled equally underfoot. The flames roar out their rage like beasts claiming sovereignty over this burning and benighted land. In front of the wall of smoke and heat are the bullet men, swinging clubs, smashing and striking. People fall before them and do not rise again.

Everything goes up in an instant. Rickety wooden shacks kindle with a whump and tongues of flame rasp the sky. Plastic tarps melt and slump. Burning tents billow, fanning the blaze. The olive trees burn from the base up, simmering as the fire works its way into their heartwood then erupting all at once into flame. The trunks burn away as if felled by an orange-red chainsaw and the trees are loosed down the hill, tumbling terrifying Catherine wheels of flame, shedding embers which seed new conflagrations. But the scariest part is the noise.

The noise is something Omar has never heard before. The fire is *howling* like a pack of wolves, a roaring bellow that sounds at once like triumph, predators closing in for bloody conquest, and a keening noise as if mourning something precious now lost for ever. The shrieking drowns out all speech and sound. With a following wind and a slope in its favour, a fire can move as fast as an Olympic sprinter. It closes in towards them, the wall of flame rising and rising.

Everybody runs for their lives.

Chapter Twelve

MARWA

Asha sits on the narrow student bed, shifting uncomfortably from the uncertainty as much as from the lumps, as her new friend taps at her keyboard with rigorous focus and long acrylic fingernails. She doesn't quite get what's going on, but she can see that Marwa has a plan. It's a plan rooted in pain.

Marwa's cousin, Nour, a queer activist who fled Sisi's post-Arab Spring crackdown, was held in various UK detention centres for over two years, shipped frequently across the country from place to place without warning. Marwa visited Nour as often as she could find her, which wasn't often. She scans again the torn and tear-stained letters her cousin wrote her on pages ripped from old exercise books, and her rage rises anew not only at what was done to Nour but her cousin's stubborn insistence that this must all be some kind of mistake, this couldn't possibly be what Britain was really like.

But in the end, it was all worthwhile. Nour fulfilled all the necessary criteria, jumped through all the endless loops. She had a good and diligent lawyer, which by no means everybody has. One final residency hearing. Just a formality, her lawyer said. A rubber-stamping exercise.

Nour was deported two days before the hearing. She was dragged screaming out of her cell at five a.m., a bag was placed over her head, her hands were cable-tied behind her back, and she was put on a special deportation flight from Stansted to Cairo with an unknown number of other Arab Spring dissidents. Nobody has heard from Nour or anyone else on that flight since that day. It's very probable, in fact almost certain, that Marwa no longer has a cousin.

This experience has made Marwa both intimately familiar with the UK detention system and very, very happy to try to fuck it up by any means necessary.

There's only one solution. Asha can't go into the intake unit. She's far more likely to get locked up than to get to talk to the guy she needs to talk to. So the guy will need to come out. Or be gotten out.

Which sounds like no mean feat. Luckily Marwa is enterprising, fearless, and has absorbed the key lessons British society teaches its young these days, which are: 1) Nobody cares about you. 2) *Everything* is a scam. 3) Don't believe a single word the motherfuckers say.

She starts digging.

꩜

ROBERT

They pass a hairdresser called Crimping Ain't Easy. No regulation in this criminally misgoverned nation is enforced like the mandate that all hairdressers' names must contain a bad pun, though this one at least is a little more contemporary. Robert wonders if there's some kind of meeting you're forced to attend when you buy your first set of clippers. Perhaps in the dim and distant past there was a woman who innocently named her shop 'Jenny's Hair' and was burned at the stake as a witch.

The proprietor is a large man who appears to have given himself the worst haircut in human history to make his customers feel better about their own life choices. The lights go red and Robert has the chance to take the guy in properly. He's wearing a silver lamé jacket and leopard-skin stack heels which match the colours of the faux-hawk he's pointing to and grinning like he's just scored the winner in the Champions League final. Robert shakes his head. Whatever gets you through the day.

Robert takes another look at Michael's pencil drawing of the mystery girl, which he's propped up on the dashboard like some weird compass. The good news is that Michael has genuine artistic ability. The bad news is that a pencil sketch from memory of a photo of a black girl by a white man who never met her is the only lead he has. This is, objectively, insane.

The drawing is pretty detailed though: the girl looks like a real human being, the sign is clear, there's some kind of statue in the background. He sneaks a glance at Danielle to see what she's thinking, but she's had her face in her phone ever since they left the house. He tries to suppress his irritation and judgy 'youth of today' stereotypes.

'What you thinking about?' asks Danielle, without looking up from the screen.

'Why all hairdressers have bad puns in their names.'

'Perhaps there was a meeting.'

And Robert remembers again just how much he loves his daughter.

The trouble is, he doesn't know if she loves him back, at least not the same way. He doesn't really know what Danielle thinks. Nobody does. She shuts everything up in the big underground bank vault of her heart and slams and bolts the giant steel doors to which nobody bar Liam has ever had the code. Always has done, but even more so since her brother died.

Robert sneaks a glance at his daughter's profile as she swipes windows on her phone. Truculent. Determined. Stubborn, in the classic way of the younger sibling who was always overlooked, cast into unfair shadow by Liam's bright sun. The only way she could be heard as a kid was simple refusal, sitting down and shouting 'NO!!', and by God did she shout.

Cherry has always claimed that Danielle has his face and he can see it at a surface level, but the jaw is all Cherry and so is the resilience, the refusal to be cowed. Robert knows deep down that the bedrock of his soul is more like mud, that if pushed hard enough he will yield. As far as he can tell, Danielle's soul is miles and miles of solid granite that would blunt BP's biggest excavating drill.

Danielle picks up the drawing, studies it for a moment, chucks it down again with a snort, presumably at the ridiculousness of their quest, and goes back to her phone.

'What are you thinking about?' he asks her.

She shrugs. Nice try, Dad. But you can't get into the big bank vault of her heart by knocking on the heavy metal doors. You have to be stealthy. Bide your time. See if there's some secret way in through the back which nobody knows about.

'Where we going?'

'London.'

'I figured that out. Specifically.'

'Specifically, we are going to my old place of work. You remember it, right? From when you were a kid?' he asks, faux casual as Danielle's eyes bug out of her head like something from a David Attenborough insect documentary, while at the same time steering around a scaffolding lorry that has stopped on a dime on double yellows then instantly reversed backwards at speed for no discernible reason other than because it's driven by scaff guys.

'Your old place of work, as in the police station?!'

'Correct.'

Robert has always been a good driver. The thumping in his chest and throat isn't from the scaff van.

'The police station where you got assaulted? That police

station?' enquires Danielle. Robert is all the way round in his seat before she's finished speaking.

'Who told you that? Did your mother tell you that?' Danielle shrugs again. 'Because that's not what happened.'

'OK. Whatever.'

'It's not what happened.'

'Right. Obviously. That's why you need to keep saying it didn't happen.'

'I was not "assaulted". I am not a victim.'

'But that's why we left London? Right? Because someone punched you in the face?'

'We left London for a lot of reasons, Danielle. Green space, better schools—'

'Because someone *in the police* punched you in the face?'

There follow several minutes of silence as Robert rigorously keeps his eyes on the road and Danielle's gaze goes back yet again to her phone. But eventually she returns to the subject she can't stop thinking about.

'How could you do that? As a black man? Be part of fucking copaganda?'

'Are we sure we wanna have this conversation now?'

And just like that, the volcano erupts. Danielle is up out of her seat as far as the belt allows, waving her arms around in the small confines of the car, screaming, knocking Robert's driving glasses off.

'No, you're right, obviously let's not talk, let's NEVER fucking talk, about fucking *anything*! God fucking forbid we ever *talk* about anything in this family! Let's just sit here in silence and pick at shit meals and watch shit TV and pretend everything'll blow over and never, ever admit we are all in so much fucking PAIN.'

'Danielle—'

'I am in so much pain, Dad.'

Suddenly it's fuzzy in Robert's field of vision, like he's looking through a smeary windscreen. It's begun to drizzle, that must be it.

He turns on the wipers but it doesn't seem to help. The steering wheel wobbles strangely between his hands. It's all he can do to choke out a reply.

'I know.'

'And I know you're in pain too because I can *see* it, rolling off you in waves. But you won't admit it, even to yourself. She can. She knows what she's done and she's doing whatever mad shit it takes to help her cope. But you won't do anything to even let yourself feel and it's killing me to watch it. It hurts me so much.'

The smeary windscreen is getting smearier. Robert needs to pull over.

⚜

MARWA

Like the prisons they kept Nour in and absolutely everything else in British public life, the intake unit has been outsourced to spectacularly useless cunts. Specifically, to the most spectacularly useless cunts in the entire private sector, a title for which there is Olympic-level competition. One of those ugly corporate neologisms that *everyone* knows are comically inept but which, no matter how often they fuck up passports and transport, healthcare and school fare, miraculously keep getting large government contracts from ministers who then go to work for them six months later. This is not great for functional public services, but excellent from Marwa's point of view.

In addition to being terrible companies, they're terrible places to work, which garners them terrible workers. Pudgy people in nylon uniforms, white shirts in colour but brownshirts in mentality, who don't give a shit about the job and insofar as they possess a coherent *Weltanschauung*, it's 'Kick unquestioningly down and suck unquestioningly up.' So all she needs is something with authority, a scary and official-looking missive from the higher-ups, to scare these small-time thugs into opening Abdi Bile's cell door. The question is what. She reflects on something she recently learned at uni.

Marwa's IT lecturer is a bald dickhead called Steve Rowbotham. Steve Rowbotham believes shit facial hair makes up for his baldness and is a Man United fan despite coming from Leicester and regards Elon Musk as one of the great heroes of Western civilization. Last week Steve was waxing irate about the phenomenon of 'typosquatting'. This is where a fraudster tweaks the domain name of a corporation, switches letters or adds an extra character, then registers the tweaked name as a new site. From it they send bills, invoices, requests for passwords etc., to the corporation's customers, a surprising number of whom are unlikely to check the email address. Looks legit. Here's my money.

Marwa thought this was clever and hilarious and filed it away in the back of her mind for potential usage. There is a reason she's not getting the highest grades in her class (though to be fair most cyber criminals start off by studying IT, before they realize poacher is a lot more fun and lucrative than gamekeeper). But even she did not expect to be typosquatting merely a few days later. Impressive practical application of learning. Should definitely go into her assessment folder.

She digs into how the court system works. Who would release an immigration detainee, and on what basis? She's a fast learner. A couple of hours later she thinks she has a decent basic handle on it. The domain name for the disciplinary arm of the courts, the basis for granting or denial of liberty, is *hmcts.gsi.gov.uk*. The person who represents these kinds of institutions is called a clerk.

It's the work of a few minutes for Marwa to register the domain name *hmcts-gsi-gov.org.uk*, as invisible a tweak as she can think of, and set up an email account from it. It's a slightly longer but by no means arduous task to mock up a pretty convincing mirror of the original website, as backup. Not all the links go anywhere, but she doubts anyone will check them.

She registers the new site in the name of Steve Rowbotham, just for a giggle in case anybody comes looking afterwards, then begins to compose an order in the unbearably pompous style of his emails, which she sends to the processing department of the intake unit.

From: steve.rowbotham@hmcts-gsi-gov.org.uk
To: Whom It May Concern
Dear Sir/Madam,

By way of personal introduction, I am the newly appointed senior clerk to the court, with specific responsibility for immigrant detainees. [She deletes *Pleased to meet you!*, first the exclamation point, then the whole line, as being too female.]

I write with urgent reference to detainee [here she inserts in capital letters Abdi Bile's real name, which he had told Asha on their phone call].

Please be advised, as per Article 475 subsection 7 paragraph 5 of the most recent applicable legislation [Marwa ponders looking this shit up for actual laws, but it's a hostage to fortune and the whole point is to scare these pricks by referring to something they know nothing about in a highly authoritative manner], *that this case has now been resolved in the detainee's favour, and he has received immediate leave to remain in the United Kingdom* [a little spasm of pain through Marwa's heart as she imagines her cousin receiving such a letter. Too late, way too late].

Said detainee should forthwith [Rowbotham classic] *be released from detention into the recognizance* [she got this word off US cop dramas and is not one hundred per cent sure it works or if it's even what they do with inmates over here but fuck it, it sounds intimidating] *of the appropriate security personnel with immediate effect.*

Please contact me post haste [another Rowbotham classic] *in case further clarification is required.*

Kind regards,
    Stephen Rowbotham, MSc, PhD, EE [Marwa's phone company], *BSE* [a weird disease involving cows she remembers her dad telling her about]
    Chief Clerk
    www.hmcts-gsi-gov.org.uk

That should work. At least on the kind of people who work in privatized prisons.

And now for the uniforms. This is the bit Marwa is looking forward to. She may have let her family pressure her into doing an IT degree, but her first love at school was drama. She's a natural performer. At Winifred Holtby Academy in Hull, they still talk about her Juliet in awed tones.

She starts Googling fancy dress shops.

❦

DANIELLE

The drizzle is a steady rain now, the classic British rain that lingers clammy-handed and unwelcome like the last pissed guest at the party, and the warmth and body heat in the little roadside café are making the windows steam up. Danielle finishes swiping through the last few windows on her phone, puts it face down and wipes a clear space in the fog with the tail of her baggy flannel shirt.

She doesn't really like flannel shirts, classic Dad wear, let alone ones that don't fit properly, but this is different. It's baggy on her not because she's trying to hide anything, she likes her body for the

161

most part, but because it was Liam's favourite shirt. And so now she hardly ever takes it off.

She looks out into the world. In a little bit her dad sits down opposite her, wiping his mouth with his napkin. She reaches over and puts her hand on top of his.

'Better?'

'I'm fine. I just needed a minute.'

'Don't apologize.'

'I'm not apologizing. I'm explaining.'

'Fairs.'

Her dad sips his coffee and looks at her like he's not particularly enjoying this turning of the tables, taking life advice from someone who hasn't lived yet, his seventeen-year-old offspring. Which she can understand. But she's waited long enough for him to work it out for himself.

'You're allowed to hurt too. She's not the only one.'

Robert wipes his face. Shame burns through him. Bent over the toilet in the back, someone banging on the locked door as salt water pours down his helpless face, stomach twisting and spasming, bowl flushed of everything he's eaten for days but his gut still expelling a horrid clear liquid, like heroin addicts told him happens after your first hit. All of it completely beyond his control. Now it feels as though some carapace, a protective shell, has been ripped away and it's raw and scary and stings like hell.

'I don't think I like this much, Dani. If I'm honest.'

Danielle takes both his hands.

'It's called being human, Dad. You should try it more often.'

He tries to laugh it off. 'How would you know what being human is? You're seventeen.'

She drops his hands like hot coals and gives him the gimlet eyes of death again. Robert is actually afraid for a second. Should a fifty-year-old ex-copper be afraid of his own daughter?

'To answer your question . . .'

162

'Go on.' She leans forward. He's never gone here before.

'I took a job with the police because it was a professional occupation, and your grandmother wanted me to have a professional occupation, not just bum around making money any which way. Something where nobody could say we didn't deserve to be here, we weren't doing our bit. I wasn't bright enough to be a doctor or a lawyer like your uncle, but I could do that. Read people. Predict people. Help people. I don't think that's a bad thing, at the end of the day.'

'Help people?! In the fucking police?!'

'That's what I tried to do. In my career. Others in the same job, maybe less so.'

'What about Mark Duggan? Chris Kaba? Azelle Rodney?' She could go on and on, but he cuts her off.

'They would've done more of that if I wasn't there. Guaranteed.'

'Or maybe they got away with even more shit with you as their beard?'

'I could give you examples. Of things I stopped.'

'I can give you examples. Peter Foster.'

'Who's that?'

'William Kean. Timothy Brehmer.'

'I don't know who they are.'

'Wayne Couzens.'

'Oh.' He knows who that is alright.

'They're all police officers who murdered women, Dad. And then their fucking mates beat the fuck out of other women when they went to a vigil for the girl Wayne Couzens murdered while he was *on the job*, where he was known *in the Met* as "The Rapist". Now tell me why that list isn't as well known even as the first one?'

A flush heats his cheeks. It's something he's never really thought about because he doesn't personally have to, and that's embarrassing.

'D'you know what the government said you should do as a woman, if you think you're about to be murdered by a serving police officer? Flag down a fucking *bus*.'

Once Dani gets started, she is relentless. He stirs the dregs of his coffee forcibly but says nothing.

'They get me both ways, you know? They get me both ends.'

'Of course I know.'

'Do you *get it* though? This country *terrifies* me, man. Every single thing I'm supposed to respect, that's supposed to protect me – the police, the government – they carry on like they hate me and they want me dead. Which is quite hard, day to day. Living in a society that just fucking hates you. Let alone when your dad is, or was, complicit in it. And that's before we even get to my fucking mother.'

'What *is* it? With you and her? You always used to be close. Closer than she was with Liam.'

⌁

CHERRY

A bang on the door.

Another bang on the door.

Liam doesn't answer.

Cherry, exhausted beyond human comprehension, face and uniform spattered with gobbets of blood hardened into small black-red rubies, knows she should shower first. Have a cup of tea. Take a breath. She knows at some abstract rational level there's no reason to home in on her son, that whatever he's going through, or *says* he's going through, isn't worth this, this unfathomable rage, this depthless fury. And yet she can't stop herself.

Three more dead today. Three more on the list of those who

didn't make it, of those she failed and betrayed, a list of which she honestly cannot remember more than the past three days but she knows is very very long.

A fifty-seven-year-old man clutched her arm and pleaded with her with wild eyes through the breathing tube not to let him die, his kids are out there waiting for him, he had them late and it's just him and them and he can't miss out on them because they are his world and he must take them home, he's promised them that he will take them home. He died three hours later and it fell to Cherry to tell his two children, fourteen and twelve, who were indeed out there in the waiting area and had been since their dad was admitted the previous night with an oxygen saturation of 73, that their father will not be taking them home today. That he will never be taking them home again.

An eighty-seven-year-old woman with dementia, who caught the virus in hospital after she burned herself badly on a pan, screamed at the top of her lungs, wrestled Cherry with incredible wiry strength and ripped out her intubation. They had to sedate the woman to reinsert the tube, and she fought that all the way too, and by the time they could get it back in she was dead. Mercifully so. Cherry can't know for sure but it felt like the woman wasn't fighting her, she was fighting some horrid trauma from her past. An assault, if Cherry had to guess. Hell of a way to go, whatever it was.

The blood from the old lady's ripped-out intubation caused the sprays of blood across Cherry's face and uniform. When all this shit started, she would shower religiously before leaving the hospital, scrub off every twist of virus, every trace of what she'd been through. She would put on a fresh change of clothes and do her make-up with neat rigour, all to keep her family as separate from the horrors of her work as possible.

But now she resents keeping them pristine and insulated, the impossible extra burden of pretending everything is 'normal', of making dinner and polite conversation. The TV murmuring its soothing banalities in the background where half an hour ago there was unspeakable agony and chaos and pain. Why is her life swamped by this, while they're on Zoom calls in bed with a cup of tea? The resentment is building and building and has been for months.

The third death was a twenty-three-year-old boy. A semi-pro footballer, been out on a mate's stag do a couple of weeks before. Bit of a cough, nothing major, then the shocking vertiginous plunge down into the abyss. He died in absolute wild-eyed terror at the real-ization of his own mortality, something he had never once thought of, something he absolutely should never have had to think of. It doesn't happen often even now, someone of that age dying, and when it does it shakes the whole hospital.

But Cherry is not shaken. She is *furious*. She's so spent in every corpuscle that it's all she can do to set one foot in front of the next, she wades the corridors through a thick green subaquatic fatigue, but now she drives home in a pulsing adrenaline rush of rage.

How dare her son, her perfectly healthy, treasured son, in his comfortable bed in his comfortable house, turn in on himself like this? So they cancelled his uni course. They furloughed his part-time job. So what? So fucking what? They will still be there when this is over. But the other kid won't. He has everything in front of him. So did the other kid, but he's fucking dead and Liam is wrapped in his duvet and the rage courses through Cherry's veins and she bangs and bangs and bangs on her son's door and she knows she should stop herself but she can't.

DANIELLE

Danielle knows none of this. All Danielle sees when she opens her bedroom is her mum, crazed and bug-eyed and still in her uniform which is covered in Covid and someone's fucking *blood*, hammering on her brother's door. Her mum who is never here while the rest of them are locked in the house going stir crazy. Who has nothing for them when she does come home because she's nobly expended it all on some randoms. Who snaps at them over fuck all, who plays the victim, who pretends she doesn't want any reward for her 'sacrifices' but constantly demands all their attention and love and pats on the back. The *ego* on this bitch. Danielle is sick to fucking death of it.

She has spent all day trying to build her brother up. Liam is a beautiful soul and an unbelievable talent but naturally fragile, volatile like reactive compounds. (Danielle is the only black girl in A level chemistry. She doesn't even like chemistry, she just likes to do shit people don't expect her to do.) He needs structure to climb high. Without his uni and his job, he's barely clinging on by his fingertips.

And so they've been making plans, things for him to do, even though everything is shut and locked down and ceased and terminated. Distanced workouts in the park with free weights and mates. Volunteering, mentoring excluded kids online. They'd sounded really excited to have him. Set times and set places. A routine, a way of making sense of the world, something to ward off chaos and despair. And now *she's* back to fuck it all up.

It's chemical, why can't her parents see that? These old school motherfuckers. Just because other people are hurting doesn't mean we aren't hurting too. And you can't 'man up' to a fucking chemical imbalance. She works in fucking *healthcare*.

So Danielle steps out of her room and raises her voice to her mother, who raises her voice back. And then Liam finally opens his bedroom door. Something about his piteous appearance – face drained of blood like a hanging carcass, a devil sick of sin, dark pools under his eyes – seems to send her mum properly over the edge. She yells at Liam. He shouts back. Danielle starts to scream. And that brings her dad up the stairs.

Her dad who's been slumping into a depression of his own, in her opinion. TV on, volume up. Got much greyer in the last few months. And something is happening between her parents, something intangible mutating before her eyes, as he tries to calm her down and she turns the full furnace blast of her rage on him. A switch of power, her mum feeding off the pain and misery of the family like a succubus and her dad shrinking, melting away, retreating back down the stairs again.

So that's when Danielle hits Cherry in the face.

～～

Her dad takes his hands away from hers and straightens up.

'You hit her in the face?'

'Uh-huh.'

He looks her dead in the eye for a long time and she thinks he's going to punish her in some way, but then he turns away, shaking his head.

'She's never mentioned it.'

'How very noble of her.'

'Dani . . .'

'What?'

'Just . . . Everybody's hurting, you know? Everybody.'

'I know.'

'*Do* you?' He looks right inside her for a long moment. 'Sometimes when it hurts most is when you have to think of other people.'

'I did. I was livid at you for running away just as much as I was livid at her. But I let you off.'

'How very noble of you,' he says, doing quite a decent impression of her and somehow getting away without a fork in his eye.

'Cos at least I could see that you were hurting.'

'What the hell do you think she's doing all this for?' That's a right hook to the solar plexus for Danielle, who is suddenly forced to see the world and her mum from a slightly different angle. She sits back, looks grumpily away.

168

Her dad grins wryly. 'Have I really?'

'Have you what?'

'Got greyer?' He tries comically to catch his own reflection in the space she cleared, but it's mostly steamed up again.

'Just For Men is in Morrisons aisle three, Daddy, that's all I'm saying.'

They laugh then. Robert taps out a tune on the rim of his cup with his spoon, finishing with a machine-gun rattle that attracts disapproving glances from the two ladies on the next table. He pulls Michael's drawing out of his inside pocket.

'My old station is the closest one to that street sign which is still open. There are people there who like me. And I think they can help us find this girl, and therefore your mum, before other people do. So that's the plan. Alright?'

Danielle shrugs. 'I dunno, Dad.'

'What don't you know?'

'I think we can do better than that.'

'What d'you mean?'

She picks up her phone and shows it to him.

Chapter Thirteen

MARWA

Danny Hodges glares at the piece of paper once again. 'You sure about this?'

'Yes, mate. Like it says on there, yeah?' The kid in front of him scratches his armpit. He can't be more than twenty. Soul patch, both ears pierced, slouching, chewing gum and staring at a spot in the middle distance over Danny's shoulder. Total disrespect. Cunt looks like he got his uniform from a fancy dress shop, for fuck's sake. These private security companies get shittier by the day.

The raghead bird next to the kid steps forward. *Her* uniform looks like she's been hired as a stripper for the world's most discount stag night. What is it with these people? Try to be at least a little bit professional. She shoves a finger at the paper.

'It's all clearly specified in the order. We don't have a lot of time, so if you can process him asap it would be appreciated.'

There's a steel gleam in her eye which brooks no argument. She sounds like she's from fucking Hull an' all, for all that she looks well foreign. Danny's from Grimsby. Grimsby don't get on with Hull, for reasons lost in the mists of time but almost certainly to do with fish. Cod in particular. Danny doesn't like this one bit.

'I'm gonna check. Wait here.'

He turns on his heel and leaves the two 'officers' alone in the reception area. The minute he's gone, Marwa kicks Eric hard in the back of his calf.

'Ow! The fuck was that for?'

'Try to be a little bit professional, yeah? Stand up straight and swallow the fucking gum!'

Eric is Marwa's on-off boyfriend, quite literally for about eighty per cent of the time they're together (what Eric lacks upstairs, he more than makes up for downstairs) but also on at uni and off when she goes home between semesters. Her family are quite strict and wouldn't be happy. With a white guy in general but Eric in particular, and to be totally honest she can see why. She would bin him off, but the only other place she can get a footlong that satisfying is Subway and money is tight.

Marwa didn't want to involve Eric in this, but she correctly surmised that even a dim-witted white male would be better received than she would be alone. They hired the uniforms from the fancy dress shop the previous day, after Marwa finished mocking up a logo and letterhead for the fictitious private security company they're claiming to represent. All they had left was the 'His 'N' Hers Police StrippoMatic Set', which isn't ideal and is also quite mental. His 'N' Hers? Why would *both* of you dress as police strippers? Hers is a lot closer-fitting than she'd prefer, especially in this environment, but perhaps that's to be expected given the basic premise.

Eric stands up straight and swallows the fucking gum. He really likes Marwa. One day he'd like to meet her family. He thinks they'll really like him when they get to know him.

Danny Hodges returns, face like thunder.

'Checks out. Order's in the system.'

'Right, so if you can—'

'I've never heard of you lot,' says Hodges suspiciously.

'We're new.' Marwa, peremptory, dismissive.

'New?'

'Like, not old?' adds Eric, trying his best to be helpful. Hodges peers even closer.

'Why are you taking him?'

'Like it says in the order, he's got leave to remain,' says Miss Hull (Sharia Law Category).

'That doesn't happen this quickly.'

'Well, it has in this case.'

'And when it does, they don't release them into further custody. They just let them go.'

'Perhaps he's dangerous. Really not your concern, is it, officer? Do you want me to report back that you refused to fulfil the order?'

Marwa and Hodges go nose to nose for a long moment, until she whispers the only thing that will break the deadlock.

'They're our fish.'

'What?'

'You're Grimsby, right? They're our fucking cod. Now go get the detainee.'

The convulsions that cross Danny Hodges's face as he tries not to strangle this bitch and/or spontaneously combust are a sight to behold. But in the end, what can he do? He knows something is amiss. But the order is in the system. And people like Danny live for the system. They would rather die than betray the system.

Hodges disappears for an absolute age, during which Marwa's nerve almost fails her and she nearly runs out screaming, but eventually he comes back trailing a short, stocky guy who radiates a certain pugnacious self-assurance, blinking in the light like someone who's recently spent time in dingy confinement.

Abdi Bile is released into Marwa's recognizance, just like on the US cop shows.

～～

BARRATT

Freddie Barratt is livid. A very disrespectful meeting with his superiors earlier. Raised voices and concerned expressions. Accusations of broken promises, of failures to deliver. Bullshit. Freddie always delivers. He's like Domino's. Better, cos the other week he waited over an hour for his pizza and when it turned up it was cold and missing the extra jalapeños.

It's not his fault those redneck beat plods can't track a car. Not his fault that the vehicle somehow just disappeared off the GPS system. Flat out vanished and has not resurfaced several hours later. That's a major problem. That was Freddie's ace in the hole.

There was a lot of talk at the meeting of Freddie handing over the investigation, of 'things getting out of our control'. Of Senior Investigative Officers being brought in from outside. Rumours of one SIO in particular. A certain hush and awe in his bosses' voices as they talked about her. Terms like 'rising star', 'nails', 'takes no prisoners' being bandied about. Patricia Something.

Freddie Googled Patricia Something. Black, of course. Double-barrelled surname, neither part of which he can pronounce, both about a foot long. Must take her about five fucking minutes to sign it. Lots of chat in her *POLICE* magazine interview about how proud she is of her mixed Nigerian-Ghanaian heritage.

They just fucking do this to taunt him, don't they? Where's Freddie's fucking interview in *POLICE* magazine? And what would happen if he did one and went on about how proud he is of *his* heritage, ten generations of white Britons who served their country and did their duty and now apparently don't belong here as much as Patricia Double-Barrel and her Nigerian-Ghanaian relatives who arrived five minutes ago? As if he can't guess.

The bitter bilious surge of resentment, that old friend and

companion, perhaps the emotion Barratt is most familiar with and certainly the one he most trusts, churns in his guts.

It's alright, Freddie. There's always another answer. Always another string to pull, for the smartest guy in the room.

He reaches for his phone again.

✹

JAKUBIAK

Andy Jakubiak dry heaves into the kitchen sink, which is comfortably larger than the bath in any hotel room he's stayed in, though his experience only extends to Premier Inn and Travelodge. Finally his insides seem willing to stick to their end of the bargain and stay inside him, and he raises his head.

His eyes light on Radka, who is rooting around in a fridge so big that if it was in Zone 2 someone would put a bed, toilet and shower inside it and rent it out for £1500 a month. She withdraws a tub of something that looks like a large clod of tiny eyeballs. She hungrily scoops a large spoonful of the gelatinous mess into her mouth, then another. Instantly Andy is dry heaving again.

'How can you *eat*?!' he asks incredulously, when he has once more attained dominion over his internal organs. Cherry is perched on a stool with a greenish pallor and a similarly sceptical expression.

Radka shrugs. 'Each to their own. It made me hungry.'

'What the fuck is that anyway?'

'Chia seeds. Soaked in milk.'

'What seeds?'

'Ancient food of the Aztecs.'

'No wonder they died out.'

'That was more smallpox and colonialism.'

174

'Yeah, but also the fucking food, clearly.'

'I would prefer a KFC to be fair, but Fiona won't have it in the house.'

Radka finishes the tub in astonishingly quick time and leans back. 'Now, who would like maybe a cup of tea?' she enquires once again, ever the gracious hostess, and before she's even finished the sentence Andy says, 'Three sugars. Four. As many sugars as you have, basically.'

It's only when all three of them are sitting comfortably at the mahogany table, albeit in separate time zones given the size of it, stirring their teas with both hands thanks to the volume of sugar in them, that Radka asks, 'So now what?'

Cherry launches into her usual spiel, but before she's even got properly under way, Andy interrupts her.

'No,' he says authoritatively.

'What are you talking about? We—'

'I've been thinking,' he says, and a smile warm and inexorable as a sunrise crosses his face. For the first time in his life, wannabe detective Andy Jakubiak is about to commit an actual act of detection.

'Go on,' Cherry says, the smile blooming on her face too in anticipation.

He puts his hands down on the table with a definitive thunk, as though he's holding a straight flush.

'The other detainees.'

⫘

DANIELLE

'I started with a reverse image search,' says Danielle.

'Sure,' responds Robert, nodding authoritatively.

A grin upends the corner of Danielle's mouth. 'You have no idea what that is, do you?'

'I mean, you know, it's not . . . Refresh my memory.'

'A reverse image search is when you put a picture of someone into a search engine, to try to find out more about them. Identity, contact details, stuff like that.'

'You can do that?'

'Uh, yeah? What did you do as a cop to find people?'

'Ring up contacts, check surveillance footage, old-school shoe leather.'

'Alright, *Life on Mars*. Things have moved on a bit since the seventies. There are several different sites you can use. TinEye's probably the best.'

'But don't you need to . . . put in . . .'

'Upload.'

'The picture itself? To search for it?'

'You do.'

'Well then,' says Robert, satisfied that he's beaten back the rude tide of technological advancement. 'We don't have it.'

'Which is why I started with a physical description and worked back. That's another step, different site, you don't need to know about all that. That gave me a load of hits of actual images, and there's various ways you can refine the search down from there. Here are the results from TinEye, Bing, Yandex and Google.'

She shows him various windows on her phone. His jaw sags.

'There's also something called SocialMapper which goes through people's Facebook, LinkedIn, Instagram and Twitter for image matches, and another thing I've not used before but which seems quite good,' she breezes briskly through more screens as though she's some kind of highly paid private security operative and not a seventeen-year-old girl studying for her A levels, 'called KarmaDecay for some weird reason, which finds the sources of photos, and drawings actually, on Reddit and some other places.'

She sits back calmly in her chair as he goggles at her.

'What?'

'How do you know all this?'

'Everyone my age knows all this. Anyone who's ever been ghosted by a boy, anyway. I guarantee your mob have a lot more at their disposal.'

'Former mob.' Robert relocates his jaw and sits forward. 'So you found her? You know who she is?' he asks, unable to keep the excitement out of his voice.

A beat. 'No,' says Danielle, though she doesn't seem particularly cut up about it. 'All that stuff is predicated on her uploading the image to some social media site or other. If she doesn't have social media, or if she only sent it to him by text or whatever, there's nothing we can do. Nothing I can do, anyway.'

Robert shakes his head and, somewhat patronizingly, retakes control of the conversation.

'Well. Dani. I am amazed. I am honestly so, so impressed. Thank you for all your hard work. When we get to the station, I want you to show . . . What are you laughing at?'

'Dad?'

'Yes.' A certain anticipatory humility creeps into his voice.

'What else do you see in the drawing?'

JAKUBIAK

'What other detainees?' asks Cherry.

'There were six other people on his boat that night.'

'How do you know that?' she asks, and shame and defensiveness jostle on Andy's face, and she raises her hands in a sort of apology. It's long past time for that now. 'I mean—'

'Because six men were booked into the intake unit the following morning. Coastguard picked 'em up. And when they got there they started kicking off. It was the other guys from his boat. Shouting about murder and describing Barratt to the guards. That's why we went to the morgue, because Barratt's mate called him up and told him we were in shit and to get rid of the evidence.'

'Right. OK. Maybe I'm being dim, but I don't really see how that helps? You want us to go to the intake unit and talk to them?'

'They'll have made phone calls. To lawyers, friends, family. Somebody will have called this girl. Guarantee it. There's no fucking way, if this lad was clutching her photo that tight, that he didn't tell someone about her.'

'Right. But . . .'

'I've been inside there before. There's only one payphone. And they keep a record of all the numbers called, and by who.'

'Whom,' says literary pedant Radka faintly, not wanting to check the flow of inspiration.

'We get the numbers the six of 'em called, then we cross-check the names and addresses to which the numbers are registered. That's the main way the police find people now. There's a database. We find which of the numbers is closest to the street sign on here.' He taps the photo. 'And that's her.'

Cherry puffs out her cheeks. 'Andy. Mate. I don't wanna burst your bubble, but it feels like something of a long shot—'

'You asked me if I had a better idea than just driving around like cunts.'

'I mean, I wouldn't exactly call it—'

'This is a better idea. Can I borrow your phone, please?' he says to Radka. 'I'm gonna call the intake unit.'

'Won't they know? That you're . . .'

'Doubt it. Departments don't really talk to each other. But there's only one way to find out.'

He holds out his hand to Radka. A man on a mission. Radka

looks at Cherry, shrugs, pulls her phone out, puts in the passcode and hands it to him. He takes it, then turns away with a sudden shyness.

'Sorry, I need to do this in another room. I have to . . . I have to talk a different way.'

Andy disappears. Cherry and Radka put their hands to their hearts and simper.

'Aw. Sweet.'

'Possibly still a little bit racist. But sweet. Incidentally,' adds Cherry. ' "I apologize also"?'

'What?'

'When we were in there.' She gestures in the general direction of the garage. 'You told him, "I apologize also." Where's that from?'

Radka looks at her incredulously. 'Have you never seen *Thelma & Louise*?'

'OH MY GOD!' shrieks Cherry Bristow.

DANIELLE

Her dad, former police investigator extraordinaire, peers so closely at the drawing that he bumps it with the end of his nose, then turns it sideways, first one way then the other. She tries hard not to giggle, but in the end not hard enough.

'The mad thing is, I would've dicked all over you as a police officer. If I didn't also have a social conscience.'

He looks grumpily up at her. 'Nobody likes a know-it-all.'

'Specially when they do, in fact, know it all.'

'You are irritating. It's some kind of statue.'

'It's some kind of statue. Holding quite a funny set of tools.' She swipes to her last window and pushes her phone at him, with the reserved triumphalism of a chess grandmaster who doesn't normally knock over her opponent's king *this* quickly.

'Draughtsman's tools, it turns out. There's an app called Visual Search that lets you look for objects within images. But I'd have got there anyway. Can't be that many statues in north-west London.

'That is Thomas Parker Jackson, Dad. Architect of a fair bit round there, back in the day. Who knew that statues of rich dead white men are a good thing, actually?

'Thomas's is on Jackson Street, NW 10.'

JAKUBIAK

Cherry and Radka are most of the way through recapping the plot of their favourite film at ear-splitting volume when Andy bursts into the room, his already substantial chest swelled even larger with pride.

'That was quick.'

'One of them's out already.'

'Really?'

'Bloke I spoke to couldn't do enough for me. Something well sus about it, he said. The release. Wanted to help me track him down. He looked up the calls the guy'd made. There was only one.'

He holds Radka's phone out to them with a huge grin. It's open to Google Maps.

'Registered to an address on Jackson Street, NW 10. An Ethiopian restaurant.

'The girl's name is Asha.'

PART THREE

The Third (and Still the Second) Burial

Chapter Fourteen

ASHA

The wind whips through the thin jacket she borrowed from Marwa, tangling it round her like a torn sail round a mast. Salt stings her face. A cold drenching rain has soaked through her clothes and she's shivering. She can't get sick. How will she work if she gets sick?

She looks over her shoulder at the stocky figure standing a few yards back from the shoreline, body angled back towards the road, hands gesturing, doing everything he can to pressure her to leave without having the balls to say it to her face. The fury at him, clean and pure and all consuming, rises inside her once again. She squats down and examines some of the stones (how is this a *beach*?!) for a long time. Perhaps Omar was here. Perhaps he crawled out of the sea, exhausted but alive, right at this spot. Perhaps he was rescued here by kind strangers and taken to somewhere warm and comfortable. Perhaps his body washed . . . No. She won't think that. Not until she has to.

She puts one of the stones in her pocket with a sort of reverence. Out of the corner of her eye, she sees Abdi Bile throw up his arms in frustration. This makes her happy.

But soon the little warm flame of happiness blows out in the wind and rain. Truth be told, she has no idea what she's doing here, other than punishing Abdi Bile. She's all cried out. She sobbed and sobbed on Marwa's narrow student bed, shaking and shuddering in her friend's arms until Marwa's shirt was soaked through and the cheap dye of her costume ran and she's not getting her deposit back from the fancy dress shop.

But the tears are all gone. And after they'd approached a few random people along the shoreline, a guy with a sailboat and a couple of local fishermen, to ask if they'd seen anyone matching Omar's description, Marwa had to go too. Back to class, dragging Eric with her and promising to do anything she can, just give me a call. But what else can any of them do? Marwa told her about something called the coastguard, but there's no way Asha is going anywhere near officialdom, men in uniform. They're already at risk enough as it is, standing out on the shore, talking to random English people who could be anyone, work for anyone.

Reluctantly she makes her way back towards Abdi Bile, who is vibrating with barely suppressed anger and fear, and probably to be fair with cold.

'We need to go.'

'Then go.'

'We're exposed here. They can see us from miles around. The prison will be looking for me.'

'I need proof.'

'Proof of *what*?!'

'Proof of what you're telling me.'

'How are you going to find that?'

She shrugs. 'Maybe I don't give up on people as easily as you do,' she says, knowing exactly how much that'll hurt him.

His face twists in fury and he opens his mouth wide and shows her his tongue. A chunk has been sliced off as neatly as with a cleaver. The red gelatinous mess in its place pulses slightly.

'I wouldn't let them leave. The people who rescued us. Even when I was numb from cold and my teeth started chattering so hard

I bit off a piece of my own tongue. I made them go round and round in a circle, looking for him. Omar is dead.'

She shrugs again and pushes past him.

'When did you last see him?' he calls scornfully after her. The barb catches in the skin of her back and pulls her up short. 'Maybe you don't even know him any more. I was with him last *week*.'

She turns around, the hurt evident in her face. Asha has never been good at hiding her feelings. 'He was my best friend,' says Abdi Bile.

⚜

ABDI BILE

A derelict building on the outskirts of Rome. Some kind of factory, long closed up and abandoned. Waves of immigrants come and go, all ages, conditions, religions and nations. Some of them have been living here for years, drifting through the sclerotic Italian bureaucracy, lodged in the system like gobs of fat in an unhealthy heart, trapped in this twilight life, half in the world and half in darkness.

The Sudanese with their huge piles of knock-off handbags and fake jewellery splayed out on street corners in the *centro storico*, on enormous blankets that can be scooped up in a flash when the cops come, running away like comedy burglars with giant bags of swag. The tourists haggling with them, luxuriating in their petty power. Life at the margins, life always on the run. Never a moment to relax, or a place to belong.

He won't settle for any of that. He wants what everybody else who happened to be born here seems to have. He is eighteen and naively arrogant enough to believe he can have everything he sees on the TV – because if they didn't want us to have it, why would they show it to us? – and moreover that he can get it all by himself.

So he castles himself into a corner of this decaying hole, his battlements made from plywood he scavenged from a tip. He ignores the rats that leap and skip over his legs like boisterous kids, puts his back against the crumbling concrete, and refuses all offers of help and advice. There are plenty of Somalis and Ethiopians and Eritreans around, some even from near his home village, but who knows what they want? His money? His arse? Better to keep your fists up and your valuables close.

Things have already happened to him on this journey, especially during his time in Libya, in Al Mabani, 'the Buildings'. Things he refuses to think about, things he cannot afford to remember. A great black void swirls at the core of his being, threatening to suck him in and destroy him the moment he acknowledges it. Even repressed, the events of the Buildings have left an indelible mark on him: his implacable and explosive rages, his vehement distrust of strangers.

Al Mabani is where the Libyan coastguard operate from. The Libyan coastguard are the best organized, best equipped smuggling gang in the world. This is because they're paid tens of millions a year by the European Union to repress the flows of refugees by *any* means necessary. They detain and torture migrants in a range of spectacularly vicious and creative ways; or, at least they do until those same migrants find enough money to pay them for a ticket across the ocean. Unlike the people who fund them, the Libyan coastguard are not stupid. They get paid to stop migrants by one side, and they get paid to transport migrants by the other. It's always great to be the middleman.

Tonight the vibe in the old factory is extra weird. There's always volatility and strangeness here, whether it's water pouring down the walls in limpid algae-green sheets after rain, or arguments over the meagre food donations distributed by local volunteers, or

scuffles with the police and the far right, both of whom are perman-
ently camped outside looking for a fight. One of the volunteers says
Italians have always been the people who leave, the ones who set
sail looking for a better life, not the hosts of others, and it's hard
for them to adjust. But tonight feels more unsettled, more dangerous than normal. A fuse somewhere is about to be lit.

A tall wiry kid strolls up to him with a bouncy, hitchy stride.
He's been around the place for the last few days. Charismatic. Easy
in his own skin. Casual lopsided grin, body all angles and lines like
a bundle of gathered sticks. Also Somali.

'Elections, man. That's the problem.'

'What the fuck does that mean, "elections"?'

'Easy, brother. I'm not your enemy. Italian government
elections.'

'Fuck do I care? Leave me alone.'

The wiry kid slides down next to him as though invited rather
than disrespected. He scrutinizes him carefully and the grin widens.

'You know who you look like? Abdi Bile. The runner. You look
just like him. Well, your face. You're a fat fucker though.'

'Fuck you, man.'

'You do though, you have the same face.'

'Yeah, well, you look like you had a stroke.'

'It's a compliment! Who doesn't want to look like Abdi Bile? My
father's hero.'

The ghost of a deep sadness crosses the kid's face underneath
his jauntiness. He sticks out a hand.

'Good to meet you, Abdi Bile. I'm Omar.'

And just like that, Abdi Bile has a new name, and a new friend.

'What's this shit about elections?'

'The guys here say this is when it always kicks off. The pricks in
charge want to show how tough they are by giving us a kicking.'

The newly christened Abdi shrugs, but his castle walls suddenly
seem thinner than before.

'What do you want me to do about it?'

'Not a thing, brother. Keep your eyes open, I guess. With two of us it's easier.'

'Maybe it's just talk.'

'Maybe. You eat yet?'

Omar brings over some of his food. Cautiously, Abdi reaches into his stash and brings out some of his own. They share. They compare journeys. Omar winces at Abdi's account of the Buildings. He went the other way, through Turkey ('psychotic place, man, real fucking shithole'). Got as far as the newly built wall on the Hungarian border ('serious crazies up there, proper Nazis') but a heavy armoured presence meant he had to backtrack, try an alternative route across the Adriatic and up through Italy. The French–Italian border crossing at Ventimiglia is a notorious soft spot, open and shut in waves depending on the political moment.

Omar pulls out a photo, laminated in peeling plastic. A beautiful girl, hair cascading down her back in ringlets, smile as wide as the ocean. Asha. The girl he loves, the girl he's going to meet in London. Abdi feels an intense stab of jealousy. He has nothing and nobody, not like that anyway.

The presence of absence kicks him in the guts. He covers it up by taking the piss.

'Laminated? I'm sorry, I didn't realize it was 1997.'

Omar kisses the photo. 'Anything can happen to a phone. Lost. Stolen. Dropped in the water. We are crossing the ocean, you know. And then pooof, all your photos and memories gone. Can't go wrong with a laminated printout. Plastic is for ever, brother.'

Later Abdi drifts into uneasy sleep, troubled by strange dreams. Huge machines grind the earth before him, gouging out giant trenches and pits that bar the way to a destination he cannot see. Thunderous crashes as the machines steadily work their way towards him, their ominous progress shaking the ground beneath his feet.

He wakes groggily to realize the shaking is real. Omar grasps his shoulder urgently in both hands.

'Up. Now.'

From down the corridor he can hear screams, destruction, the thump of heavy boots. Instinctively he reaches behind the plywood for his possessions, but Omar yanks him away.

'*Now.*'

They run. From behind them a young woman screams in abject terror. Clubs thud flesh. Glass shatters.

They enter a different space, a long low room. The police have already been here. People crawl in ones and twos along the filthy concrete floor, clutching their heads and moaning. A horrid sound beyond pain, as if they're fighting for their souls. You can see where they were caught unawares because in neatly spaced rows, about the width of a sleeping body apart, there are bloodstains where their skulls were smashed in. Abdi feels sick.

A phalanx of armoured policemen enters through the other door. A modern Roman legion, body armour matte and bulging, visors glinting like giant insect eyes, heavy shields and clubs. They spot them and lurch forward as one.

'This way.'

Omar shoves Abdi through a gap he didn't realize was there and out onto a decaying fire escape. The sudden night air and the vertiginous drop four floors down make Abdi wobble and clutch at rusty struts. They begin to clatter their way down to safety, great hunks of flaking metal shearing away, the whole structure swaying terrifyingly as the riot police crash about above their heads, chasing them down.

Three floors. Two.

Down the last flight of stairs and there, smoking on the bottom step, helmets off, are two cops. Skiving or there to round up stragglers. They snatch their clubs hurriedly and charge up. Abdi is in front. He freezes and tries to back away, but the phalanx is stomping down towards them from above, the steps bucking under their weight like a tiny boat at open sea. Trapped. The first cop reaches them, narrow vulpine face curled into a snarl of teeth. He raises his baton. Abdi Bile raises his arm, closes his eyes, waits for the inevitable.

There is a thud, but he feels nothing. He opens his eyes. Omar has his hands over his mouth and blood running between his fingers. He's taken the hit. He has taken the blow that was meant for Abdi. Omar takes his hands away. Most of a front tooth is missing. He spits blood and phlegm and tooth fragments into the face of the cop.

A great fury seizes Abdi, like nothing he's felt before. No one has ever voluntarily taken pain that was meant for him. No one has ever proven to him that he deserves his trust.

He smashes a fist into the eye of the vulpine cop. The guy staggers back. It happens again. And again. A great surging torrent of punches and kicks erupts from the deep molten ocean of rage inside him, Abdi watching almost as a detached spectator as his body unleashes a windmilling avalanche of violence from which the two policemen can only retreat. They back away, stumble, fall headlong. A corridor of freedom appears. The armoured phalanx gets closer, two floors above them. One floor.

The boys sprint between the fallen cops and into the safety of darkness.

ROBERT

'Why did you have kids, anyway?'

They're on the M25 and Danielle is firing the heavy artillery. It's like the First World War in the car but with less mud and irritating poetry: the explosions, the shrapnel flying. Robert feels shell shock coming on. But at least they're talking, there is honesty, more than there's been for months, years maybe.

'You don't wanna have kids?'

'Fuck no. Children, yeah, are noisy, ignorant, selfish, entitled little pricks who are terrible for women's bodies.'

Robert puffs out his cheeks and widens his eyes. It's definitely a take.

'I will give you the last one.'

'They're like tiny Tory MPs, except people don't laugh when you say you want to kill them.'

Fucking hell. She's upgraded to nuclear weaponry.

Robert glances across at his daughter. Combative, chin out, in that moment the very spit of her mum. Love rolls through him again like a thunderclap, followed by uncontrollable and unexpected laughter. He collapses over the steering wheel, tears in his eyes, the tension and pain of the last months not already vomited out in the café toilet transmuting into gurgles and cackles.

'What? What are you laughing at?'

'Tiny Tory MPs??!!'

'I'm serious!'

Danielle crosses her arms under her chest and tries to act sullen and offended at her dad's laughter but pretty soon it overwhelms her, her resistance dissolving into shared hilarity. Their guffaws and howls last on and off for two junctions.

'They are though!'

'Mate . . .'

Eventually they calm down round Cobham services, catching their breath in time for a coordinated boo as they pass Chelsea's training ground, home of the world's most disgusting and racist football team. Robert and Danielle sit companionably for a little while, enjoying the meditative rumble of tyres on tarmac.

'I thought the same, when I was your age. About having kids. Perhaps not quite like that.'

'Yeah, but was the fucking world on fire when you were my age?'

'Point taken.' Robert scratches his neck. 'Must be hard for your lot. You shouldn't have to think about stuff like that. The future. Should just be able to live.'

'Don't think I've ever been able to just live. Not ever.'

'Really?'

'In all *this*? How?' A moment. 'Were you?'

'Yeah.'

'When?'

'About your age, I suppose. Bit older. Rave times.'

'Rave times?! You were a cheesy quaver old skool raver?!'

'Big time.'

'You?! My dad? What were you, undercover?'

'Before I was a cop. Lived for it.'

'Get to fuck.'

'Language. Spent about two years basically living here. The Orbital. Still all comes back to me whenever I drive it. All the raves were off here somewhere, down some little slip road or hidden in a field.'

'What was it like?'

'Well.' The smile that crosses Robert's face at the memories is like a beach sunrise, an irresistible warming glow. 'We'd pull into one of these lay-bys or a service station, anywhere there were payphones, and we'd wait in the dark. Dozens and dozens of cars, hundreds sometimes, all waiting for the signal, the word about where the crew had set up the rig. People sat on hoods smoking spliffs, wandering from car to car introducing themselves, "Easy geezer, where you from, mate?", handing out flyers for the next rave, offering round cheap Es and mardy speed—'

'Dad!'

'What?'

'I do not need to hear about you taking pingers!'

'Do you wanna hear the story or not?'

There is a crafty disbelieving smirk on Danielle's face that suggests she very much wants to hear the story, whatever she says, so Robert carries on.

'The civilians staring at us and us staring back, feeling like a different species, arrivals from a more enlightened planet. All the talk was tribes and freedom. Cos we'd cracked it. All the barriers coming down. All the fear going away. The weight off our backs and the hope and the happiness. Thatcher had finally fucked off and the world was going to be better for everybody.'

Robert suddenly finds himself welling up, a lump in his throat. Over a fucking party from long ago. Embarrassing. He blinks and looks the other way and hopes Danielle hasn't noticed.

'Go on,' she says, and she has.

'The anticipation. The sense of possibilities, of not being fenced in any more, of being set free. That was the best bit, even before the rave itself. And then whoever it was had the crew's number would call it from one of the payphones, no mobiles in them days obviously, and they'd get the coup and they'd jump onto the roof of their car and they'd fucking *scream* out the destination, and we'd roar back like mighty warriors, and everybody'd jump in the cars and head off in this massive convoy, down country lanes and through industrial estates until we found the field or the warehouse where it was happening. All kinds of incredible things happened in there, things that made me who I am in a lot of ways. And then before you knew it it'd be sunrise, and you'd be lying on the grass staring at the rising red and orange glow with people you loved and cared about, and you'd think nothing could ever be bad again. Nothing could ever be bad again.'

Danielle doesn't say anything, and he sneaks a glance at her, and she's looking at him with amazement and a little bit of awe and such pain in her face, such an obvious need for the hope and belonging he once had, that he takes her hand in his and she doesn't even take it back.

'How'd the cops feel about that?' she eventually wonders.

'It weren't prominent on my application form.'

They drive along for some moments, still hand in hand, both peering out of the windows with new eyes, seeing the faint glow of magic beneath the roadside KFCs and shredded tyres and smashed tail lights, the residue of lost joy below the everyday grime.

'Met your mother in a rave,' Robert adds casually.

'Shut UP!' shrieks Danielle, and chucks his hand down.

'Do you wanna hear the first thing she said to me?'

'Ugh, NO! Obviously not!'

She stares out of the window. Something sombre settles on her like a fine dark mist. She speaks quietly.

'Would you still have had kids if you'd known?'

'If I'd known what?'

'That one of them would die. That Liam would kill himself.'

Robert stares ahead for a while.

'You're not thinking about what could go wrong. You're only thinking about what could be beautiful.'

'Would it have changed your mind though?'

Robert looks at his daughter with genuine surprise.

'No, of course not. It's a risk you take. Any form of love is a risk you take. Otherwise it wouldn't be love, would it? It wouldn't mean anything.'

She looks at him and her mouth wobbles. He winks, signals and pulls off the Orbital, former repository of hopes and dreams of a better future, and onto the M4.

CHERRY

They set out on the road again, but a few things are different. For one there's been a kit change, badly needed given all they've been through physically as well as emotionally. Cherry is now tastefully attired in a pair of (OK, slightly tight) designer jeans and a black merino sweater which is stylish yet practical. Between them, they cost more than her monthly wage. Radka reckons Fiona won't miss them. Jakubiak's bulk made him a little bit trickier to fit, but he's scored a pair of the tennis coach's tracksuit bottoms and one of Alasdair's 'loose fit' Japanese selvedge denim shirts, which is painted onto him like some kind of weird denim bondage gear.

Andy did a bit of Googling and found out where the GPS was in her car. He insisted he could take the telematics box out manually, but that plan came to a screeching halt when she caught him watching a YouTube video in Russian subtitled 'How to Remove Black Box with Only Small Damage to Car'. And in any case, that's the car the police will be looking for. So they've gone for an alternative mode of transportation.

It seems counter-intuitive to Cherry to be driving a pink, glossy soft-top convertible when they're trying to be inconspicuous, but Radka persuaded her. For one thing, she said, that's exactly the kind of car they *should* be driving. Someone in a vehicle that screams, 'LOOK AT ME!' cannot by definition have anything to hide. Also, because it only has front seats it has a surprisingly capacious boot, and given the state and smell of the body that's really the only safe place for it, wrapped and bundled in a heap of old bedsheets. She felt a familiar pang of guilt as Andy manhandled the poor dead boy one more time, into the dark recess. Hold on, fella. Nearly there. We've got you.

Radka waves them off cheerily, looking forward to the absolute hell that will break loose when Fiona returns home and finds her little runabout, a car of which Alasdair has simply *never* approved, is missing. It's a wrench for Cherry, watching Radka grow smaller in the rear-view mirror. Someone she's only known for a few hours, but whom she already feels could be a true friend. How hard it is to make true friends after the age of about nine. They'd had so much fun trying on Fiona's things, clothes Cherry wouldn't dare even pick up in the shops normally in case she got coffee stains on them somehow. It reminded her of when she was eleven or twelve and she and her mates would ransack her mum's drawers after her parents had gone out.

But nonetheless here she is, a bandit queen on the run, driving a convertible (with the top up obviously, she's not completely insane) through the badlands of, erm, South-East England. It's pretty hard to stage a road movie in a country that only takes about four hours to drive across, traffic depending, but she's never felt more *Thelma & Louise* in her life. Except there are three of them, and one of them's dead.

Jakubiak is looking out of the window, head propped in his hand, not saying much, and for a while she worries that he's having belated second thoughts about the whole enterprise, but once again she's underestimated him.

'What would you do differently?' he asks quietly.

'What? With this?' She circles her hand around the car and laughs. 'I dunno, fucking *everything*?'

'With your son.'

Ooof. That's a gut punch. She sits back in her seat. She doesn't want to rush a reply.

'Why do you ask?'

'I'm just wondering. What I could've done. With my dad.'

And suddenly she feels a tenderness towards this man, this boy really, that she would never have imagined feeling in a million years.

'That's totally different, Andy.'

'Why?'

'How old were you when you last saw him?'

'Eleven,' says Andy Jakubiak, with a sense of shame, as if he's the one at fault.

'You were a child.'

'Yeah, but, if I'd—'

'You were a child. You did nothing wrong. It was up to your dad. He was the adult. As was I.'

'But—'

'What he chose to do,' and she wobbles, and struggles, and holds it together, 'what *he* chose to do is not your fault. It's not your fault, and it's almost certainly got nothing to do with you at all.'

'Maybe I wasn't good enough. Smart enough, nice enough.'

'It maybe feels better if you can think that, mate, because then you feel more connected to him in a twisted way, but it is down to us. The adults. We are the ones. And to answer your question, that is what I should've done differently. I should've remembered that even though Liam was six foot two and county eight hundred metre champion and a massive pain in the fucking arse sometimes, he was still, at the bottom of it all, just my boy.'

Andy is looking out of the window and won't look back at her and she can hear him weeping quietly. She ponders touching him on the shoulder, but it seems at once too much and too little.

Instead she drives on.

They creep across the M25 at a quiet junction and begin the stealthy crawl through the blasted heath of South London, the green and leafy bits to begin with, gradually entering more familiar territory. Cherry has decided the indirect route is best, rather than heading straight for the address. Sneak up on them. Just in case. And perhaps she wants to glimpse old haunts, summon up the spirit of her dad to help her on her quest.

This is where Cherry grew up, though things have changed a *lot*.

Probably more than any other part of London, the South has been recolonized by the forces of capital. Once an abandoned no-go zone marked 'Here be dragons' by all right-thinking members of the bourgeoisie and thus left blissfully to its own devices, in recent decades South London has been subject to a reign of developmental shock and awe. Carpet bombed by evictions and sell-offs, defoliated of its natural life forms by the vicious Agent Orange of gentrification. Forced displacements, destruction of communities and demolition of housing on a scale normally only seen in the late stages of a war.

The incentives were pecuniary, but the motivation was control. The powers that be couldn't have got the fractious, resistant, working class black communities of Brixton and Loughborough Junction out of their homes with a fucking tank, if they'd been ill-advised enough to turn up in one. Yet the market, the marvellously malevolent market, managed it with barely a scuffle. And the difference it makes, the transformation, is extraordinary. South London was a poor city once. A radical city, familiar with its history, truculent and contemptuous and liable to bare its teeth on minimal provocation. And now, like everywhere else, it is a place full of people concerned above all with material things. And that strikes Cherry as a genuine tragedy.

Being back is weird. A feeling of being home and yet very far from home. The strange concatenation of shabby and wealthy. Of tired kebab joints with the letters peeling off and shiny new restaurants called self-conscious shit like 'You Know, That Little Italian Place?' Minicab firms with grilles over the windows, exhausted drivers asleep on their arms, next to car dealerships with pricey 4x4s lined up on the forecourt as sleek and plump as freshly caught salmon. The familiar and the unfamiliar, the sacred and the profane. A choice selection of double takes, wolf whistles and hilariously the occasional boo remind Cherry of what she's driving.

Suddenly something in the road arrests her musings. People. Lots of angry people.

⚜

ASHA

'We don't know he's dead,' says Asha for the twentieth time. She shakes off Abdi Bile and plunges into the crowd thickening by the second on the pavements as evening comes, spilling out onto this busy street packed with pubs and clubs and bars. Exactly where Abdi doesn't want to be. Asha ploughs on, driven by spite and fury, temporary scar tissue holding a broken heart together, uncertain where she's going but knowing that like the shark, she will drown if she stops moving.

Abdi catches up to her and hauls her back. She whips around with real fury in her eyes.

'Let go of my arm!'

'Do you think I didn't do *everything*?'

'I don't know what you did. I don't know you.'

'You're disrespecting me.'

'Let go of my *arm*.' She wrenches it away. One of the watching drinkers, fascinated by the unusual quarrel, shouts, 'Gwan, darlin.'

'My family borrowed a lot of money for this,' he growls.

'So what?!'

'Nearly a year's income. Sold sheep and goats too. The least I can do is repay them.'

'THEN GO!!' she screams. Other drinkers turn to watch. Panicked, Abdi flaps his hands trying to quieten her, but she will not be quiet.

'You made me get you out!! When you could just have told me on the phone and saved me so much time and money and pain! So now you're free! Go and work and send money to your fucking family!'

'I can't,' he mumbles.

'Why not?! I don't need you! I'm not some helpless woman.'

'You are all I have left of him.'

That brings her to a sudden standstill.

'He saved my life. If I couldn't save his, then I gotta look after what he cared about.'

A new understanding dawns in Asha's eyes. And then something bad happens.

They are standing outside a pub. A huge echoing barn of a place, not so much a drinking den as an intoxication station, part of an (in) famous chain owned by a worthless bigot with a spectacularly low opinion of his clientele to which they seem determined to live down. A uniquely British institution so specifically configured to get you drunk as fast as possible they might as well cut out the middleman and pass you a hose connected to the beer barrel. The football is on, the noise is loud, the vibe is raucous.

A couple of its most alcoholically committed denizens are clustered on the step above Asha's head. One of them, a hod carrier whose wage has recently gone up to a hundred and forty a day ('Happy days!') and who's been celebrating by drinking it all in one go since ten a.m. this morning, drunkenly nudges his mate, who giggles and nods and dares him. The hod carrier stretches out his arm and yanks Asha's hair hard.

She shrieks at the top of her lungs.

Abdi follows the only instinct he trusts. The guiding impulse of fists. The gout of blood from the hod carrier's nose is impressive, as though someone's turned on a high-pressure hose. It fountains through the air like a scarlet Alhambra, before spattering down noisily over the pavement and Asha's hair.

She screams again.

Two policemen are walking down the other side of the street.

They are in fact Community Support Officers, the notorious 'plastic plod', but Asha and Abdi aren't to know that. Not with the head-to-toe hi-vis and the big labels. And even the plastic plod suspect, from the combination of screaming women, violence and blood spatter, that something is amiss. Elite policing instincts.

They start to give chase.

Chapter Fifteen

Let's call her Romilly.

Romilly could easily be (and is) called Martha or Olivia, or Julian or Philip, or even Humam or Shaistah or Femi or Ronke. It really doesn't matter. There are many Romillys of all shapes and sizes, though largely only one class.

Romilly went to a good though not elite private school, then one of the less egregious Cambridge colleges. Romilly is a decent person. She would like to do something useful in the world, though she also wants fitted kitchens and career advancement and these two things are fundamentally incompatible. But she doesn't know this yet. And so when she sees her uni cohort applying to big banks (money laundering) and high-powered law firms (reputation laundering) and Goldman Sachs (Goldman Sachs), she turns up her nose and takes the high road. She applies for, and is accepted into, the Civil Service fast stream. She does really well. Exceptionally well, in fact. And so when the time comes, she has her pick of departments.

Because she is a decent person, and would like to do something useful, and because she doesn't know *anything* about what it's really like, she chooses the Home Office.

And that is when things start to go swiftly downhill.

The Home Office is not like other government departments. All government departments in the endless vicious age of austerity are at war with the people they're in charge of, tasking with cutting and diminishing and making their lives as difficult as possible, even if the civil servants might rather do the opposite. But still, if you're a civil servant in Education, you're spending time with people who generally like education. If you're in Health, you're working with people for whom health is at least something of a motivating factor.

The Home Office is not like this. The Home Office, not to put too fine a point on it, FUCKING HATES EVERYONE. Everyone is a threat. Everyone is a danger to national security or a chancer trying to 'game the system' or somehow linked to 'criminal gangs'. Most of all, everyone is a potential risk for a nightmarish front-page splash in the *Daily Mail* and a mahoosive bollocking from the Minister of State. So fuck 'em all, it saves time. You're familiar with Orwell's 'boot stamping on a human face for ever' maxim, yes? Actually the new Home Office logo.

This is not an ideal working environment from Romilly's POV.

And then there is the Minister of State herself. The Home Secretary is a brown woman. The previous Home Secretary was also a brown woman. This is because conservatives, though vicious greedy clowns to their bones, are somehow less dumb than centrists about identity politics.

The previous Minister got to work at 7.30 every morning, sometimes still in a bulletproof vest with HOME SECRETARY printed on it in large white capitals, which she'd worn on last night's immigration raids. The Minister had targets on her whiteboards and pie charts on her laptop for arrests, detentions, deportations. The people subject to her targets were not referred to as migrants or refugees, or indeed as people, but as 'stocks and flows'.

If there was any deviation from the targets, which there always was because they were insane and unachievable, the Minister screamed and threw markers and coffee mugs and staplers and called people cunts and layabouts and traitors. A formal investigation found her guilty of bullying staff in no fewer than three different departments, which is a record even under this government. The only person who lost their job as a result was the one who did the investigation. This is England.

The new Minister is miraculously somehow worse, though less inclined to bulletproof clothing. Morale at the Home Office is the only thing lower than its approval ratings. Romilly has put in for transfer on numerous occasions, but other departments have stopped taking its refugees. Ironically.

The only way out is up, and the only way up is to hit the targets.

So when Romilly gets a call from a man with something of a reputation for informal, hush-hush, below the line enforcement, a police officer to whom she's never spoken directly but has heard *plenty* about from Border Force, she doesn't want to take it. But then she remembers the good white shirt ruined by green marker ink, and the spreading bruise beneath. With trepidation and reluctance, holding the phone in her fingertips like it's a bag of shit she's about to throw in the bin, she picks up.

'Mr Barratt.'

'Freddie, please.'

'What can I do for you?'

'Well, love, you can help me help you, now you mention it.'

Freddie Barratt sketches out a situation. He's on the trail of a major people smuggling operation. Tentacles all over the country. Proper prime time, big numbers. He's got a hot lead (it's just amazing how much of their real life vocabulary people derive from bad TV shows, thinks Romilly idly) in a certain part of London. He tells her where it is, and describes the type of migrants he's looking for. Probably Eritreans from his experience, maybe Somalis. Ethiopians as an outside bet.

What's she got on her databases for those groups in that part of town? Social clubs. Community organizations. Restaurants and other classic places of work.

And of course, when it comes on top, he'll be more than happy to let the Home Office lead the way. Kick in the doors, make the arrests, drag the lot of 'em out screaming by the hair. She can have all the credit, the camera time, the numbers. All he wants is the satisfaction of a job well done.

He would like to be there though. When the arrests are made. Purely for professional purposes.

Somehow Romilly fancies she can smell this man's rancid breath down the phone line. She looks up from her desk and glimpses one of the twenty-four-hour rolling news channels the Minister has insisted on streaming into the office. A puffy-faced man in a lifejacket, despite standing on dry land, is describing the arrival of refugees on the British shoreline in the tone of a bored pest control officer telling an unhappy restaurateur that the rats are back. From the Minister's office comes an enraged shrieking and the sound of breaking glass.

Resignedly, she begins to tap her keyboard.

ROBERT

The dark cloud under which Robert left the London police force seems to have dissipated. His assailant, an extravagantly moustachioed detective superintendent known to all as 'the Walrus', waddled off this mortal coil some years ago. The Walrus was a hardcore Ulster Unionist and ex-RUC enforcer, whose two favourite topics of conversation were his aversion to 'unnatural mixing across the divides' and the day he served as Keith Blakelock's pall-bearer. Robert was the only black man in his unit. It never went well, but from the minute Cherry popped in unannounced to take Robert out for lunch, the denouement was just a matter of time.

But the heavy tread of the Walrus no longer resounds along the polished corridors of the station. There are still older types whose faces close when they catch an unexpected glimpse of Robert, but many more broad smiles and outstretched hands and hugs and a general sense that a wrong needs to be righted. Danielle, who had to be virtually dragged through the door, is amazed to see how widely her dad is known and respected and loved. And Robert feels himself expand and flourish, refreshed like a wilted plant whose roots have been immersed in cool water, now he's back somewhere he knows what to do, what to be, where he has a purpose.

He's asking around for a guy called Charlie, and eventually they're outside an imposing closed door. Robert flinches slightly and hesitates before knocking.

'Come in.'

He smiles when he hears the voice inside, which Danielle doesn't understand because the voice is female. He opens the door. A brunette woman sits behind a desk. Robert's smile falters.

'Sorry, I'm looking for—'

'Robert!'

'Charlie?'

The woman sprints from behind her desk and fully leaps into Robert's arms. He laughs and catches her. The woman hooks her arms behind his neck. Danielle's eyes goggle out of her head.

'Gastric bypass surgery!' shrieks the woman. 'Couldn't have done that ten years ago, could ya?'

'Not without breaking both arms, no,' says Robert. The woman slaps him lightly. 'You look great,' he adds.

'As do you. As ever.'

'Not that you didn't . . . always . . .'

Danielle coughs lightly. Robert sets the woman down.

'Danielle, this is Charlie Maserati, an ex-colleague. Charlie, this is Danielle. My daughter. Not sure if you remember her.'

'I do indeed.' The woman takes Danielle in with a shrewd appraising glance, like a farmer eyeing up livestock for its pedigree. She holds her hand at hip height. 'The last time I saw you, hun, you were about yay high.'

'Fascinating,' deadpans Danielle. 'Also blatantly not your real name.'

Charlie reaches onto her desk and flips Danielle her work ID card. In black capitals, next to a barely recognizable headshot of the same woman with three chins and blurred rubbery features, is the name CHARLIE MASERATI.

'It's officially Charlotte, my parents are Italian, and my ex-husband was a feeder. I cannot get you a discount on sports cars though, sadly.'

'Ex-husband?' Robert raises an eyebrow.

'We will discuss.' Charlie takes the ID card back.

'Did you ask for the Walrus's office on purpose?' asks Robert, looking around and finding only bad memories.

'No one else would take it. You know how superstitious cops are.'

Robert shrugs slightly in puzzlement.

'Didn't you know?' She pets the desk like it's a dog that's done well. 'He carked it right here. Heart attack midway through an Ulster fry. Mouth full of bacon rasher.'

'It's the way he would've wanted to go.' The two of them snigger like schoolkids.

'Booked myself into the bypass clinic the next day. Also binned the ex. Even I can take a hint from the woman upstairs. Anyway, my friend: to what do I owe the pleasure?'

'We're looking for someone. Wonder if you can help.' Robert unfolds Michael's drawing. 'What have you got for restaurants, bars, shebeens, anywhere an illegal is likely to be doing cash work, based around Jackson Street, NW10?'

Charlie peers closely at the drawing. Notably she doesn't ask who the girl is, or why they want to find her. 'Who did this?'

'A guy my wife knows.'

'Does he want a job? Our sketch artist just got his nose broke by an armed robber who said his court picture made him look thick.'

'You're not serious.'

'It did make him look thick, as it goes. But then he is thick, so not a lot the artist could do really. We caught him on the bus home after he knocked over Billy Hill's on the High Street. Wouldn't be quite so bad, except that bus literally goes past the police station. All we had to do was flag it down. You've just robbed eight and a half K, splash out on a fucking Uber. Anyway,' she says, tapping Michael's masterpiece, 'what are we thinking? Somali? Eritrean? Ethiopian, maybe?'

'That's where I was gonna start, yeah.'

'There's actually an Ethiopian restaurant on Jackson Road itself. Let me see what else is about.'

Charlie starts tapping away at her keyboard. Robert bends over the desk to see what she's come up with, and Charlie takes the opportunity to check out his arse. Danielle catches her doing it. She catches Danielle catching her and winks. Danielle is somewhat surprised to find herself reciprocating with a grin.

'There's another person of interest we'd also like to find,' says Robert almost incidentally, straining for normality but not quite getting there.

'Oh yeah. Who's that?'

'Um, Cherry. My wife.'

Charlie straightens up smartly and stares hard at him.

'You're gonna have to break that one down for me a little, Robert.'

He sighs. 'Where to begin?'

The phone on her desk rings. She reaches for it.

'Yeah?' Terse and urgent barking on the other end. Her expression changes. 'Fuck.'

～⁓～

CHERRY

'It's a demo,' says Andy uncertainly, and right away Cherry can tell he's wrong. She's been on plenty of demos in her time. Anti-war marches, with their combination of jolly politeness mixed with nervousness at going outside the comfort zone, like a Church of England garden party that's decided to invite the Hells Angels this year to spice things up. Lots of respectable, middle-aged citizens in macs and sensible shoes, drinking tea from their own flasks and saying stuff like, 'Well, they simply *can't* ignore this many people,' no matter how often they do.

This is not that. This is not that at all. A torrent of people of any gender and ethnicity you can think of, almost all of them young, is flooding onto the main road as though a water main has burst (something the locals are used to, thanks to Southern Water). There is not a witty placard in sight. Instead there is ragged hoarse shouting and fists raised and a bubbling, vengeful fury you can taste on the wind. This is pure, raw, undistilled anger, nebulous inchoate rage seeking form, seeking a mode of expression. This isn't about whatever it's about. It's about something long-standing rising up from the dark and deep, from the repressed and crushed and quashed, and the cause of it will not be the end of it.

Several girls are in tears. Others have their faces twisted with rage. Boys jab the air or smack a closed fist into an open palm. The

209

traffic has ground to a halt as more and more people gush into the road and surround the cars. One or two horns sound, but most people in South London are smart enough to recognize trouble when they see it and keep their hands to themselves.

A knock on Cherry's window, almost polite. A pretty black girl with tattoos and what they called picky dreads back when she was her age is waving and smiling, framed by friends. Cherry smiles back and rolls the window down.

'You won't be able to get through there, darling. Too much people.' The girl points in the general direction of the swelling tide. 'Turn around if you can.'

The thing that strikes Cherry is just how young they all are. They barely look capable of carrying the crushing load their society has dumped on them, with their eggshell faces and freshly hatched bodies. They look as if they'll crumple under the weight. Could she have handled all *this* when she was that age? She very much doubts it, and she thinks she's tough.

She recalls the things she thought were so important and massive back then, and how insignificant they seem now compared to all the shit this generation have to deal with: the planet burning, and their elders' venomous hatred of them, and the promise of absolutely no future at all except getting rigorously dry-fucked by offshore dark money and its political flunkeys for ever and ever.

'What's going on?'

'They killed Matthew.'

The girl's face is full not so much of anger but a profound sadness that exceeds her. A sadness that reaches far beyond this incident and these kids and way way back into generations, has its taproots deep in the fertile stinking muck of British history. And then she briefly tells Cherry the story.

There was a community centre nearby. A warm space for people who couldn't afford to heat. Hot meals for people who couldn't afford to eat, made up from donations and dumpster diving. It hosted English language classes, and spoken word nights of frankly debatable quality. It was the brainchild of a guy called Matthew, a community celebrity of the type you only really get in South London. Looked a bit like the rapper from Arrested Development, though that's going back a ways. Tall, big glasses, wavy locs, less meat on him than a butcher's pencil as the saying goes. Not even thirty. A gentle soul, just trying to do a bit of good.

The thing is, the centre wasn't supposed to be there. Legally. It was housed in an abandoned Jobcentre (a serious upgrade in serving the community on that score), on a site which developers had had their eyes on for some time. They'd asked for permission to stay, for grants to put in a bid on the place, for council assistance, but all the main local councillors work for Lendlease. And so last night, in the middle of bingo (a particular favourite with the older Jamaican ladies, and thus rammed), the riot cops charged in. Matthew went to meet them, hands upraised.

The police are claiming he tripped over some debris and broke his neck.

'But we have this,' says the girl, and passes her phone through the window. Suddenly Cherry notices how many of the kids around her have their faces in their phones or are passing them around, pointing at the screen in furious denunciation.

She can't watch more than a few seconds of the video. The threshing of limbs, and the scuffling, and the police yelling out their bullshit alibis, and the frightened outraged voices of old church-going ladies screaming, 'He can't breathe! HE CAN'T BREATHE!', is all at once so shockingly unexpected and so horribly familiar that the last few days and the last few years all come streaming back in torrents. She blinks hard and shoves the phone back without looking. The girl is distressed.

'It's OK! It's OK! I'm so sorry, I didn't mean—'

'It's alright.' Cherry has recovered herself. She smiles at the girl.

'It's alright. It's not that. Well, it is that, but . . . It's a lot, you know? It's all just . . . a lot.'

'It's a fucking lot,' agrees the girl, smiling back.

'Good luck,' says Cherry, and means it.

'Thanks, lovely,' says the pretty girl. 'I *love* your car, by the way.'

'Thank you. I stole it,' says Cherry, deadpan, and the girl pisses herself giggling.

A sudden bang on the window. Jakubiak jumps. A finger points at his head. 'Cop.' A second bang. A face snarling.

'Ay! You man! Bare look like cops, you know!'

Jakubiak goes to roll down the window but Cherry yanks his arm back. Somebody in the tide of people now engulfing the car pulls the face away. 'Low it, fam,' disappears on the wind.

Cherry puts the car into reverse and backs out of there.

ROBERT

It's weird watching it with no sound, in black-and-white. Distant, unreal, like an old movie. But the timestamp says ten minutes ago. The rear window shatters as the bottle with the burning rag flies through it. Nothing happens for a strange while after, the violence inside fermenting, biding its time.

Then the side windows explode, as if punched out by soft fists. Flames creep out through the broken glass like young tigers emerging from a lair. Tentatively at first, then growing in confidence and strength, licking the paintwork off with their rough tongues, clawing the body apart, an exultant display of orange and black power. Hands of bystanders start to rock the burning vehicle, shaking it from side to side, adding oxygen to the conflagration. The flames rise higher. The windscreen blows out. The police car erupts.

Danielle whoops and screams. Robert rips his head around to glare at her. Charlie puts a hand on his arm and stifles a giggle. She really shouldn't laugh given the circumstances, this is very serious, but this girl is *so* his daughter. People step back from the heat of the flames, which roar in triumph at the sky, fully grown now, claws outstretched. The people start to run, the burning car suddenly alone, isolated. Then the engine explodes.

Charlie turns off the CCTV footage. They take it in for a moment or two.

'Where was that?' asks Robert.

'Neasden.'

'Neasden?! Thought you were gonna say Harlesden way, Stonegate estate or something.'

'Gentrified now. Kind of.'

'Nothing's happened in Neasden since the early eighties.'

She shrugs. 'Apparently it has today.'

'I thought you said the guy was killed South? This Matthew?'

'He was.'

'Then what is this doing West? Let alone fucking Neasden.'

'Language,' chides Danielle with a smirk.

'It's much worse down there, from what I'm told,' says Charlie. Her phone goes again. She picks up, doesn't even listen. 'I'll call you right back.' She puts it down. It rings again, somehow more insistently.

London is a highly, highly regionalized city, less so since mass gentrification but still comprised of separate citadels. North, West, East and especially South, segregated by the river but above all by loyalties to localities, regional enmities, ancient divides. Some people still go their whole lives without crossing the river. Postcode beefs are still a thing, brawls over arbitrary administrative areas, a problem the authorities are solving by evicting as many poor people as possible and selling their housing to sovereign wealth funds. Conflicts and protests tend to stay local. They do not usually jump across areas, let alone whole precincts and zones of the city.

Something is fucked up. Something weird is happening.

Charlie and Robert look at each other. 'It could get quite dangerous out there, I reckon,' she says flatly.

Robert makes a choice. He gestures to Danielle. 'Better hurry up then.'

Charlie's phone has not stopped ringing. She picks it up and an urgent stream of jabber leaks out. She doesn't try to stop him. But as he's closing her door, she says, 'Robert. Take care, please.'

Halfway down the corridor, smirk still on her face, Danielle says, 'I like her.'

'Shut up please, Danielle.'

☙❧

MARWA

Marwa sits waiting for her IT lecture to start, phone in hand. It feels so weird to be back in the banal sterile surroundings of the lecture room after all her recent adventures. She gazes around at the stained whiteboard and creaky seats that flap up to reveal coagulated stalactites of ancient yet somehow still sticky chewing gum, and wonders if she dreamed the whole thing. Perhaps she did; she's just texted Asha for the fourth or fifth time, but the girl has not replied. Marwa's a bit worried.

Her lecturer struts in. Bald Steve, with his ridiculous cock of the walk swagger like he's about to launch a major venture capital investment in Silicon Valley, not teach first years at a coastal ex-poly surviving on fees paid by Chinese students who barely speak English and whose parents are plainly using them as a form of human money laundering device.

He turns what looks to Marwa like the grimace of a man dealing with a severe case of haemorrhoids on her friend Emma, who is sitting next to her. Presumably he thinks it's a winning smile, but Emma shrinks away and buries her face in Marwa's sleeve. Steve has sent Emma late-night emails of an explicit nature, off which you can smell the stink of Famous Grouse through the computer screen but which Emma is too nervous of his likely revenge to report.

Through the open door enter two police officers, a man and a woman, moving purposefully. Marwa stiffens and her heart jumps into her throat. She looks for the fire escape but in classic cheap-ass uni style it's been boarded up for ages. She shrinks back into her seat and tries to disappear.

Steve sees the officers coming and smirks. He wonders which of his students they're here for. It would be amazing if it was the cocky Muslim. Take her down a peg or two. She certainly looks nervous. The pretty blonde won't have mentioned the ill-advised whisky-fuelled missives, she's not the type, he's confident of that, which is one reason he went for her in the first place. Nothing ventured, nothing gained.

'Steve Rowbotham?'

'Speaking! Which one is it? The Muslim girl?'

'I'm sorry?'

'If you can make it as quick as you can, I've got a class to—'

'Could you come with us please, sir? You're under arrest.'

As the police bundle away Steve Rowbotham, who gesticulates furiously at a baffled Emma, Marwa takes her hands from her mouth and gives in to wild and uncontrollable laughter.

ASHA

She leans her head against the damp chilly glass, exhausted. They're still catching their breath from the escape from the plastic plod, whom they'd soon lost dodging through the dense (in every sense) crowds, but suddenly Asha is overwhelmed by all the accumulated stresses and tensions and terrors of the past few days. How is it barely a day since she came here?! She looks at her reflection in the night-time window of the train and she looks like she's aged years. Drained, depleted, her face a grey pallor. She turns away and stares at the tabletop for a long time.

The buoyancy, the energy and excitement that have carried her this far, feel like they're drifting away and something more serious, something with consequences, is taking its place and she doesn't like it. This was all such an adventure. It wasn't real, in a way. It was just a relief and a release and a dream, and she's never really thought about the future. How long she would stay here. What her life would be like. Will she still be scraping dishes and hiding from the police in two, three, five years' time? How will she feel then?

She thinks of Khadija's bitterness, her frustration with her shadow life, and she shivers. She loves Sharp Tooth but she doesn't want to end up like her. No place to belong in this new world, yet reviled by her own kind for not giving due thanks for it. Insufficient gratitude is the migrant's great heresy. Ingratitude for fifteen-hour days and constant endless phone calls saying your auntie is sick and your cousin wants to go to school and the animals are starving and can you send more money? More more more. This limbo life where the only reality is the next shift and the next remittance. Always dreading the knock on the door, the dawn raid, and yet in some dark twisted place almost wishing for them too.

This is the life awarded to the winners, the survivors of the great modern odyssey of migration, and the least you can do as one of them is show some fucking appreciation.

And of course all these new dark thoughts are coming from one place only.

'He's dead, isn't he?' she says, still looking at the tabletop, so quietly that Abdi Bile doesn't really hear her.

'Huh?'

She looks him in the eye. 'Omar's dead.'

He doesn't break her gaze. 'Yeah,' he says simply. 'Has to be.'

She stretches mournfully across the sticky plastic table and puts her chin on her hands. She can feel the tears building again but this is almost too big to cry over, especially here. She will have to take her grief somewhere private and quiet and break it down into bite-sized pieces which she can begin to swallow and digest over time, like one of the big snakes.

'I will have to call his mother. And his sisters. At least they can read *surah yasin* and *Janaaso* for him.'

'How many sisters does he have?'

'Three.'

'And the father is dead.'

'Mmmm.'

He winces. He knows how tough that will be for all of them.

'One of the sisters will have to leave too. Maybe all of them,' says Asha reflectively. Then: 'I feel like I failed him, you know?'

'You? What the hell else could you have done?' he says, almost roughly, seemingly somehow offended.

'I don't know. I wish I'd said more.'

'When?'

'The last time I spoke to him. Before he got onto the boat. But he said it would be bad luck.'

'We were about to leave.'

'I know.'

'The tide was coming in.'

'He said. But—'

'Hard to get a boat full of men out against the tide. But he did think it was bad luck. To fear the journey too much. It could make bad things happen. He was going to call you first thing when we hit land.'

She nods, sore of heart but grateful for little nourishing scraps of detail, tiny memories. Then she says, almost too soft to hear, 'I'm sorry.'

'What?'

'Don't make me say it again. One time is all you get.'

'What are you sorry for?'

'I took it all. All the pain. I gathered it all up for me and I wouldn't let you have any. You were his friend too.' She stares out of the window. It's raining again.

He doesn't speak for a moment or two. 'Yeah, but I made you get me out of that shithole.'

She laughs. 'Yeah, you did, you dickhead.'

'I could've told you what happened over the phone. I didn't have to use you like that.'

'What the hell else could you have done?' She mimics his tough guy voice. He shrugs, hard nut as ever but she can see he's grateful to be at least partially forgiven. And she feels gratitude to him for the first time. 'I didn't realize you were looking after me because of him. Thank you.'

'What else can I do? You are all there is left of Omar on this earth.'

'Don't say that. It hurts.'

'Sorry.'

'And it's pressure. I can't live for him. I can only live as me.' A beat. 'What are you gonna do? When we get to London?'

'Look for work. Avoid the police.'

'There might be something at my place. A cook just quit. You can ask Zelalem. He's the boss. He's a prick but he's OK.'

The rain picks up against the window. The train rattles on through the darkness.

⁓⁓

CHERRY

The fires are everywhere. Bright blossoms of orange flame. There was an enormous one as they crossed the river, Cherry's not exactly sure where it was, looked like Bermondsey way or off towards Wapping. Hopefully something belonging to Rupert Murdoch anyway. Thick ribbons of smoke weave along the Thames. Black tendrils snake around the shiny glass temples of the City like an invasive species, dirtying up the financial dominion which has polluted this country for so long. Dark sepulchral nebulous ivy, here to pull down the battlements of the old regime.

The howling of sirens from all directions. Police vans full of grim faces tear across bridges in one direction, then a few moments later roar up the other way, blue lights flashing, horns blaring, the cars unable to get out of their way. Roadblocks and diversions. Cones and lights. Queues and crashes. Panicky figures in hi-vis waving their arms madly this way and that. An overwhelming sense that control has been lost. And Cherry Bristow driving through the heart of it all, in a bright pink soft-top convertible with a body in the boot.

Finally they pull up outside the Ethiopian restaurant. Somehow the banality of it shocks her. The Holy Grail is just a converted terrace on a hectic dirty road, a handful of place settings behind a grubby plate-glass window. There is a small fire close by, in a skip by the looks of it, but the smoke from a much bigger conflagration frames the church a few streets away. Shouting drifts closer. Sirens.

As Cherry gets out of the car, a short, greasy man rushes from the door carrying sheets of plywood and a hammer and nails to board up the window. He sees her, drops his load and strides over, wagging a finger in urgent denial.

'We are closed.'

'It's not—'

'No food. Closed. See?' He gestures at a white sign in the window. When she doesn't move immediately, in a sudden panic the man begins to shove Cherry back towards the car.

'You go now. Go!'

'Get your hands off me!'

Jakubiak emerges from the car like a hungry bear from its winter den. The greasy man stops in his tracks and backs away. Cherry takes the opportunity to reason with him.

'We're looking for a girl called Asha.'

The man shows a little courage. He stops retreating and addresses her, wagging his finger again.

'No. No Asha.'

'She works here.'

'NO ASHA. Please. You go now. You go.'

One of the grimy windows above the restaurant flies open and a girl sticks her head out. For one dazzling moment of joy Cherry thinks it's her, but the face shape is all wrong, the energy is much spikier. The man yells something at her, but she's not having it at all.

'Shut up, Zelalem,' the girl says in English. She turns her attention to Cherry. 'What you want?'

'Are you Asha?'

'I am Khadija.'

'But you know Asha? She works here?'

The man yells again, but withers quickly in Khadija's basilisk glare. She turns back to Cherry, takes it all in: the urgent woman, the hulking man, the madly out of place pink sports car. Something registers. She nods.

'Is she there?' asks Cherry. The girl shakes her head but doesn't dismiss them.

'Why you want her?'

'We have something she needs to see.'

Chapter Sixteen

DANIELLE

This is the most amazing thing Danielle has ever seen.

The crowd is an electric eel, pulsing and crackling with vitality and rage. Bolts of lightning shoot from it, sending shivers of life into its participants and shivers of fear into the police vans parked across the street, afraid to intervene. It is a living organism, multiplying by the second like cells under a microscope, growing into it knows not what, something beyond normal evolution. It is Frankenstein's monster with the bolts through its neck and the tingle in its veins, but beautiful not ugly and far more than the sum of its spontaneously cobbled-together parts. The beautiful monster flexes its new-found muscle tissue, cracks its ligaments and tendons, feels its power, senses its tensile strength. Wonders what it is now, and what it can be in the future.

The boot is off the neck. The arm is off the throat. The chain is cut, the leash is slipped.

The feeling is like being at the top of a roller coaster as it starts its lurch into the unknown: heady and captivating, yet with the pit of your stomach falling away from fear and adrenaline and glee. People look at one another with disbelief, almost a sense of shyness, seeing each other in a new light, as new humans. We don't connect like this. We don't see each other *as* this, as joyous additions not threats, locked as we've been into our individual jail cells of rise and grind and hustle and get my flowers. We are cut off from the blood flow of human connectivity. And when it is restored it hurts at first, like the pain in your arm when you've slept on it the wrong way.

Danielle spins around and around, trying to take it all in, hungry for revelation, greedy for enlightenment. Dark smoke and the acrid smells of burning plastic and metal. Unreal, hallucinatory snapshots. Knots of blurry human shadows clutching fire. A broken water main gushing forth. A man standing on the stump of a toppled street lamp, roaring at a cheering crowd, clad all in black and wearing a strange beaked mask as if from an Italian Carnevale. A plague doctor, here to purge the body politic of a virulent and long-lasting disease. To apply leeches and let the blood of the dark melancholic humours of late-stage capitalism.

She listens in on a babel of arguments. Some are banal, crude — where to rob and how to get away with it — because every tide of revolution drags a flotsam of chancers and wasters whom the powerful use to smear it. But there are more important discussions too, constructive, philosophical. Should we burn, or should we build? Which comes first? Can you have one without the other?

Moments like this, cracks in the wall, lacunae in the system where radical change is momentarily possible, are never prepared for. They loom suddenly out of history like monsters from the dark, unexpected and fearsome, and they must be caught and broken like wild mustangs, to be ridden into the future before they disappear, before the steel cell door clangs shut again. But what to do first? And how to decide what we will become?

A beautiful boy with golden eyes emerges from the ruck and swirl, accompanied by his mates. The mates plunge on but the beautiful boy locks eyes with Danielle and stops for a moment.

'Alright?' he says.

'Alright?' she says.

She takes an instinctive step forward. A strong hand grips her arm. It's her dad. When she looks back, the beautiful boy is gone.

～⁓≈⁓～

ABDI BILE

This is *definitely* not the London Abdi Bile had been told about, where he'd banked on making his fortune. For a start, most of it appears to be on fire. He and Asha gawp out of the train window in disbelief at the dense skeins of black smoke twisting up into the dark sky, the glowing reds and blues of the police vans screaming back and forth like drones around a shattered beehive, panicked and displaced. A calm and golden harvest moon shining strange above it all.

Theirs is one of the last trains to arrive, after much grinding and delay. The authorities are stopping all services: trespassers on the lines, they say, fires on the tracks. Wild rumours of crashes, of bloody punch-ups and stabbings on board trains, whip around the station like litter in high wind. Yet Pret and Oliver Bonas are still open, people queueing patiently for flat whites and scented candles. A strange conjunction of order and panic.

As they get off, Abdi and Asha have to squeeze through a wall of besuited commuters blocked from reaching their platforms by a hi-vis fence of rail employees and police. The untrammelled terror in the suited faces, the white rolling eyes and spittle-flecked shouts, remind Abdi Bile of the more middle class migrants he encountered on his journey here. The urban, affluent Syrians especially: ripped from a comfortable life and plunged into a turmoil for which they were completely unprepared, emotionally more than practically. These things happen, sure, it's a hard world. But they just don't happen to *people like us*. But why shouldn't they? Abdi's lip curls in a certain contempt.

224

They drill through the solid wall of the crowd and emerge onto the street, where they begin the long walk to Asha's place of work and the possibility of employment. A large fire is burning a few streets down, red trucks at oblique angles shooting jets of water, yet white men in blue suits and pink shirts still cluster round a pub on the corner clutching beers and phones. What kind of place is this?!

Asha's phone goes. Her face lights up as she answers. Abdi Bile look away, hears a gasp and the crack of something hitting the pavement. He looks back. Asha is ten metres ahead, sprinting as fast as she can, ploughing people out of her way, physically knocking them into the road.

'Asha! ASHA!'

Twenty metres. Thirty. If he doesn't go this second, he will lose her.

Abdi scoops up the cracked phone, puts it in his pocket, and begins to run.

⁂

ROBERT

'*Don't*,' says Robert.

'I wasn't doing anything,' protests Danielle unconvincingly.

'Yes you were. Don't disappear, please. If you go off on your own, I'll never be able to find you.'

He roots himself to the spot and tries to take it all in. All his years of police training and experience make this . . . thing, whatever it is, stick in his craw and his gorge rise. He's policed outbreaks of disorder like this before (though nothing on this scale, if he's being honest), even cracked heads a few times when it was felt by senior ranks to be necessary for the safety of the wider public. It doesn't sit right with him, smashing things up, messing with other people's lives. There are better ways to express your dissatisfaction, your dissent.

But then he looks into the eyes of his daughter, and he sees a light of ecstasy that goes beyond the usual predilection of the rebellious young for sticking up two fingers at the system. Goes beyond even the immediate buzz and thrill of occupying the streets. The light in Danielle's eyes is the light of justice. The light of truth. He thinks back to his Orbital raves. The absolute conviction they had all felt as one that a better world was coming. It had to be, because they were making it out of whole cloth right where they were. And maybe this is the equivalent now, the best these kids can do in the world they've been given.

And Robert himself is all churned up. The other week he was reading about a glacier on a mountain famous for climbing accidents which has started melting and disgorging the long-frozen bodies of explorers and guides and mountaineers, some almost as fresh-looking as the day they went missing but in the clothes of fifty or seventy or a hundred years ago. This is Robert's soul. He can feel massive sheets of ice grinding around in there, slowly turning to water, releasing long-held burdens, destabilizing what he had thought was solid and permanent.

There was the thing today with Charlie. He'd always liked her and she had always liked him, that was clear to both of them from the off, gastric bypass or no gastric bypass. Big-time professional and personal boundaries, so be it, nothing to be done. But there was something there today that wasn't there before, and has not been there with Cherry for a long time. Robert has never considered, even in the worst of times after Liam, letting go of his grip on his marriage. Loyalty has always been his touchstone. But there are things that have happened, things Cherry has said and done, not in this recent insanity but before, things far more banal yet hurtful which he is starting to think about, starting to feel . . . Ice floes shift and creak inside him.

226

How could he ever get across to Charlie that it's not because of the surgery though? Because that would be embarrassing, if she thought it was just because of her weight that he didn't—

There's a sudden blur as a girl with long bouncing ringlets rushes past. Robert doesn't see her face. Danielle yelps and turns and runs after her. Robert catches up to his daughter in a few strides.

'I *told* you not to—'

A stocky kid about Liam's age collides with the pair of them, almost tumbles to the floor, rights himself and continues running after the girl. Danielle rips angrily at Robert's arm and pulls away, gesturing urgently after the pair of them.

'It's her. It's *her*.'

Robert's eyes bug out. The two of them begin to sprint.

CHERRY

The four of them, Cherry and Jakubiak and Khadija and Zelalem, are taking Omar's body out of the car, hidden under the sheets. The stench of the corpse is unbearable even outside, but nobody complains. Even Zelalem finds a sombreness. Jakubiak looks purposeful, almost fraternal. Khadija has tears streaming down her face.

Suddenly Cherry straightens up. A figure is running down the road towards them as fast as she can, head upright, arms pumping. Decent technique, muses Cherry, from some far-off place long ago. Could do with relaxing her shoulders a bit. Even before she's close enough to see her face, she knows it's the girl from the picture. A vast weight lifts off Cherry's spine and her lungs open. Her knees buckle and tears spring to her eyes. The rest stop and look in the same direction.

Then Cherry's jaw drops and she cranes her neck forward. Behind Asha, like some deranged 4x400m relay team that have completely lost the run of themselves, is a stocky guy about Liam's age, and behind him are her daughter and then her husband. All running in her direction as fast as their legs can carry them.

Cherry gawps and stands stock-still and waits for them all to arrive.

➤➤

ASHA

Innaa Nahnu nuhyil mawtaa wa naktubu maa qaddamoo wa aasaarahum; wa kulla shai'in ahsainaahu feee Imaamim Mubeen.

Verily We shall give life to the dead, and We record that which they send before and that which they leave behind; and of all things have We taken account in a clear Book.

Omar's body is laid out on dining tables. The windows have been boarded up, the outside world excluded as best it can be, and lighted candles and incense give some semblance of sacrality to the front room of a restaurant. But it's the chanting that makes it seem at least a little bit holy. The imam reads the *surah yasin*, the *surah* of creation and resurrection. He places particular onus, as might be expected, on the restoration of life.

Wa Aayatul lahumul ardul maitatu ahyainaahaa wa akhrajnaa minhaa habban faminhu ya'kuloon. Wa ja'alnaa feehaa jannaatim min nakheelinw wa a'naabinw wa fajjarnaa feeha minal 'uyoon.

There is a sign for them in this lifeless earth: We give it life and We produce grains from it for them to eat; We have put gardens of date palms and grapes in the earth, and We have made water gush out of it so that they could eat its fruit.

The men wash Omar's body with bowls of warm water. Abdi

228

Bile takes charge, exactly as she would expect of Abdi Bile, doling out orders to men three times his age and crashing back and forth out of the kitchen with new towels as though he's been working there for years. She smiles, because now she can see why Omar took him as a friend. Abdi had stood for a long moment, staring down into Omar's dry sightless eyes with eyes equally dry, but his hand gripping the dead boy's shoulder so hard it seemed as though he might tear it off. Then he nodded, and began his tasks.

None of the men makes any comment on the state of the body, or blinks at the smell, though the incense helps. Asha doesn't know where they came from, all these men, or how they got here so fast. They don't eat at the restaurant. She's never seen them out in the street. Yet here they are. She doesn't even know how they heard, amidst all the chaos outside.

But then it's the same at home. Asha remembers the day of her elder brother's death, how men flooded in from miles around, from far-off villages hours away on foot. People don't keep in the heat back home; the body is buried the day they die. The mystery is how other people learn about it.

Women are not supposed to wash a man's dead body. Women are not supposed to be part of the burial ceremony at all, but Asha told Khadija she wanted to, and Khadija booted in the imam's door, and two minutes later, considerably paler than before, the imam let Asha in.

Asha closes Omar's eyes and mouth. She straightens his arms and legs. She rubs them with a white *carfan* and then applies the red *adar*, the perfume of burial. Lastly she ties his legs, neck and head with white cloth to keep them in place while the men begin to wrap the body in white cotton, starting at his feet and working up to his head. The face is kept free. And when the body is covered afterwards with the green cloth embroidered with gold for the *Janaaso*, the goodbye prayer, a rent is made in it over the face so that it can keep contact with the earth. Omar will be buried not far away, in a plot the community use, as soon as they can get him through the streets.

The rhythmic chanting of the imam, and the answering *duas* of the men, soothe Asha and root her, and slowly she begins to lose the horror and the disgust, and then the guilt at the disgust, that had gripped her when she first saw the state of Omar's body, and was forced to confront the reality of his death. The rage and sadness and disgust drain away. She begins to feel grateful that he is here and she is here.

She breathes slowly and deeply, and watches the cotton be wound. The imam finishes the surah.

Fa Subhaanal ladhee biyadihee malakootu kulli shai-inw-wa ilaihi turja'oon.

So glory to Him in Whose hands is the dominion of all things: and to Him will ye be all brought back.

※

OMAR

Omar's spirit watches Asha prepare his body for burial. The corpse is a strange distant unpliant thing now, a lump bloated and unrecognizable, nothing to do with him at all. It is just an object, merely the former receptacle of the human, and he puzzles when he recalls his desperate desire all through his recent journey, from the cutting-up room to the strange cars, to get back inside it.

A fog seems to be growing in the room. Something swirls in the middle of it, a thickening nebula first pale lemon, then bronze, now tarnished gold in colour. He knows the portal is for him, that soon he will go to it and it will take him on somewhere and he is not scared of that, though he doesn't know what awaits him. But this is his last time to watch Asha, and he wants to take it before it ends.

His heart broke when she ran down the street to him, and he stepped forward arms outstretched and lunged for the embrace longed for across so much time and so many worlds, and nothing happened. Like a sliding of planes, like a needle refusing to thread. Substance brushing through absence. And he knew that would happen, he knows what he is now, but it didn't make it hurt any less. All he wanted, more than anything in this world he is about to leave, was a final touch.

And now he's getting it. He watches her quick busy hands run over his ruined skin, cleansing and preparing, soothing and acknowledging. Such beautiful hands. Delicate yet strong. He always liked Asha's hands. He can't remember if he ever told her that.

He knows it is time. He steps away. He keeps his eyes on her hands.

Omar steps through the golden portal, and into peace.

CHERRY

Cherry stands on the flat tar-paper roof of the restaurant, staring out across London. Blazes spark orange and magenta across the night as far as the eye can see, winking open and spreading their fragrance like flowers in springtime. She remembers breathlessly watching the LA riots on TV after the Rodney King beating, eyes glued to the screen, heart in her mouth. ('Can't we all just get along?' he famously enquired afterwards. Rodney King died traumatically at forty-seven, so the answer was very clearly 'No'.) Wondering what it meant, and what would happen next. She wonders too what this will mean, how the world will change after this. Because surely it *has* to.

She did it. Against all the odds, she brought him home. She finished her odyssey so he could finish his. She learned his real name: Omar. Asha, who is also real, a flesh and blood girl, a human being somehow sprung to life direct from a picture and whom she had held in brief chaotic embrace, had told Cherry the identity of her charge, of the boy she had rescued from oblivion. So now Omar is being remembered and cried over and commemorated, not slung into a mass pit to rot to forgotten bones. She's never been prouder of anything she's done in her life.

The funeral incantations rise from below and mingle with the steady susurration from the streets, the singing and cheering and yelling and the breaking of glass and the occasional soft whoomp of a car catching fire. It all melds into one great song of solace, a scary and thrilling and powerful and necessary consolation. A commemoration of Omar, and Matthew, and all our many, many recent dead, many known but many nameless, all lost to Coronavirus and austerity and racism and immigration policy and the rabid psychotic cruelty of our malicious, mendacious, profoundly evil ruling class. And she did a tiny bit of this. She played her part. All she's ever wanted to do.

And yet she doesn't feel triumphant, or exultant, or overjoyed. What she feels mostly is sadness. The sadness that comes at the end of any great quest, the sense of anticlimax that the journey can't go on. And instead normal life, that crude and dull domestic abuser, comes roaring and belching in through the front door, picking its nose and scratching its arse and mocking, 'Aw, did you miss me?'

But also the unmistakable fear of now. Now what? That's the real question. The question she never had to consider because of the urgent adrenaline of her task. But suddenly that task is over and real life, and even more than that real *people*, have caught up with her.

A strange stand-off with Robert in the grimy street. The

realization and the gratitude that he had come all this way in pursuit of her, to protect her, and yet now he'd found her he seemed to have nothing to say. And she couldn't find words either. She realized with a guilty start that she'd barely thought of him since their last call, and what does that mean? That she regards him as part of the past, the past she was running from? Has her insane odyssey really changed nothing between them?

It was easier with Danielle, in a weird way. It doesn't surprise Cherry one bit that Danielle is here with her father, in fact she suspects he wouldn't be here without her, and a warm cosy feeling towards her daughter spreads through Cherry's chest, which she is pleased to discover is a sense of pride. And something appears to have changed in Danielle's gaze too. Maybe a sense of understanding? Or respect at the sheer scale of Cherry's madness? There will be time to talk it all through, when the chaos around them recedes.

Or will there? Will Cherry be in a cell and the only time they'll have to talk will be during visiting hours?

What is next? And what is left?

She peers down into the crowded street. So many young people, all kinds of backgrounds, mixing and mingling, almost a festival vibe, something bacchanalian and celebratory amidst the flames. She picks out Danielle in the throng, talking animatedly to a good-looking light-skinned boy. They're both clearly very into each other.

A sharp stab of jealousy runs through Cherry. Again the desire for that young life, that first-time excitement, those rushes of untrammelled, uncauterized feeling she knows she can never have again but can't bear to give up on for the banal horseshit that's all she's offered now. Cherry Bristow doesn't know how to go back to the ordinary world, assuming the ordinary world will even have her.

DANIELLE

The boy with the golden eyes is called Damian. Danielle spotted him from the upstairs window and pointed him out to Khadija, who elbowed her repeatedly until she finally called out to him. He stopped and looked up and grinned a mischievous grin and beckoned to them to come down. A little bit more back and forth and the two of them were thundering down the stairs, drawing irate glares from the men at the funeral, hoping the boys would still be waiting when they got outside. And they were. Khadija is talking to one of Damian's mates, a tall white guy with excellent hair. They seem to be getting on great despite linguistic limitations. Danielle is with Damian.

The vibe here is different than it was near the police station. Less crackling and vengeful and Old Testament, more joyous and exultant. Celebrating taking back their space, their streets. 'TAKE BACK CONTROL!! TAKE BACK CONTROL!!' hollers the crowd mockingly, waving looted beers and spliffs high in the air. A herbal fragrance predominates. Someone has a bike-powered generator and speakers and is pumping out old-school tunes to which the crowd sings along.

This is her. This is where she belongs. She's a London girl. Dragged away before her time to the sticks, even if she can barely remember it here in truth. But this is where she belongs, not just in the city but *this*, all this, the madness and the vibes and it all going off. The crowds and the rage and the joy and the people standing up for themselves. These man know what the fuck is going on. The boys back home are alright, some are even pretty, but they don't know shit and they don't seem to *care*. More than anything, Danielle has always wanted to be part of something with meaning.

But what she *really* wants this second is to link Damian. She says something funny and he laughs and a thrill shoots up her spine, a bolt of pure electric excitement. They get a few centimetres closer, almost touching now. Her heart thuds in her throat and her eyes flare. She hopes she's not sweating. She steals a glance at his hands. Beautiful hands. She imagines them around her waist, up her back, other places.

Somebody elbows him in the back. Damian stumbles to the side, raises a hand in forgiveness. Then the guy does it again. Damian turns with a fist half-cocked (and Danielle would be lying if she said that didn't thrill her a little bit too) but the guy puts both hands flat on Damian's chest and apologizes profusely. Somebody is shoving him too. And somebody else is shoving that dude. The whole crowd is being pushed around.

They stand on tiptoe, crane their necks to see the cause.

Some kind of van.

⌒⌒⌒

BARRATT

Just a few more minutes.

Freddie Barratt sits in the lead vehicle as the convoy of vans grinds slowly through the crowds of scumbags and rioters, twitching with glee and hard with anticipation inside his body armour. He has been watching the parade of African men stream into the restaurant on the CCTV screens inside the van with avid hungry eyes, a savvy investor watching his stocks soar, counting the ticking profits.

Keep coming, fuckers. Roll up, roll up. They'll all be fucking illegal, every last one, and he has them all in the bag.

It couldn't be working out any better. The bigger the take of illegals, the bigger his pull with the bird from the Home Office and her chickenshit bunch of pen pushers and pie-chart slaves. That should give him plenty of leverage over his super and the regional brass wrt any inconvenient questions about the last seventy-two hours or so. And the nurse bitch is there, and Jakubiak too, dressed like a fucking homo for some reason. So that pretty much does them in as reliable witnesses.

Even his forecasts for London are coming true all around him. What he said would happen for donkey's years is unspooling in front of him in real time: the woke and the niggers and the trash setting fire to the world around them, because that is all they are good for.

Everything's coming up Freddie. He rocks back and forth in his seat, scarcely able to contain his excitement.

⤞⤝

ROBERT

Cherry calls Danielle's name, but her daughter doesn't hear her. She shouts louder.

'She's fine. Leave her be,' says Robert, who made the decision to let his daughter go in pursuit of his wife, and wonders once again if it was the right one.

Cherry shoots him a look that he's become all too accustomed to over recent years: unreasonable irritation at his reasonableness. Impatience. Disappointment with him. For a while now he's shared her disappointment, her sense that he's not the man he used to be. But this time there is a twang in him that doesn't normally resonate, like a hamstring pull of the heart, an anger and a frustration of his own.

He didn't really know what to say when suddenly, bizarrely, inevitably, there she was, standing on the street large as life, holding the stolen body. He hadn't thought what he would do, or feel, when and if he actually found her. His only purpose had been in tracking her down. And so they'd stood awkward as shy teenagers while the chaos of the riot and the funeral and everything else went on around them. Then she'd disappeared, and it had taken him a little while to find her up on the roof.

He looks down again at Danielle and her prospective beau, and a huge warm grin splits his face. Go on, girl. Cherry shakes her head and mutters something under her breath. Eventually he turns to her.

'So, are you coming home?'

She doesn't answer straight away, and then she makes a joke of it.

'Maybe via Holloway Prison.'

'Holloway closed.'

'Did it?! When?'

'Few years back.'

'That's how uncool I am these days. Not even up to date with the prisons.' She sort of half-turns to him. 'I don't know yet. I'm sorry. When I'm coming back. If.'

There's a pause.

'Right.' He nods. 'Fair enough.'

Sort of the response she's expecting, by the looks of it. And then he drops the hammer, and he would be lying if he said he didn't get a little pleasure as well as a deep sadness out of it.

'I don't know if I'll be there.'

Now she fully turns to him, whips around in fact. There is shock and disbelief in her face. She goes to say something except Robert suddenly isn't looking at her, he's looking at the street below.

Something's wrong. The people are jostling, agitated, more condensed and concentrated. The impetus is all coming from one direction. Danielle is getting shoved and crushed.

Several large vans are moving through the crowd, bumping and hitting people, paying no heed to angry shouts, fists against the metalwork. The vans are white with red and yellow diagonal stripes along the lower sides. They look like police, and a few people start to bolt in case they are police, but then they stop when they read the words. High on the sides, above smoked glass windows, in large black capitals, are the words HOME OFFICE: IMMIGRATION ENFORCEMENT.

He starts to move but she's beaten him to it.

'DANIELLE!' screams Cherry, and begins to run.

꩜

CHERRY

They'll bury her.

Everybody knows, or everybody who *cares* to know knows, what happens to immigration enforcement detainees. They bury them. They'll inter her in a concrete holding cell. Brick her in with paperwork and procedure. Entomb her with administration and rule changes and failed appeals and no access to lawyers. They'll dig her grave in Yarl's Wood or Brook House or Harmondsworth or somewhere even less well known and further away and harder to reach. And then one fine day, years down the track, they will dig her up and deport her.

They will bury Asha alive. And she will never be seen again.

That's the only thought on Cherry's mind as she charges down the fire escape.

She crashes through the back door of the kitchen and bursts into the restaurant and the funeral ceremony, Robert close behind. The men protest, the imam takes a step forward, but she's through them before they can stop her and up to Asha.

'We have to go.'

And at the moment she places both hands on the startled girl's shoulders, Danielle crashes through the front door.

The only word on her lips is, 'MUM!'

Cherry and Danielle exchange a look with a whole library in it, a look they both instantly get in full even though anyone else would need to do a PhD to break it down. Of course they don't get on, thinks Robert idly in that frozen moment. They're the same fucking person.

Cherry points back through the open front door.

DANIELLE

Danielle turns back the way she came. The Home Office storm troopers are trampling through the crowd, clobbering people with their truncheons, intimidatingly bulky in their body armour, heavy helmets and opaque visors. Mutant humans, half-man half-beast.

'It's a raid!' she screams, but it's hard to be heard above the tumult, the shouting and singing and the breaking of things. Damian and his mates are the only ones paying attention to her, and they're not quite sure what's going on. Damian has a half-smile on his face, as if maybe it's some kind of joke. The mutants are nearly at the door.

Danielle does the only thing she can, the thing she's learned how to do from the history books.

'IT'S A RAID! IT'S A RAID! IT'S A RAID!' she screams again, at the very top of her lungs, and she throws herself into the knees of the lead officer, who trips and crashes to the floor.

CHERRY

The men are fleeing the funeral, pouring through the kitchen and out the back door into a grubby storage area full of empty tins of grease, over a rickety wooden fence and away into a narrow alley that runs between houses into the next road over. The speed is incredible, they're almost all gone already. The imam stands perfectly still, face calm, hands raised in the air. The poor fucker's been through this before, thinks Cherry.

She grabs a baffled Asha by the shoulders.

'We need to go.'

'Where?'

Cherry points back towards the kitchen, the way the men are fleeing. 'That way.'

ROBERT

Danielle has lit a wildfire. The word rips through the crowd, which is dry tinder already seasoned, that there is yet another indignity taking place, yet another cruelty inflicted upon ordinary people by a state that hates them. If you keep telling people at every opportunity how much you fucking despise them, you think they are worthless scum who deserve nothing but suffering, and furthermore that that suffering is their own fault for not being born better . . . Well, one day, they will take you seriously. And then look the fuck out.

People mass in front of the door to the restaurant. They block entry to the Home Office enforcers. They take the shoves, the blows, the kicks and punches and baton strikes on behalf of people they have never met, whom they don't even know, and yet they stand strong, rise in a kind of violent glee to confront the heavy boots and the batons, because what they are resisting is wrong and they know it is wrong and that's all there is to it.

Which is fucking great and all, thinks Robert, but it's my fucking daughter in there. Robert is in the heart of the ruck, shoving, stamping, kicking, a scrum-half trying to rip a trapped ball free, when he sees a flash of her shirt. Liam's favourite shirt. He reaches down for Danielle and is suddenly yanked back by the throat. An armoured officer has grabbed his collar so hard that it's cutting into his neck and making it hard to breathe.

Robert twists around and looks up into the grinning face of Frederick John Barratt.

Barratt reaches for his belt of weapons, the grin never leaving his face. He removes a Taser, which he brings slowly and irrevocably, despite Robert's panicked struggles, up towards his victim's eye.

The Taser is almost touching Robert's eyeball.

Suddenly Barratt disappears.

JAKUBIAK

He'd enjoyed the riot, which is not something Andy Jakubiak would have expected to say forty-eight hours ago. Really enjoyed it, to be fair. People kept passing him lukewarm cans of Red Stripe and other looted bits and bobs, which initially he'd been a bit awkward about accepting. But then he'd said, 'Excuse me sir, are those items *stolen*?' in his best pompous policeman voice to some guy, who'd pissed himself laughing and offered Andy a dab or three from a little glassine bag of ecstasy.

Some of the lads back at the station have been known to help themselves to the impounded items in the lock-up at times, the drugs especially. 'Strictly for the report, mate! Gotta check the quality!' a coke-eyed sergeant called Marvin had cackled down the corridor, chewing furiously on his own lips. Andy had never had the balls. But all for the best, because now he has discovered in the best possible circumstances that MDMA is awesome and people are basically amazing.

And so Andy Jakubiak was wandering around in a pleasant haze, working out what else was different inside him, what else he had discovered on his journey, when the Home Office vans ploughed into the crowd and a snatch squad erupted from them. At the front of the snatch squad was a man who, body armour or not, Andy would recognize anywhere. And the pleasant haze vanished.

He tailed Barratt through the press and mass of the crowd, watched him disappear into the scrum and pounce on a victim. It's the black guy who came running up to them in the street when they took out the body from the pink soft-top. Cherry's husband, can't remember his name. A weird sense of loyalty to Cherry, his kidnapper and yet at the same time his true mentor, surges through him.

Andy Jakubiak pulls Freddie Barratt off Cherry's husband and yanks his helmet off. He takes a long second to appreciate the look of shock on Barratt's face, like a connoisseur savouring the subtle depth of flavour in a particularly rare vintage wine which he's been saving for just the right occasion.

And then he breaks Barratt's jaw in four places.

CHERRY

Cherry straddles the wooden fence next to the alley. She holds a hand down to Asha. The girl hesitates.

'Come on.'

Of course she's hesitating. Why wouldn't she? Cherry has no idea where she's going, no plan, no thought but to get Asha away from evil.

The thing is, if she hesitates, if she *thinks*, even for a second, she will stop too. And that's why they have to go. Now.

'Come the fuck on.'

Asha reaches up for her hand.

'Mum.'

She looks back. They both look. It's Danielle.

Her shirt, Liam's shirt, is torn and hanging off one shoulder. Her face is badly scraped, her left eye is swelling up and a steady trickle of blood runs from her split lower lip.

'I'm coming too.'

Cherry looks at her daughter for a second, and then she nods. She pulls Asha up and over the fence and down into the alley behind, then does the same for Danielle. Finally, she drops herself over.

The three women begin to run.

Chapter Seventeen

OMAR

The seven of them are pushing the boat out off the rocky shoreline, knee deep in the cold water, fighting against the incoming swells, when Omar's phone goes.

'Let me get this.'

'The tide's coming in!'

'Let me just get this real quick.'

Abdi Bile throws up his arms. Omar answers the phone, cradling it against the roar and splash.

'I'm coming,' he says, before she's even spoken.

'Baby, it's me,' says Asha.

'I know. I'm coming.'

'I love you.'

'I love you too. I need to go. The tide's coming in and we have to get the boat out.'

'I'm scared.'

'There's nothing to be scared of.'

'Just talk to me for a minute.'

'Baby, it's nothing. A puddle. A little stream. The more we talk about bad things, the more we make them happen.'

'I just want you to be here.'

'I am. I will be. I'll call you in a few hours.'

'You promise?'

'Of course I promise.'

'How can you promise?'

'I can promise because I love you.'

'I love you too,' says Asha, and he can hear the smile in her voice.

'I promise you, Asha: there is nothing to be scared of.'

'OK,' she laughs. 'OK. I trust you. Call me the second you land.' And she hangs up.

Omar smiles widely at his phone.

Abdi Bile scowls at him. 'Anything else, dickhead? Wanna send a few emails? Maybe write her a fucking letter?'

Omar grins at him. 'Push the boat out, fat man.'

It takes a few goes to get the little craft up and over and through the white-capped waves, but then they're in and they're out, away from the shoreline and out to sea, and Abdi waves his phone, the little blue dot of them surrounded by endless lighter blue. He points them in the right direction and the boat begins its journey.

The boys sail into the future.

Acknowledgements

You can blame the existence of this book (as opposed to the content, which is obviously my fault) on two great women, my agent Eugenie Furniss and my first editor Hannah Chukwu, in combo with my current editor Simon Prosser. It was Eugenie's idea that I try prose fiction. Long ago, before I got sidetracked writing plays for prisoners and other people, I'd vaguely considered like every other literate person on earth having a crack at a novel. Novels however are quite long and the thought of writing four hundred pages which might turn out to be quite shit did not appeal. Eugenie read my play *Lampedusa* (which is comprised of two prose monologues) and told me to write ten thousand words and she'd judge if it was good enough for me to carry on. Decide for yourself if she got that right.

Hannah was the first person in novel world, maybe anywhere, to get my writing in its entirety. I don't lack for confidence but it was amazing to have someone else believe in me the way I do. My work is unusual and it takes a special person to swim against the currents of orthodoxy. Simon has been just as supportive and committed, and the whole Hamish Hamilton crew including Ruby Fatimilehin and Rosie Safaty have been incredibly skilled and professional. I've done a lot of work in theatre beyond writing (including directing my plays, which I suck at) out of necessity, so it's been a revelation to work with smart people who produce great stuff quickly. Their cover design is masterful and summons up the many convergent currents in the book in a single image.

Big shout out to Laurenz Bolliger at Hoffman und Campe in Germany, who was actually the first person to commit formally to the book and is a pretty cool guy into the bargain. Shout out also to Greivin, Rafa and Marco at the Campanario Biological Station, Osa Peninsula, Costa Rica. I wrote the second and final draft of this book (I work extremely fast, again you can decide if this is a good thing) while volunteering at a remote research station in the Costa Rican jungle, on a laptop on its last legs powered by solar panels on the roof. We'd get up at 4.30 a.m. to beat the heat, clean the station, sweep the trails, help visiting researchers investigate scarlet macaws and the *mono congo*, then Greivin would let me knock off in the afternoon and redraft my novel. Strongly recommended as an extreme form of writers' retreat, though not ideal if you prefer electricity/hot water/a bed not made of planks or don't like bullet ants/physical labour/multitudinous varieties of highly poisonous snake. I hope we get a Spanish translation so the boys can read it.